BEHIND
THE EYES

ROBERT
SADLER

All characters, names, locations,
and events in this novel are used
in a fictional manner.

 Bahamut Publishing
ISBN: 978-0692460597

Vist the author's website at
AndABlankPage.com

Cover illustration created by
Peter Faylor of Strange Things Art.
StrangeThingsArt.com

This novel is dedicated to everyone
who reads even a single word of it.
That means you.
Yes – this book is dedicated to you.

Thank you.

ONE

The last time I left my home, I suffered a heart attack. I survived. Four others, including a seven-year-old boy, did not.

I try to keep myself locked up where I can't hurt anyone, but the world we live in isn't fit for recluses. Everything's "out there," and even an old-timer like myself, someone who has help and care, can't avoid society forever.

I knew the dangers of leaving, and what could happen, but I had no choice. I usually call Cameron before I run out of my meds so she can refill them for me, but my mind is a rusty machine. So I weighed my options, staring out the window at the driveway I'd only stepped on three times. I didn't want to venture out. I told myself I could hold out another day. Bullshit. My blood sugar levels dove; my vision blurred and my breathing slowed and my stomach turned. Rational thinking and desperation beat my stubbornness. I needed my damn insulin. I figured I could handle it. I was up for the challenge.

When I stepped outside, rain hit my face for the first time in twelve years. It felt good, but I worried about pneumonia. I pulled my hood over my head and walked. My back and legs hurt like a bitch, and my feet kept slipping out of my slippers. I must have been worth a good laugh to the drivers speeding by. A seventy-year-old man in a hooded sweatshirt, oversized khakis, and slippers, shuffling along like I could tip at any moment. What the fuck was I thinking?

By some miracle I made it to the pharmacy. I stepped in the wobbly line of fuzzy people with soft faces. I judged my chances of reaching the register at about forty percent.

Those odds didn't work in my favor. My legs buckled. I tried to use an M&M display to keep my balance, grasping at the yellow character's eyes, but the cardboard collapsed under my weight. I fell to the ground. The dozen or so people in the store jumped to attention. A few crowded around me, two knelt down beside me, and one told me to stay put. All their voices and movements and thoughts and lives swirled in my head.

The lady with the green dress pulled her child closer. His name was Phillip. He thought I looked like his grandfather, who had died during a triple bypass surgery ten months earlier. I suppose I did.

A teenager named Zach Miller used the chaos to his advantage, hurrying out of the store with two boxes of condoms beneath his shirt. He hoped to use them that night at Tony Nickelby's party, with a girl named Samantha Freeman with whom he'd had a crush on since the sixth grade.

The pharmacist cleared the crowd away from me. He told me to breathe, as if I didn't know that's a good way to stay alive. He took off his white lab coat and bunched it into a ball to place beneath my head. I tried to yell, to tell him to stay away, but I was too late. As his hand touched the back of my head, a surge rushed through me. I saw his life. All of it. In a split second I knew things about Michael Vincy that he had long forgotten. I saw his children. His wife. The college freshman he fucked every Thursday night after her economics class, at the cost of stolen Vicodin and Adderall.

My tired body couldn't handle the sensation overload. Pressure built in my chest. I recognized the feeling from a lifetime ago, when I had watched an elderly lady in a park drop dead of a heart attack. I remembered sharing her panic and feeling the knot under her ribcage grow until it brought both of us to our knees. Now I had a heart attack of my own. I reached for the sky. The pharmacist grabbed my wrists and pushed them down. He fought to keep me still. My heart seemed seconds from exploding. I gasped for air.

Tim Fitzgerald, a paranoid Iraq veteran who had been at the front of the line, clutched his chest. He looked around, mouth and eyes wide, wanting someone to notice. No one did. They were all busy worrying about me. He sat on the ground and rocked back and forth, trying to calm himself and get air into his lungs.

Lindsey Tripp, a regretfully childless chair of a nonprofit retirement home, felt it next.

And the little boy, Phillip.

Then his mother.

Then Michael Vincy.

○ ○ ○

I woke up in a hospital bed, full of tubes. Police officers surrounded me. One had a pad open, ready for a statement. He said that aside from me, seven people suffered a heart attack in that pharmacy. Four died, including Phillip. His mother survived.

That's why I don't leave my house.

I wasn't always like this. At the start of my story, I had no story to tell. A boring, unemployed web developer – that was Will Deslar. I couldn't hear the supermarket cashier call his customers douche bags, assholes, and fucktards. I couldn't get sick if the man two tables away from me in a restaurant had an allergic reaction, and he couldn't sneeze because of a tickle in my nose. I didn't absorb conversations from two apartments over, I never found myself swept away in another person's daydream, and I never saw myself through foreign eyes. I could leave my house and no one would die.

Then my wife hit me with a baseball bat.

TWO

Julie paced. She bit her upper lip. She slipped her hands into her pockets, then out again, then through her hair, then back into her pockets. She peered through the rear door of The Perfect Cut for the third time in two minutes. All those signs, yet I suspected nothing. In defense of my disregard, my wife had understandable cause for anxiety. We were minutes from robbing a jewelry store, and although that may have factored into her nervous tics, the main cause was this:

She knew what I had coming to me.

"Where the fuck's Lincoln?" I said, once again glancing at the green light on her CB radio. "He was supposed to call us five minutes ago. I'll give him two more minutes, then I'm done with this."

"There you go again," she said, turning away for a fourth glance into the store.

"What's that supposed to mean?"

She faced me, annoyed. "It means I get it, Will. You don't want to be here. You're pissed. You've made that perfectly clear from the start. But guess what – we're here and we're doing this, so suck it the fuck up." The rare vitriol lingered from an explosion between us the night before.

So much for, "I'll never mention it," I thought, but said, "You're right, Julie. I *am* pissed. For Christ's sake, we're not criminals."

"I've heard this spiel a million times," she said, holding her palm up to stop me. "You can only pull the 'responsible adults' card so many times. When are you going to realize that we're *broke* adults? With a kid. You think I'm doing this for fucking entertainment? I'm doing it for Marcus."

We froze as a car approached the front of the store. The sound was unexpected; night made that area of Mansfield, Massachusetts silent. My mind jumped to the worst-case scenario: cops. *Where do we go if they come around back?* Julie and I looked at each other wide-eyed as the sound of rubber on potholed pavement grew closer. The faint bass of a rap song put us at ease.

When the vehicle passed, I exhaled and turned to Julie. "I'll tell you one thing – when this is over, I never want to see Lincoln again. You understand me?"

"Don't talk to me like you're some kind of authority figure," she said, stepping toward me. "And don't put this on Lincoln. You're a grown man. You made a decision. All I've heard from you is a bunch of bitching about being dragged into this, but you haven't offered shit for an alternative. I waited for you to get another job, Will. I couldn't wait forever."

"I knew you'd fire that shot," I said, then threw my hands up in surrender. "You're right again! It's my fault we've sunk to this level. You win." I turned away from her. "I don't know why I'm even arguing anymore. Who needs morals, right? Not the fucking Deslars."

"Morals don't pay the bills. They don't put food in my child's mouth. This" – she pointed at the store – "is our last resort." The CB radio on her hip chirped before she could continue.

Lincoln's voice crackled through. "The alarm's down. You have five minutes."

Easy to say from the safety of your Lexus, asshole.

Julie brought the radio to her mouth and pressed the button on its side. "Got it. We're going in now."

I sighed and pulled a two-foot-long miniature baseball bat from my belt. The light wood felt heavy. I watched Julie retrieve her own, and doubted that it weighed as much to her.

My own face met me at the glass door. The combined effects of my sweatshirt hood, the cap underneath it, and my weapon masked my usual innocent appearance. The look irked me. The strange face told me to walk away, to keep my clean conscience.

No. Your family needs this. Marcus needs it. Stalling won't make the leap any easier. Do it, dammit.

I listened for vehicles, and when I heard only silence, I swung the bat. With that, the strange face shattered. I cringed as glass sprinkled the ground.

Julie reached in, unlocked the door, and went straight to work. Her first priority was, as I had predicted, a necklace that she had fallen in love with during our reconnaissance visit. She had talked about it for weeks, and I could almost see her mouth water every time she did. Her excitement powered the swing that smashed her prize's case.

I headed for a display that held engagement rings. Our bats broke glass with an unplanned synchronicity that would've given the impression of experience. I shoveled rings mixed with glass shards into my canvas bag, thankful for the leather gloves Julie had thought to buy. I skipped over the chains and earrings in favor of bracelets. A black velvet pedestal made the stones on top of it fight for my attention. I demolished the carefully arranged display and swept them all into my bag.

I couldn't fight the exhilaration. I tried, but each handful equalled weeks, months, or even years of programming at a desk. Then the thrill withered to shame. Rings represented meals I couldn't provide. Every bracelet reminded me of missing paychecks. Case after case taunted my shortcomings, and each swing built up my resentment toward myself. I stopped, exhausted and satisfied with the contents of my bag, and looked at Julie's. It bulged like a child's on Halloween.

"We should leave," I said as she hammered another case. She didn't hear me. "Let's get outta here," I said louder.

"Can't yet." She brushed the contents of the case into her bag and turned to me. "We didn't get the safe."

"Fuck the safe," I said. "I want out of this place."

"We can't go back to Lincoln without those diamonds." She looked at her watch. "We still have three minutes."

"God-fucking-dammit, Julie."

"The quicker we do this, the sooner we leave." She reached into the pocket of her sweatshirt and pulled out a plastic bag. It held a peach-sized ball of green putty and three fuses. She didn't wait for my consent before disappearing into the pitch-black back room. I heard her fingernails tap the wall, feeling for a switch. The room lit up when she found one.

When I caught up to her in the office, she already had the blob of plastic explosive out of the bag. She pressed it to the hinged side of the four-foot-square safe's door, making sure to force some into the creases like Lincoln had instructed. I fidgeted with my bag and looked around the office while she twisted two of the fuses together and stabbed the putty.

"Lighter," she said with her hand out.

"You have it," I said.

She reached inside her sweatshirt pockets and rose in a panic. "Please tell me…" She patted her pants and nodded in relief. "Thank God." She knelt back down and held the lighter's flame to the tip of the twisted wick. The end sizzled and threw sparks. She stood and hurried back to the front of the store, hitting the light switch as she passed me. "Come on. You wanna lose an eye?"

I followed her and turned back around when I reached safety. In the darkness of the office, the sparks bounced flickers of light off the walls. I heard the hiss, and the longer it continued, the faster my heart pounded. The fuse ran out, and a deafening boom lit up the room with an intense orange glow that immediately died behind smoke, dust, and darkness. My ears rang. My eyes struggled to see through the afterimage of the blast. I coughed.

Then something struck the back of my skull.

The impact rippled through my body as I landed face-first on the razor-lined floor. A sharp shock ricocheted through my head, like my brain had short-circuited. The pain weakened and slowed until it stopped just behind my eyes, where it fizzled out. When I thought I'd pulled through, another shock hit, stronger than the last. I pressed my head to the ground and shut my eyes as I waited for the internal lightning storm to fade.

When it did, I opened my eyes to find that the ground was no longer in front of me. The picture no longer came from my own vision. I hovered above my body, watching myself writhe on the ground. I remember thinking I was experiencing one of those out-of-body experiences coma patients talk about.

I wasn't.

An arm entered the frame. The wrist at the end of it wore Julie's watch. The hand beyond clutched her miniature baseball bat. The bat rose, then came down on my head.

I woke to the sound of stomps and sirens and the bright shine of flashlights all around me. I looked, with my own eyes, at my hand on the ground in front of me. Blood flowed from dozens of small cuts. Red streaks curled around my fingers and forearm. I tried not to envision what my face looked like as I pulled my cheek from the shards. Voices yelled at me, and after a few dazed seconds, I realized that they came from police.

I never imagined I'd ever feel the cold metal of handcuffs on my wrists. "I'm a decent man," I wanted to yell at the officers. "A husband, a father, a college graduate. An honest person." But I didn't. It wouldn't matter – they would never see me as any of those things. I had secured my status as scum.

With the cuffs locked, four hands grabbed me and yanked me from the ground. My shoulder popped. They underestimated my weakness and gave me no support when I reached my feet. I dropped hard, startling them all in the process. They swore as they cut themselves in the shuffle of lifting me back up.

Fresh air hit my face. Blue lights blinded me. Dozens of voices talked at once. I was relieved when the cruiser's door slammed, isolating me from the chaos. I counted how many had responded to the call. Twelve units, just for me. I wasn't in the mood to laugh, but I recognized the humor in it. They had brought a pack of wolves to catch an ant.

THREE

"Welcome."

The chubby, baby-faced correctional officer made a grand, sweeping gesture with his arm, as if introducing me to my new mansion. He (Bruce) had been friendly enough, but still exuded an intentional vibe of superiority. I assumed he revised that attitude around more intimidating prisoners.

I stepped into the tiny space. The dry air made my throat raspy. I coughed as I looked around. Solid gray concrete made up all six sides of the box. A bunk bed with a metal frame stood tall in the corner, feet away from a toilet with a sink built into the tank. *Fantastic.* Two rusty, steel-wire shelves jutted out from the wall. One held a couple books, a toothbrush, and two pictures. One picture showed young, twin girls hugging a Disney Pluto mascot. The other showed an infant boy in a crib. The second shelf was bare, waiting for my belongings.

The cube would serve as my home, at least until my trial. I planned to plead guilty. No point in fighting the charges. Police found me lying in a ransacked jewelry store. No bullshit story would sway a jury. I told the police everything I knew. They searched my house and found no trace of Julie or Marcus. Same with Lincoln's two properties. Julie's mother Maureen, who had been babysitting Marcus during the robbery, told the cops that Julie had come home early that night and rushed out of the house with him. She had no more information. The interrogator told me that an AMBER Alert would be issued.

Bruce flipped through his chart. "Let's see. Your cellmate is…" He ran his finger down the list until he found my cell number. "Benjamin Short. Lucky you."

An inmate appeared behind him and leaned on the bars to the cell. The man seemed disturbed, but looked too frail to be dangerous. He was at least 70, with purple veins covering every inch of bare skin.

Bruce noticed my unease and chuckled. "Good news – that ain't Benjamin Short. That's just" – he put his hand over his mouth and hacked up a mean cough – "that's just Crazy Dave." He turned to the man. "Go on now, Dave, there ain't nothing here for you. The new guy ain't looking to hang out with nutballs." Dave didn't seem to comprehend a word, but he stumbled away regardless. Bruce turned back to me. "Short's probably downstairs playing chess. Go ahead and get acquainted with the place." Then he left.

I slumped onto the bottom bunk. *Julie and Lincoln would laugh for days if they saw me now*, I thought. I pictured them sifting through diamond rings and bracelets, talking about all the things they would buy with their new fortune. I saw Marcus beside them, asking when I'd be back. *He must be a confused mess.* Before I got laid off, Marcus would wait for me at the door before I got home. At five o'clock he'd drive Julie crazy, darting back and forth between her and the window overlooking the driveway. *What's she telling him now?* The thought of never seeing him again sent tears to my eyes. I wiped them. *You have to stay stone-faced. No weakness. Not in here.* The tears ignored my command.

A deep voice startled me. "You're up top."

I looked to the door of the cell and saw a black man in the same gray jumpsuit I wore. He was large. Not fat, but built. Tall. About thirty-five years old, forty at most.

"Huh?"

He stepped into the cell. "Bottom bunk is mine, you got the…" His words trailed off when he saw me wipe the salty water from my face. "Shit. Five minutes in this place, and you're already crying?"

"Sorry," I said. I don't know why I apologized.

"Don't be sorry," he said, waving me off. There was sympathy in his voice. I hadn't expected to hear that for a long time. He sat on the bed beside me. "Most won't admit it, but everybody has one real good cry the first time they get thrown in here. Most wait longer than five minutes, maybe do it at night." He shrugged. "But hey, to each his own."

I rubbed my face on my shoulder. "You're Benjamin?"

He put his hand out. "Benny."

I shook it. "Will Deslar."

"You got lucky, brother. I'm just about the best cellmate you could hope for."

I had no trouble believing it. "Good to know. So why are you in here?"

He laughed, exaggerating a bit to show how ridiculous the question was. "Lesson one: don't go around asking people why they're in here. They don't like that. No one wants to be identified by something they're trying to get past."

"Sorry."

"Lesson two: stop apologizing to me. I ain't gonna bite. There's plenty of things to worry about in this place, but I'm not one of them. Unless you fuck with me, of course." He grinned. "I'm obligated to add that last part. Comes with the territory."

I did my best to humor him with a smirk. "And lesson three?"

"Haven't made it up yet. Don't you worry, though – I'll think of something."

○   ○   ○

That first week kept me deep in the dark. My mood grew cold

to match everything around me: the air, the concrete walls, the metal bars, the stares, the routine. Each day held less promise than the one before. I hadn't just lost my freedom; my life disappeared with it. Julie and Marcus were all I had. Dead parents. No siblings. The few aunts and cousins I knew meant little to me, and I meant less to them. I was alone. Rotting.

They deserve to rot with me, I thought, every time Julie and Lincoln invaded my peace. I hated them – less for what they did to me than for what they did to Marcus. They snatched him from a normal life, forced him to spend his childhood on the run. *How could you do it, Julie? No amount of luxury is worth that sacrifice.*

The unrelenting mental venom wore me down, and my depression worsened. Four days in, I snuck a towel back to my cell and stashed it under my mattress. I did the same the next day, and the next. I collected five of them, hoping that I would work up the nerve to knot them all together, tie them around my throat, and end myself.

Benny didn't see me collecting my noose, but he saw my pain. He kept telling me that I would adjust, that I would feel better. I didn't. I only descended further. I slept the majority of each day, and when I did leave my cave, I did so on a mission for another towel.

The nerve I needed arrived on the seventh day. I sat alone in the cell, at the edge of my bed. My mind tore into itself. *You deserve this. Every fucking bit of it. You failed Marcus. And by the time you get out, he won't even remember your face. You let that happen, you sorry fuck.*

An argument outside broke my self-flagellation. Two assholes fighting over whether to watch Maury or Jerry Springer, most likely. The clapping of shoes announced the arrival of the guards. I heard a swear-laced scuffle. Six or seven inmates leaned over the railing, trying to get a view of the action below. I didn't care to join them.

I slid off the bed and lifted my mattress. Underneath I found only the bare metal frame. My collection had disappeared. I spun in the cell, confused and enraged.

"I took them," Benny said, appearing at the cell's entrance.

"You had no right," I said through clenched teeth.

He countered like a boxer. "And you do? You have the right to leave your boy without a father?"

I backed against the wall and dropped to the floor. I covered my face with my hands. My fingers shook and tapped my cheek and forehead. I didn't know how to feel. My emotions crossed. Confusion, fear, anger, embarrassment, anxiety, hopelessness, pain, melancholy – they all simmered together under the surface.

"It's not getting better, Benny." I kept my head down as I spoke. "You said it would get better."

He closed the gap between us and squatted down to my level.

"I've been in here eight years now," he said, restating the answer to a question I had asked him days earlier. "I got twenty-two to go." When I didn't look at him, he rose and sat on the edge of his bed. "The reason I'm here…" He hesitated, debating with himself about whether or not to continue. "I killed someone. Someone real close to me." I raised my eyes. His forehead tightened. "I live with that guilt every day. Every fucking day, man. I know you're blaming yourself for all this. For where you're at. That's good, you *should* blame yourself." He leaned closer, put a hand on my shoulder, and squeezed lightly. "But you gotta follow the blame with forgiveness, brother. You think I've never considered leaving here with a rope and a step stool? Shit, there must be at least a dozen sad motherfuckers in this place thinking about it as we speak. Some will do it eventually. Most won't. *I* won't. And you know why?"

I shook my head.

"'Cause in twenty-two years I'll be free, and this will be a memory. What kinda time you looking at? Six years? Seven if the judge has a stick up his ass? Most guys in here would kill for that bid." He stood and extended a hand down to me. I took it and let him pull me from the floor. "Lay down for a while. Think of your son and what you're gonna do to make things right when you get out. Do I need to sit here and watch you?"

"No," I said. "I'll be fine."

He flashed a wide smile. "That's what I like to hear. Listen, I'll be playing chess with the boys." He turned and pointed down to the opposite side of the first floor. "Right down there. If you need anything – anything at all – come down and get me. I mean it."

That was the first time Benny saved my life.

FOUR

This is how Julie introduced herself:

"Hi everybody. My name's Julie, and, um… I'm a shopping addict."

The Shopaholics Anonymous group met in a church basement twice a week. The circle of 16 people huddled under the watchful eyes of a hundred Jesuses, Marys, and Holy Ghosts. I sat among them, sipping my stale coffee, glad to not need their services. I listened as a mother talked of an urge so strong it made a Gucci purse come before her teenage son's football dues. A poker addict who had missed his Gamblers Anonymous meeting spoke of his six-digit debt and the constant need to fear every shadow he passed. After the fourth or fifth addict, the stories began to follow a template (maxed-out cards, depression, naïve family).

Then Julie's turn came. She wore a generic gray sweatshirt, zipped up with the hood on, like she wanted the "Anonymous" part to be literal. Dark strands of hair escaped the sides of her hood and rested on her chest. She fiddled with them as she told her vague, edited story. I didn't pay much attention to her words, too distracted by her face. I spent her five-minute speech plotting how to approach her afterward.

I never got the chance to put my plan into effect, however. When the fifteen-minute break came, she took on the task.

"Hey," she said, lighting a cigarette as I approached her with my opening line.

I looked behind me.

She laughed. "No, you. Are you gonna speak? To the group, I mean. "

"Oh, no. I'm not, uh… I'm not a shopaholic."

She pointed the tip of her cigarette at me. "Denial's the first roadblock."

"No, really," I said. "I'm a web developer. My company is building your group a new website."

"This isn't really *my* group," she said. "It's actually my first time with this one."

"OK, we're building *this* group a new website. I'm here to learn the audience. The designer should be here too, but he's probably at home drinking beer and playing video games."

"How exactly does a volunteer church group pay a web development company? Through indulgences?" She laughed at her own joke.

"It's pro bono, actually."

"That's noble" she said, taking a puff.

"It's just my boss's way of sleeping better. I'm Will, by the way."

"Julie," she said, exhaling smoke through her nose.

"So tell me, Julie – how is SA working for you?"

She stepped backward into the church's dim parking lot lamp, then unzipped her sweatshirt.

That was easy, I thought, before I saw the purple shirt underneath. Its shimmer dulled everything else in the vicinity.

"This beauty was a hundred bucks," she said. She beat back my raised eyebrows with, "Yeah, I know – stupid. Just bought it today, so if the program's working, it needs to work better."

"At least you have good taste," I said.

She zipped up. "I'd like to think so."

A period of silence followed, during which I weighed the pros and cons of making a move. Everything about her raised a red flag, but I hadn't been laid in months, which is a powerful catalyst for bad judgment. I decided it couldn't hurt to try.

"So, what are you up to now? Wanna grab a drink?"

She bit her bottom lip. "I don't know…" She lifted the bottom of the sweatshirt, once again revealing the vice beneath. "I should really finish this meeting."

"Of course, of course," I said. "We could go afterward. You know, unless you're not interested. Which is fine, you know, if you're not. That's cool."

"Wow, you were doing so well up to that point." She smiled as she dropped the butt on the ground and killed it with a clap of her heel. "You know what, Will? I'd love to get a drink. You get points for even asking after hearing me talk at an SA meeting. That's commendable. Or dumb. Probably dumb."

"Or brilliant," I said. "You see, I figure a shopaholic will wanna pick up the tab."

Her smile encouraged me. She turned and walked back toward the church, then looked over her shoulder at me. "You coming back in?"

I did go back in. Then we went out for drinks. Then she spent the night.

FIVE

I woke, alone in my cell. Habit made me look for an alarm clock to tell me how long I'd been out. I found none, but guessed that it hadn't been more than two hours since Benny left me to rest. A chess piece tapped a board downstairs, and I assumed that he was near it.

I sat up, and as I did, I heard a crinkling noise. I looked at my lap and found a sheet of lined notebook paper, filled with a hand-written note. The penmanship looked like my own, but it couldn't be – I'd been sleeping, and beside that, something about it looked awkward, like someone had attempted to forge my handwriting. The pen strokes were sloppy, jotted in a hurry.

I picked up the paper and and read it.

I don't know where I am. Who I am. But I know you will Deslar. Ive seen you in my mind like you live inside it. No – it's like I'm in yours. We're in each others. I know what happened to you in that jewelry store. Youve been lying to yourself about what you experienced when she hit you when you saw yourself through her eyes.

It was no hallucination. And I know what you planned to do with those towels. Thank God Benny stopped you. Your death would mean my own.

Im sorry. This must be jarring but there's just so much to say. Ill back up.

I've been kidnapped. I'm writing this from a basement bedroom. The door is locked & barred from the other side. I dont know how I knew to write this message or how it reached you but I knew it would and it did. I can feel you reading these words as I scribble them. How? How can I feel that? Things are happening to me. Things I cant explain. You'll see.

Cant remember my life before this room. Been here 2 days I think. I havent seen any natural light to confirm. The walls are wood panelled, the floor is brown carpet. The room holds only a nightstand and a desk. And a bed too. And a single lightbulb hanging from a string in the middle of the ceiling. Does any of this sound familiar to you?

No. It doesn't. Fuck.

Maybe a description of myself will
o Normal height & weight
o Brown hair, 2-2.5 in long
o Normal amount of body hair
o No tattoos (unless on back)

And gashes. Partly-healed gashes all over my upper body. My chest. Neck. Face. Some are small, shallow. Others are deep into the muscle. What did my captor do to me?

Please tell me something sounds familiar to No. It means nothing to you.

I don't even have a name. I need a

ROBERT
You thought that just now. I heard it. Your grandfather's name. Ok. Robert will do for now. Hopefully my real name replaces it soon.

Ive yet to see my captors face. He's a male, I know that. He delivers food through a rectangular hole at the base of the door. Canned beans & vegetables. The room stinks. He hasnt emptied my bucket. Ive heard him talking, far away upstairs. Cant make out the words. And I think he has a son. I found crayons. And theres 2 sets of footsteps. One is heavy—the man. The other is made of short strides from a lighter body. A child, Will. In a house holding captives. Jesus Ch

Yes. Captives. Theres 2 of us. A woman occupies the next room. I hear her crying even now. You hear her too, dont you? Its awful. Ive tried to speak with her through the air vent that connects our rooms. Ive begged for any information anything about who she is who I am where we are. She's said nothing. She's afraid. I cant blame her. I'm afraid. I wonder if that monster cut her like he cut me.

Why are we here? What does he

Im I so lams ——

*Something happened something something
in my head it burns like*

*I saw something now something I didn't see
it I felt it like*

You shoot. He shoots. I drop.

I had am to stop now my head

You need to find me.

Your meant to find ——

I read the letter again. Then twice more. Each time I read faster, with more anger. *Benny,* I thought. *He's fucking with me at the one time in my life I can't handle it.*

I took the letter and charged out of the cell, down the white steel stairs. A dozen inmates sat in a semi-circle around the television, watching a Red Sox game. Six Muslims prayed on mats. The rapid clinking of my descent drew their attention. Benny and three others surrounded a chess board. Benny held his knight, about to make a move, when I slammed the letter in front of him. The pieces scattered, ending the game and startling the group.

"Whoa!" Benny said, backing his chair from the table.

His opponent shot up and grabbed me by the collar of my shirt. "We been playin' that game for an hour, you little cocksucker." His mouth housed a lonely pair of bottom teeth. A meth addict. The man was a caricature of a hillbilly cooking the stuff up in his basement. Thin, stringy hair. Skin that looked much older than he did. Odor beyond offensive. A speck of spit hit me in the eyebrow as he scolded me. "You got some balls comin' in here and fuckin' up our shit."

"Riley, stop," Benny said, standing up. He loosened Riley's grip on my shirt, but couldn't loosen the death stare. He pointed to the paper at the center of their game. "What the fuck is that? What's this about?"

"You tell me," I said, loud enough to gain more glances. Bloodthirsty inmates watched us from all angles, hoping for a fight. "Is this how you get your kicks? You just talked me out of…" I didn't want to make my business known. Benny knew the end of the sentence. "And for what? So you could prank me? To see if I'm gullible enough to take this shit seriously?"

"I have no clue what that is."

"Bullshit!"

"Hey!" A guard stroked his cuffs twenty feet away. "We got a problem, fellas?"

"We're good," Benny said to him, then returned his focus to me. "You're real fucking lucky I like you, Will. Anyone else in this place would rip you apart right now. If we're gonna continue this conversation, you better fix your tone."

His warning humbled me. "You're right. I'm sorry."

"Should knock the sumbitch out, Ben," Riley said, his nostrils flaring.

"Shut up," Benny shot back, then swiped the letter from the chess board. He grabbed my arm and led me away from the group. When we reached a wall, he pushed me against it and pressed the letter into my chest. "Now explain this to me. Like a civilized adult, please."

"I found it on my bed," I said, grabbing the paper before it fell. "It's a letter. A fucking joke that someone left while I was sleeping."

Benny snatched the paper back and skimmed through it. "This

is your handwriting."

"I didn't write it. I swear. I woke up and it was just… It mentions the towels, Benny, and what I told you about the robbery. Who wrote it if you or I didn't?"

He shook his head. "Walls have ears in here, brother. You're kidding yourself if you think I'm the only one who knows your story. Either you're writing letters to yourself in your sleep or—"

"I didn't write it."

He put up a hand to push back my protest. "Or someone's fucking with you."

"Forget it," I said. "Sorry I fucked up your game." I took the letter from his hands and retreated back to our cell.

SIX

Two months passed, and as Benny predicted, things did get easier. A few weeks in, I started to accept the prison as my new home. I left the cell on a regular basis; I socialized; I tried to live. I made a decision not to spend my incarcerated years in a mental stasis.

Literature helped the monotony. I read more in that stretch than I had in ten years of my previous life. The prison received its books from the public library when they became too old and tattered to continue loaning, or when they got donations that gave them too many copies. And since classics made up the majority of this selection, mostly because of childrens' summer reading lists I imagine, we had a rich collection. While most inmates fought over the few coveted Tom Clancy or Stephen King novels, I found myself gravitating toward Tolstoy and Kafka.

I made acquaintances playing cards and bullshitting with the more even-tempered guys, but I kept most at arm's length. The middle-class biased part of me found difficulty getting close to admitted drug dealers and gang members. Benny was the only one I considered a friend, due mostly to the fact that he'd gained my trust and respect before telling me he had killed someone.

"Thinking about your boy?" he asked me one day in the cafeteria.

I sat across from him at a table with Riley and a quiet guy named Ross, who might as well have been invisible. "How'd you know?" I had to raise my voice to reach the other side of the table. Besides a concert or a night club, I've never known a louder place than a prison cafeteria. Dozens of conversations, led by a hundred and fifty alpha males, fought for dominance.

Benny held up a finger and made me wait while he swallowed his mashed potatoes. "You always get this dazed look in your face, like your mind's in Wonderland or something."

"It kills me, Benny. I feel so fucking helpless in here, not knowing if he's all right. I swirled the gravy and potatoes with my spork until they formed a tan blob in the center of my tray. "And of course, I can't think of him without thinking of them." I didn't need to elaborate. They all knew my story.

"If it were me," Riley said, mouth full, "I'd hire one of them private investigators." His rocky first impression of me had faded. I wouldn't call us buddies, but we got along well enough. "Then, when he found 'em, I'd make sure those motherfuckers pay for that shit."

"And you'd end up right back in here, dumbass," Benny said. Riley's reputation rested on shit-talking, so no one passed on an opportunity to reciprocate.

"Not if I did it right," Riley said. "Shit, you think Deslar ain't never thought about it?" He looked at me. "Tell me you ain't never thought about gettin' even."

"Oh, I think about it every day. But it's never gonna happen. Chances are I'll get out of here and live the rest of my life wondering where they are." I looked down. "Wondering what happened to Marcus."

"Keep faith," Benny said. "It ain't easy for fugitives these days. They'll get careless. The cops'll catch up to them."

"That's what I'm counting on."

"Shit," Riley said, "first thing I'm doin' when I get outta here is findin' that bitch Nicole. I ever tell you that story, Deslar?"

I thought about lying to save myself from the guaranteed torna-do of bullshit that would follow, but I shook my head.

That pleased him. "Benny knows it, but he don't mind listenin' again. See, I sold dope 'fore I got thrown in this shit hole."

"Baddest dope dealer this side of the Mississippi!" Benny an-nounced with fake enthusiasm.

"Fuckin' right, I was."

"When you say dope," I said, "you mean…"

"Crystal, man. And mine was the best shit you ever seen." (I'd never seen any. Still haven't.) "My girl at the time – excuse me, my *bitch* at the time – tells me a friend of hers is lookin' for some shit in bulk. I don't remember numbers, but enough to make dollar signs flash in my fuckin' eyes, you know what I mean?" He laughed and looked to us for confirmation. We humored him. "You know what she had me walkin' straight into?"

"Cops?" I said.

"Even worse. Six feds waiting for me when I pulled up. I tried to hightail it outta there, but the faggots got me. Ya see, that bitch got caught sellin' my stuff a week earlier. Turns out she gave my ass up to save her own hide. Fuckin' cunt, let me tell ya. Can't wait to get outta here and give that bitch what she deser—"

A tap on Riley's shoulder stopped him mid-sentence.

He turned and looked up, agitated and ready to chew the head off of whoever had the balls to cut into his story. His attitude changed in an instant when he saw the perpetrator. The saturation drained from his face as he almost choked on saliva.

Behind him, a prisoner I'd never seen loomed over him like a king would stand above a leper. His weathered face put him in his sev-enties, but he stood like a man who welcomed anyone to fuck with him. Solid, confident, and calm. Everyone in the vicinity seemed to know something I didn't, and they all hushed to hear what the old guy had to say.

"Uh…" Riley tried to speak, but failed.

The man crossed his arms. "All out of words?"

Silence.

"Funny," he continued. "You had no shortage a few seconds ago. Here I am, trying to eat my dinner in peace, only to have my ears violated with your profanity-filled jabbering. Tell me something – do you know how many times you swore in the past two minutes?"

Riley cleared his throat. "No, Mr. Angeletti, I don't." That name sounded familiar.

"Seventeen times if you count 'bitch,' 'ass,' and 'faggot' – which I do. You kiss your mother with that mouth?" He gave Riley no opportunity to answer. "You know what that kind of talk does?" He gestured to the gathered audience. "It lets everyone around you know just how stupid you are. Are you stupid?"

"No, sir."

"Judging from what little I've heard come out of your yapper, I would have thought the exact opposite. Is that the kind of impression you want to make on people?"

"No, sir."

"Of course not. Now, do I have to worry about another dinner being spoiled by your ignorant, simple-minded drivel?"

"No, sir."

"Fantastic."

He smiled, patted Riley on the shoulder, and walked out of the cafeteria, but not before making eye contact with me. Something in his expression hinted at a hidden amusement, like he would double over with laughter the second he left the room. When he turned the corner, the crowd erupted into a mass heckling.

"Yeah, yeah," Riley said, fending off the horde of jokes. "Keep laughin', fuckers. Y'all actin' like you woulda done a damn thing different." This only brought a stronger eruption.

"Who was that guy?" I asked through the teasing. Everyone stopped and looked at me as if I had asked the silliest question imaginable. I looked to Benny for clarification. "What?"

"That's Franco Angeletti," he said. "Just got here yesterday. How the hell haven't you heard about him?"

I shrugged. "I don't know, I guess I've been reading in the cell a lot the past couple of days. Sounds familiar, though. Who is he?"

"He's a lieutenant in the Detroit mafia. He was hiding out in Boston for a year or so before he got snatched up."

"OK, yeah. I've seen him on the news."

"That man's straight nuts," Riley said. *Here come the stories.* "Nick, my buddy from cell one-two-one, told me Angeletti cut a guy's tongue out just 'cause he cooked his pizza wrong."

"Your intelligence knows no bottom," Benny said. The few men still paying attention laughed.

Ross spoke up for the first time that day. "I heard that story too. Of course, I got the brains to know it's nonsense."

Riley gave Ross the finger, then swung it around to the rest of us. "Fuck y'all. I'm tellin' ya, Nick's from Boston. He knows this shit. He told me some asshole who owed Angeletti money couldn't pay up, and cops found him hanging naked from the Zakim for all the mornin' traffic to see. Ask anyone in Boston, man. I'm tellin' ya."

I laughed more. "You really are a gullible son-of-a-bitch."

"If you're so sure, I dare you to say some shit to Angeletti. Bet you won't, you sissy motherfucker."

I pointed at him. "I dare *you* to drop a few more F-bombs tomorrow while he's in here eating."

"Hell no," he said, and chuckled. "Shit, rush hour traffic would look up and see *my* white ass hangin' over them."

SEVEN

On my 95th morning as Prisoner 16238415, the sky fell.

Benny and I sat in his bunk playing rummy. This was the norm for the early hours, since we both woke before eight o'clock, and the cells didn't open until ten. More often than not, I woke first and made it through a dozen or two pages of whatever escape I happened to be enjoying at the time. That morning, I polished off *The Sun Also Rises* before our daily card game.

"So, what exactly does a web developer do?" Benny said, putting down a nine-through-king straight. He wrestled with a decision, then discarded a jack.

"We build websites," I said. I drew an eight, added it to his straight, then discarded a six.

"I know that," he said, as he took my six and put it down with two of his own. "But how do you build a website?"

I laughed. "Seriously, Ben? You don't even know what Facebook is. I'm not about to explain HTML and PHP to you." As he discarded, leaving only one card in his hand, I added, "I never asked you what you did for work. Why hasn't that ever come up?"

"I installed hardwood floors," he said. "And went to school at night."

"No shit. What did you study?"

"Culinary arts. Spent a year at Johnson and Wales before this."

"Good for you, man. Must've been a bitch to go back to school at what – 26? 27?

"I was 26," he said. "Yeah, but it had to be done. My back would've been destroyed by 50 if I kept on flooring. And I wanted more for my kids."

I put down three sevens. "I didn't even know you cooked. I assume your aunt taught you?"

"Yeah, she gave me a good head-start. You know, I used to cook right here in this cell."

"How the hell did you pull that off?" I said.

"Well, this was before they tightened up the rules a couple years back. I used to—"

A distant tremor killed his story.

I placed my cards face-down on the mattress. "What the fuck?"

Another tremor hit. Someone fell in a nearby cell.

Benny jumped up, scattering the cards in the process, and pressed himself to the cell door. He grabbed the metal bars and tugged in blind panic. His head darted back and forth, desperate for a glimpse at the cause of the disturbance. He muttered something too low to hear.

I stood and approached him with care. "Ben?"

"We're gonna die in here," he said without stopping his hectic scan of the area.

"What are you talking about? Nothing's gonna happen to us." This new side of Benny astonished me. I felt like a child who had just realized his father wasn't a superhero.

The cell block hummed with curiosity. Most of the men kept their cool. A few, Benny included, trembled like dogs during a thunderstorm. I put my hand on his shoulder. "Breathe, Ben." As I tried to comfort him, his terror seemed to seep into me. My heartbeat quickened. Breathing became a voluntary action.

Another rumble hit, more violent than the others. It finished with an ear-splitting crack. A switch flipped inside of me. I no longer felt that I held the reins of my own mind. My calm disappeared, replaced by Benny's deep certainty of death. I held on to the bars to keep steady as spots dotted my vision. I fought through the panic attack with the realization that the next tremor could push us both over the edge.

When my eyesight recuperated, I saw that every cell mirrored ours. Every prisoner, without exception, pressed themselves against the bars as if they could push through them like dough. The officers didn't seem to fare much better, but the ability to run if the need came kept them from falling apart.

Baby-faced Bruce pulled together his wits and took center stage. He climbed onto a table on the first floor, where most of us could see him. I knew what he thought when he looked around at his audience: *Thank God it's not past ten o'clock*. He clapped his hands for silence. We obeyed. At any other time, the crowd would have ignored him at best, but not that morning. We needed something to ease our fears. Anything.

"Remain calm, people," Bruce said. "Panic ain't helping." He cleared his throat before continuing. "There's nothing to worry about."

"How the fuck you know that?"

All eyes found the tattoo-covered kid responsible for the outburst. A short-lived roar of agreement followed, but died on account of the majority wanting to hear Bruce's answer.

"It's just a small quake or something," he said. "This building's more than strong enough to handle it."

"I grew up here," I said to Benny. "Quakes are rare, and when they hit, you can barely—"

A deep crushing sound interrupted me.

It's coming from F-Block.

"That's coming from F-Block," Benny said.

This one didn't stop; it had us in its sights, and intensified as it closed in. Everyone fell silent and waited, fixated on the direction of its origin. The anticipation made my chest ache. Every breath needed concentration. Beside me, Benny held his chest and fought for air.

When the sound seemed to be on top of us, it stopped, giving a second of false promise. Then the corner of the ceiling crumbled. Cracks spread like vines or veins toward the center of the room. Bruce, who could no longer speak of our safety, watched in awe as the tendrils carved the concrete roof.

Then sunlight hit our cell block.

Concrete rained on it.

The first slab to fall crushed Bruce and his table. Dust and debris exploded from where he stood. The thick cloud smothered the light as it filled the air. The roof continued to plummet through it. Prisoners yelled. Concrete crumbled upon impact. Guards ran frantic, without a clue of what to do.

On the other side of the cell block, Riley's silhouette jumped and flailed. I heard his screams, even though the disaster unfolding between us should have overpowered them. He stopped and looked up. His arms dangled in defeat. *He hears something above him. A crack.* I heard it, too, as clear as if I had been there with him. A second later, dusty darkness took his place in the cell.

"I…" Benny rested his head against the bars. "I don't…"

"Are you OK? Benny?"

His muscles gave up all at once, and his body fell to the floor. I yelled for help, but my plea drowned in the sea of others. I knelt and put a hand on his chest. It rose and fell with his heartbeat. *He's breathing. He just fainted from the excitement, that's all.* The thought, if said aloud, would have sounded more like a hope than a certainty. I pulled Benny to his bed and managed to wrestle him into it.

"Fuck, Benny, you're a heavy bastard." When I stood after the struggle, I noticed something strange: my calm had returned. My heart felt rested, my pulse slowed. I looked out at the dusty chaos with a level-headedness that seemed to fit me better than the fear that had preceded it.

The rain of rocks stopped like a bag of popcorn in the micro-wave, with longer and longer spans between each bang. Men prayed. Concrete settled. Guards swore as they called for paramedics.

With the damage assessed, prison officials told us that our block alone had suffered three deaths and nineteen injuries. In the entire prison: fourteen dead, one hundred and eight injured.

The catastrophy wasn't the result of an earthquake. Paul Winters, the warden, released a statement to the press explaining that an explosion in the east wing had started the collapse. The building's age, along with poor maintenance through the past few decades, had allowed the chain reaction that carried the damage to the rest of the prison. The cause of the explosion was under investigation.

"You had me worried," I said to Benny, hours after the event.

Outside, men rummaged through the rubble, hoping the casualty count wouldn't grow. The occasional gasp signaled when it did. I couldn't bring myself to risk looking out of the cell.

"I grew up with quakes in California," Benny said. "As a kid, I loved them. Thought they were cool. Then I grew up, became a dad." He turned over in his bunk. "See, quakes are usually harmless – some frames will fall, or a glass will slide off a table. But every once in a while there'd be one strong enough to take down a bookshelf. Maybe even trees. That's a scary fucking thing when you got babies crawling around. Those rumbles I used to get pumped about, man – they started giving me panic attacks. I haven't felt the ground shake like that since I came to the east coast. It fucked me up."

"I could tell," I said. "You good now?"

"Yeah, I'm cool."

"Good. What do you think they'll do with us?"

"Don't know," he said, looking out at the concrete wasteland, "but they sure as hell can't keep us here."

EIGHT

Officers woke us the next morning at dawn and divided us into groups for transportation to our new homes.

"Go figure," I said to Benny as we filed into a rickety blue school bus, "just when I get comfortable here, the place falls apart at the seams."

"Look on the bright side, brother," he said. "At least we'll still be cellmates. They split up Peña and Martinez. They've lived together for four years."

"That ain't right."

"What *is* right in this fucking place?"

The temperature rose ten degrees as we stepped onto the bus. The scent of sweaty brutes already polluted the air inside. After I won the window seat from Benny in a rock-paper-scissors match, we sat and watched the rest of our group flood in, curious and hopeful about who would join us. We groaned at the sight of a few assholes we wished were going elsewhere, but rejoiced at the absence of some. Our luck evened out. I caught myself expecting to see Riley board. It stung a bit. The guy had been a prick and a damn fool, but his death left something missing.

By the time the bus neared its capacity, it fizzed with chatter. I wiped sweat from my forehead, and couldn't wait to catch some wind through the tiny slit in the window. As I looked out of it at a seagull digging in the dirt for something, all the background noise died. I looked up at the cause.

Franco Angeletti stood at the front of the bus, carrying his legendary status with him. I could see his satisfaction in the silence his arrival evoked. He was an enigma and he knew it. I wondered if he'd heard half of the rumors based on him.

He stabbed his own uncle over a poker game.

No bullshit?

No bullshit, guy.

He's worth a half a bil.

I don't doubt it.

I heard he owns a brothel. Has his pick of the girls whenever he feels like it.

Really?

Not anymore. Now that he's locked up, he's just surrounded by dicks all day.

He made his way toward the back with the perfect confidence he always wore. Four guards followed. They watched him as if no other prisoners were present. Angeletti had the choice of three seats, the third of which would place him across the aisle, beside Benny.

He passed the first seat, and as he approached the second, Benny and I held our breath. When he decided against it, we both looked down and exhaled.

You know that guido they found in the showers a week back? Trent, from 84? I hear Angeletti had one of the guards do it. No one knows what the kid did wrong.

No one?

No, he never even spoke a word to Angeletti.

You're full of shit.

No, I'm telling you, shit's real.

Get outta here.

Angeletti, knowing that all eyes targeted him, halted beside his seat and looked around. Heads turned and eyes dropped as his survey swept the prisoners. He smirked and sat.

The window seat had a new perk. Benny's large frame protruded halfway into the aisle, just inches from touching the guy. We kept our gaze straight ahead. So did Angeletti. The bus bucked forward into gear. Conversation reignited. Before long, everyone was talking. Everyone besides me, Benny, and Angeletti.

The silence that lingered in our our immediate area bothered the hell out of me. I wanted to break it, but my memory returned to Angeletti verbally destroying Riley in the cafeteria.

You're such a friggin' wuss, I told myself. *The guy's not gonna fuck with you for talking. Just don't talk like Riley talked.*

"Hey Benny, what's the first thing you'd do if you got free. I mean, like today. If something happened and you got out, what would you do?" I looked at him and inadvertently at Angeletti, who sported a knowing expression.

"You mean like I got pardoned or something?" Benny asked.

"Yeah, something like that. Or if you broke out. Whatever, man, it doesn't matter. What would you do?"

"It does matter. If I got pardoned, the first thing I'd do is go see my girls. If I broke out, I couldn't go running to the first place they'd look for me."

"Jesus," I said, throwing my hands up. "I can't even ask you a simple hypothetical question."

He flashed his signature gigantic smile. "If it's such a simple question, why don't you answer it?" He pointed an authoritative finger at me. "And if you say anything besides, 'I'd track down my son,' I'ma slap you."

"We've been over this. It's easier said than done." He rolled his eyes. "Don't give me that," I said. "I'm just being realistic. They could be anywhere. I wouldn't know where to begin."

"Your wife's got family, right?" he said. "That's where I'd start."

"I'm sorry to butt in, fellas," a voice said. My eyes panned an inch to the right, past Benny's face, bringing Angeletti into focus. "But I can't resist giving my two cents when a topic such as this arises." He stopped and waited for permission to go on. Benny and I froze for a few seconds, neither of us sure about how to proceed.

I swallowed, then spoke like a child addressing the boogeyman. "Uh, yeah. We'd like to hear it."

He leaned into the aisle like he had been thirsty for human interaction. "I knew you would. Look, there are plenty of people out there – and I may know one or two of 'em – who can find anybody in the world. What happened to your son? If you don't mind me asking, of course."

I didn't see a choice but to tell him. I spoke in short, timid bursts at first, but found my stride when I noticed his genuine interest. I told him about my recent history, starting with my layoff and ending at the present. I told him about Marcus. About how I might never see him again. Angeletti made a perfect audience, hanging onto every word, never breaking eye contact. Speaking to him was strange; you hear so many stories about a person like that, and you forget that the myth is just a human.

When I finished my story, he beamed like a man with a revelation. He leaned in further and said, "Do you believe in fate, kid?"

I hadn't expected my story to draw that response. It took me a few seconds to get on the same page. "Fate? It's, uh… It's a little too magical for my taste."

"Well," he continued, "I believe in it. Very much so. Do me a favor…" He motioned for me to tell him my name.

"Will. Will Deslar."

"Do me a favor, Will. Promise me that an hour from now, you'll rethink your stance on fate."

"With all due respect, Mr. Angeletti—"

"Franco."

"Franco. In an hour I'll be in a box with Benny, hoping he doesn't change his no-rape policy." Angeletti chuckled, startling everyone around him. Benny shook his head and smiled.

"We'll see," Angeletti said when he stopped laughing. Then, in a hushed voice that we could barely hear over the many other conversations, he added, "But if anything should happen, keep close to me. Both of you." With that, he smiled, straightened up, and sat forward.

Benny and I looked at each other and thought the same thing: *Oh, fuck.*

The bus continued along without incident. Anxiety trickled into me. Our caravan, which consisted of two busses and three squad cars, turned off of the highway. A red light waited for us at the end of the ramp. The group stopped. I turned to Angeletti for a sign or a hint. His lips were tight, holding back a smirk. *It won't be long.* His excitement was contagious. Anxiety became anticipation. I had trouble keeping the corners of my own lips from curling up. Benny saw it in me. He wanted to be appalled, worried even, but he felt it too. The light turned green. The line of vehicles took a left, then a right onto a narrow road walled with woods.

"Watch the driver," Angeletti instructed, like a narrator on a theme park ride. "This is where the fun starts."

My gaze arrived at the white-haired driver just in time to see his head jerk to the right and spray blood on the windshield. His body slumped, held only by his seat belt. Prisoners erupted. The guards fought to keep them contained. The bus came to a gradual stop on the shoulder of the road. By then, the prisoners owned it.

"Holy shit," I said.

Benny sat silent beside me, taking the scene in. Angeletti stood like nothing happened, like he was an ordinary bus rider getting off at his stop.

The rear bus collided with us. Even at no more than five miles an hour, the impact knocked most people over. The driver of that bus mirrored ours. A deafening explosion roared behind us. Everyone turned in unison to see the two rear cruisers engulfed in pillars of fire.

"Let's go," Angeletti said. "Quick. And keep close." He threw people aside as he moved toward the back emergency exit. Benny and I followed, forging our own path as Angeletti's closed behind him. An elbow caught me in the chin, but I didn't stop to soak it in. Shots rang out everywhere, inside and outside of the bus.

We reached the open rear door and were greeted by three men. They helped Angeletti with the drop and began to move away.

"Get back here, you oafs!" he said to them. The men hurried back as we hopped down. "These two are with me. Watch their asses." He turned to one of them. "Ed – you got an extra weapon?"

The bald giant, who held an assault rifle in one hand like it was a pistol, reached into his leather jacket with the other. It emerged with a six-inch metal cylinder. Without warning, one side of the cylinder shot out, transforming it to a three-foot-long baton. He handed it to Angeletti.

"Give it to him," Angeletti said, motioning to me. I took it from Ed, surprised by its weight, then realized I didn't want it. Angeletti gestured to the treeline. "All right, let's get a move on." He and his men took off. Following them never occurred to me until Benny started.

He looked back and stopped. "Will?"

"I don't want to go," I said. "I want to finish my time. Get out legit, you know?"

His face dropped with disappointment, and he said, "I need to go. I just need to. I'd hate to part ways, but…"

"We're not parting ways," I said, surprised by my own answer. "Fuck. No, I'm coming." And so we hurried to catch up.

Officers and convicts ran around the street in a panic. Men lay still on the pavement, some dead, some surrendering. The six of us advanced in a line that snaked through the confusion toward the woods.

I fell to the back, with Ed's slick, shiny dome as my guide.

To my right, a group of men circled an officer like hyenas. I heard him scream for his life as they closed in, kicking from all angles. He fought with everything he had, but I knew he'd never leave that spot. *It'll be a miracle if any of the guards make it out alive,* I thought. The prisoners weren't going to pass up such a golden opportunity, which was an unjust tragedy in that the victims were only men pushing through another workday. *You can't help him. You can't help any of them. Keep moving.* I forced myself to look away from the feeding frenzy, back to my guide.

Then a violent burst sounded to my right. Ed's head opened up.

I couldn't stop from running into him. My face drove into the space between his shoulder blades. Both of us went down. I landed on top of him, my eyes inches from the soupy mess inside his skull. I screamed and rolled off. The boom of another shot ripped through my ears. Another of Angeletti's men dropped. I tucked my head to the ground, covered it with my arms, and waited. No more shots came.

Nearby, someone yelled, "Put the gun down and get the fuck on the ground!"

I peeked out from hiding, keeping my head guarded. Ten feet in front of me, Angeletti, his one remaining man, and Benny had their hands to the sky, opposite an officer with a shotgun.

"You fucking heard me!" the officer said, out of breath and panting. "Get on the ground!" He faced away from me, down on one knee, resting the shotgun on the other. The gun shook in his hands, even with the extra support. Angeletti saw me as he obeyed the officer's instructions.

I rose, not knowing why. Officers and convicts ran around me in a panic. Some men lay still in the grass. I couldn't tell if they were dead or surrendering. Shots popped. I should have stayed down, safe from stray bullets, but I stood.

Angeletti's eyes fixed on something near me. The officer yelled again at the three of them. I missed the words, too busy tracing Angeletti's sight to the baton in my grip. I knew what he wanted. *No way in hell I'm gonna hit a cop*, I thought. *Especially one with a shotgun.*

Then I heard a voice in my head.

Take this pig's head off. The words echoed in a familiar but distorted voice. *Take this pig's head off.* I couldn't concentrate enough to identify the speaker; the scene around me overpowered my attempts to decipher it. The words came in another wave, breaking through all the shots and screams and laughs and commands. *Take this pig's head off.*

This time I recognized the speaker. *Angeletti.*

I thought I might fall over. I looked at Benny. He focused on the ground in front of him, praying that a shaky finger wouldn't end his life. I looked at Angeletti. He focused on me, hoping that I would deliver him to freedom.

Angeletti nodded to me. *Take this pig's head off, kid. Just do that one little thing, and the most powerful man you ever met is gonna owe you a huge favor. A quick swing. Then it's over.*

I felt myself melt away.

Yeah, I thought. *One little swing.* Hitting him made so much sense now, and the contrary wasn't even worth consideration. I wasn't going to let some little cocksucking pig stand in the way of my freedom. My life.

Who the fuck do you think you are anyway, waving that shotgun around like you have the balls to use it? Do you know who the fuck you're dealing with?

An itch built up inside me, like swinging that baton meant the end of all my problems. The answer to everything. My one last obstacle. The officer continued screaming at my group. I took two steps forward, just as he rose from his knee, thinking he had the upper hand. *You haven't even looked behind you this whole time. Your negligence alone makes you deserve a good fucking whack to the skull.*

"Hey!"

He turned his torso. The shotgun trailed behind it. The long barrel proved useless in stopping me as I swung. His head caved upon impact. He fell hard, face down.

My anger toward the man dissipated as I looked down at him twitching in the grass. Benny gazed at me like a stranger. I dropped the baton and stepped back, horrified.

What did I just do?

NINE

I watched the violence of the prison break shrink behind us. Angeletti, Benny, and I sat in the backseat of an old Ford Explorer that didn't look like it would make it over the horizon. Vincent (the lone survivor of Angeletti's rescue team, who I now knew by name) drove, and a man named Theo occupied the passenger seat with no more life than a block of stone.

"I know what you're thinking," Angeletti said to me and Benny. "You were expecting something nice, like a Mercedes or an Audi, huh?" I gave a weak smile and nodded, too drained and confused to care about much. "It's best to keep a low profile, boys. It's tough to dodge the fuzz in something sharp. That's what this old tank's for. Don't you worry, though – I got some toys stashed away that you'd drool over." His casual tone seemed to ignore the real world; he spoke like we'd spent the last hour watching a football game.

Meanwhile, I feared for my insanity. *What happened back there?* I tried to sort out what I did, and why, but the event had already lost its clarity, like a dream I wouldn't remember in a day or two. *He might be dead. I may have killed an innocent man. A cop.*

Angeletti noticed my weariness. "Don't look so down, kid." He slapped my upper arm. "We're free."

I tried to match his calmness. "Just tired, that's all. It's been a crazy morning."

"It certainly has," he said as he cranked the window down an inch or two, letting in a refreshing cross-breeze. His head straightened as a thought struck him. "Jesus, where are my manners? I haven't even thanked you. I wouldn't be here if it wasn't for you." He tapped the passenger on the shoulder. "Hey Theo, you should've seen this kid. The way he clocked that pig…" He looked back at me. "I'm surprised you didn't take his head clear off."

Take this pig's head off, kid. Just do that one little thing, and the most powerful man you ever met is gonna owe you a huge favor. A quick swing. Then it's over.

The words stung as they charged through my head. I remembered the way Angeleti had looked at me. The way he looked at the baton in my hand.

He wanted me to do it. He told me to. He made me.
But how?

"You need anything, Will," Angeletti said, "you just ask. I owe you big, you hear me?"

I struggled through the buzzing in my mind, then replied, "You don't owe me a thing, sir."

"I told you – it's Franco. I never liked 'sir.' Too distant. Anyone who calls you 'sir' has no…" He kept talking, but I didn't listen. Reality seemed to jumble for a few moments before my senses regrouped. Angeletti was still going when I came back to the one-sided conversation. "You saved my ass back there, kid, and I'm gonna repay you one way or another. In fact, I'll start right now. We're on our way to a place with comfortable beds, food fit for a king, and a stocked bar. You too, Benny. You guys can take a load off and relax like free men do. Whaddya say?"

My mind worked overtime to find a polite way to decline the offer. I wanted to do the honest thing; I wanted to turn myself in. The riot had nothing to do with me, and no one could stick me with the attack on the officer. I didn't think I'd see a penalty if I returned right away. That logic aside, I had no interest in spending any more time with Franco Angeletti. I'd seen enough of what he was about.

"Forget it, you're coming," he said. "I'll spoil the two of you for a couple days while you figure out your next move."

Benny looked at me for the first time since I swung the baton. He hadn't slept the night before, too riled up from the collapse. He looked tired and eager to rest. He wanted to go, but he wouldn't go without me. I couldn't say no to him. I couldn't say no to Angeletti. Then the longing for a real bed pushed my already-tilting decision.

I gave in and nodded. *One day*, I told myself. *I'll find a police station first thing tomorrow.*

Angeletti smiled. "It's settled, then."

We drove an hour before pulling up to a large cabin at the end of a long dirt driveway. I know Eastern Massachusetts well, but by the time we reached our destination, I was lost, besides knowing we were near Randolph. Through the front window of the house, I saw a brute inside at full alert.

"Glad you're out, boss," the brute said when we walked in. He stood and extended his hand to Angeletti.

Angeletti gripped it. "Me too, Earl. Me too. Look, I'm gonna get these guys settled, then we should go over a few things." Earl nodded and sat back down. Vincent grabbed a chair to join the lookout.

Angeletti led me and Benny down to the basement. The furniture was all cedar, the floor was hardwood, and the faint smell of bark made me feel like I'd soon be sleeping in the woods.

"I know you're beat," Angeletti said, pointing to two beds on the opposite end of the room. "Those mattresses are the best that money can buy. You'd swear you were on a cloud." He placed his right hand on my shoulder, his left on Benny's. "Take all the time you want, boys. I'll be upstairs if you need anything." We thanked him, and he left.

I let myself fall face-first into the mattress. I had forgotten what a real bed felt like, let alone a memory foam mattress. I thought about going back to those stiff, twin-sized bricks in prison, then decided to save those concerns for the morning. *Enjoy it while you got it.* I turned and stared at the ceiling. I sighed, knowing I couldn't pretend I never assaulted an officer.

"That wasn't me," I said without looking at Benny, who sat at the corner of his bed, untying his shoes.

"Huh?"

"When I hit the cop – that wasn't me."

"No shit." The words carried disappointment.

"I mean that literally, Ben. Something happened to me."

He kicked the shoes off and looked at me. "You don't need to explain yourself, Will. I'm not your father. Shit, I'm free because of what you did, not that I agree with it."

"Listen to me," I said, irritated by his response, but more so by my own lack of eloquence that invited it. "When I was standing there with the baton in my hand, something happened to me. Something happened *inside* me. I heard Angeletti's voice in my head. He told me to do it." I expected Benny's blank face, and pressed on despite it. "But I wouldn't have done it in a million years. You know me, Benny. I don't have that in me. Then… I don't know. I changed my mind. Or someone did. A switch flipped, and the next second I had no control."

"Let me get this straight," Benny said, foreshadowing a sarcastic remark. "You're blaming Angeletti for your own fucked up actions? What was it, psychic powers? Did Angeletti control your mind?" He stroked his chin as if in deep thought, then pretended to light up with an idea. "No, no, I got it! He knows subliminal messaging techniques, and he planted the command in your brain."

I sat up. "It wasn't like that." I hesitated, aware of my pathetic odds in this battle. *You have to try.* "I think it worked the opposite way, like I pulled in his thoughts. Or his personality. I felt like he felt. And I don't think it's the first time it's happened." Benny's annoyed stare broke any hope I had of winning his belief. "I know what it sounds like."

"You need rest."

"I'm not delusional. I'm not making this shit up."

"Get some sleep. It's been a rough morning." He turned away from me and got comfortable in his bed.

I didn't have the energy to continue. I threw myself down, closed my eyes, and fell asleep, fully-dressed in my gray jumpsuit.

TEN

This is how my life stepped onto the path of complete shit:

I showed up to work, fifteen minutes early as always, and booted up my computer. I had spent five years as a programmer for Cole Web Solutions, but that Friday morning, four months before the robbery, would be my last. While I waited for my computer to start, I poured a cup of coffee in the kitchenette.

Joel Crimmons, the office manager, stepped in with his hands in his pockets. His eyes drooped. I knew he came with bad news, even before he said, "Will, do you have a minute?"

I dropped the stirrer into the trash bin. "Sure, what's up?"

"We should talk in my office."

I followed and sat opposite him at his desk. I sipped my coffee to fill the silence while I waited for him to get to the point.

"There's no graceful way of saying this, Will. I have to let you go."

I swallowed the coffee I had in my mouth. It burned on the way down as I spoke. "Why, Joel? What did I do?"

"You didn't do anything. I fought for you, but Ted…"

"That fucking asshole."

"You're not the only one. I have to break the same news to Kevin, Nicole, and Pete G."

"Those are his best people. What the hell is he thinking?"

"He's thinking that college grads are cheaper. He says the company's struggling."

"Yet that pile of cow shit somehow finds a way to pull up to the office in an F-50. That is, the two days a month he graces us with his presence." I put my coffee on Joel's desk before my shaky hands spilled any. "Even if the company is struggling, keeping a staff of inexperienced kids isn't the way to pull it up. Seriously, that one kid – what the fuck's his name? – he's never even worked with JavaScript. Fucking JavaScript, Joel."

"I know," he said. "Trust me, I know. Between you and me, I'm gonna start peddling my resume ASAP. I'm just as dispensable as you and the rest of 'em."

"I'm fucked, Joel. Julie and I are already hurting. Even with unemployment checks, if I don't find another job…"

"Won't happen. Look, give me a day or so, and I'll type you up a letter of recommendation."

"I'd appreciate that." I put my face in my hands and let my shit luck sink in. "Fuck."

○　○　○

That night, I told Julie. We sat at the dinner table in silence when I finished. Marcus read comic books in the living room with muted cartoons on the TV. The only sound in our apartment came from his flipping pages and Julie's fingernails tapping the wood tabletop.

"What are we going to do?" she said.

"I'll find something, hun. There's demand for developers, and good ones aren't a dime a dozen."

A tear built up in her eye, ready to drop. She sniffled. "I hope so, Will. I really fucking hope so. We won't last with what I make at the bar." The tear took the plunge and settled on the tip of her nostril. She pulled the wrist of her sleeve over her hand and wiped it.

"I promise it won't come to that."

"I'm overreacting, aren't I?" she said. "I suppose we have a little time before we need to hit the panic button."

"That's all I need. It might even be for the better. Fuck Ted and his ass-backwards company."

Marcus startled us as he rounded the corner into the kitchen. He stood with his fists on his hips like a superhero at a photo shoot. "Mom, can I have a snack?"

"It's eight-thirty," she said. "You need to get ready for bed."

He put his palms together and begged. "Pleeeeease."

"He *did* clean his room today," I said. "Without being asked, I might add."

Marcus jittered in his pajamas. "I did!"

"And we *do* have sugar-free chocolate pudding packs that wouldn't keep him up."

"We do!"

"Fine, fine, fine, fine, fine," Julie said. She grabbed a pudding cup and a spoon, and presented them to him. "Your pudding, majesty."

"Thanks, Mom."

"Thank him," she said, pointing to me.

"Thanks, Dad."

"Any time, bud. No, I take that back. You'd be chock full of pudding in minutes."

Julie patted his butt. "Why don't you go watch TV while you eat that. Then I want you in bed, you hear me, mister?"

When he was gone, I stood up and hugged Julie. "We'll be fine. You know that, right?"

"Yeah," she said, tucking her head against my neck and kissing my shoulder. "I know that."

ELEVEN

I woke with the feeling that I'd swallowed half a bottle of cough syrup before sleeping. I stood and stretched, concerned that my body had grown a preference for prison mattresses.

"Morning," Benny said. "Or afternoon, I guess." He sat at the edge of his bed, fully-dressed, tying the laces of a pair of pristine white Nikes. His jumpsuit was gone, replaced by a fresh pair of jeans and a red polo shirt.

"Whoa," I said.

"I know. Crazy, right?"

I searched the room for a clock. "What time is it?"

"One. Got a couple hours of sleep in." He pointed across the room to a cedar chair. "Angeletti left clothes for you, too. Won't get far in prisonwear." He spoke as if I wanted to stay out, and I realized that he didn't know otherwise.

I sat across from him on my own bed. "I need to talk to you about that, Benny." I wished I could have gotten some caffeine in me before tackling the topic, but I needed to get it out there. "I'm going back."

"Back where?" His forehead and eyebrows wrinkled. "The pen?"

"I can't live on the run. I'm not built for that. Six years is no picnic, but it's not a lifetime. I just wanna do my time and live free."

"No shame in that," he said after a long exhale through his nose. "No shame at all. Me, on the other hand – I got 22 years left, brother. I'm 34 years old. When I get out, my girls will be grown. They'll have kids. I can't sit and rot while the world goes on without me. This is a blessing."

"You'll miss just as much on the run," I said. "You can't just walk through your front door, kiss your wife and kids, and carry on like everything's peachy."

"I'll cross that bridge soon, but now that I'm out, I can't do another day in there." His expression turned solemn. His knee bobbed up and down as his foot tapped the floor. "Look, if you're going back, then more power to you. I respect that. But I'd be a lying son of a bitch if I said I didn't want you to come with me."

It occurred to me that Benny and I had no other friends. The lives we knew before our arrests had evaporated, along with most of the people in them. Benny didn't want freedom without me, and I didn't want incarceration without him.

"I wish I could, Ben. I really fucking do."

He stood. "It's all good, brother. Do what you gotta do." He began walking away.

"Where are you going?"

"I'm sorry," he said. "I forgot to ask." He raised his hand like an elementary school student. "Mr. Deslar, can I please go take a shit?"

"Get the fuck outta here," I said. "And it's '*may* I please take a shit?'"

I dressed in my new outfit, the same as Benny's, but with a gray polo. I put the shirt beside the jumpsuit to see a perfect match. *Someone has a sick sense of humor.* I didn't recognize the brand, but the clothes felt expensive and fit like they were tailored to me. I stood in front of a mirror, pleased with the sight of myself in civilian clothes. *If only I could take these back with me*, I thought, then saw something in my reflection. A shape in my jeans pocket. I reached in to investigate. I felt paper, and when I pulled it out, I was surprised by five twenty-dollar bills and a small note. The note read:

IN CASE YOU NEED IT. ~FRANCO

A whistle came from the stairway, followed by Angeletti.

"Good," he said. "You're up. And looking sharp, too."

"Thanks, Franco. For the clothes and the cash. You didn't have to."

"Nonsense." He brought a cigar to his lips and took three quick pulls. The delicious aroma almost distracted me from my wariness of the man producing it. "I got a question for you, Will. That Lincoln guy – the prick that's with your wife…" This got my attention. "What's his last name?"

"Alders," I said. The syllables felt dirty on my tongue. Every time I spoke the name, it came up with a larger dose of resentment than the time before.

He bit his cigar and rubbed his hands together. His smile took up half his face. "I knew it. I said I owed you, kid." He took the cigar out of his mouth and pointed at me with the hand that held it. The glowing tip almost hit my chest. "And right now I start paying my debt."

He found them, I thought.

"Destiny's dealt you an ace, my friend. Turns out I've done business with Alders. I didn't make the connection 'til I mentioned your predicament to Vincent. You see, a few months ago, my boy Earl…" He put his index finger up. "Give me a second." He walked to the stairs and yelled up, "Earl! Get down here, will ya?"

A few moments of silence passed, then the floor shook as the tank of a man approached and descended the stairs. If Benny had been beside me, I might have made an earthquake joke. Earl's 350-pound build barely fit through the door frame.

He seemed to strive for unpleasantness; his face defaulted to a scowl and his attitude was acidic. Craters dotted his nose, cheeks, and chin from severe acne that he no longer had.

"Yeah, boss?" he mumbled.

"Tell Will what you told me."

"About…"

"About the last time you saw Lincoln Alders."

Earl rolled his eyes, annoyed with having to retell the story. He spoke in a dull, bored tone. "We get a call from him a few months back."

Angeletti cut in. "You already know – sorry, Earl – you already know what Alders does for a living."

"Yeah," I said. "I know too well."

"Right. And when people in his profession get their hands on a score that they can't sell through public avenues, they bring it to good folk like us. We've done business with him on and off throughout the years, so this call wasn't out of the ordinary. All right, Earl, go ahead."

Earl continued. "So he tells me he's got some jewelry to unload. Says it's worth a quarter mil at least, but he'll let it go for 200. Now, me and Vince are thinking that this is too fucking good to be true, so—"

"Can you go one damn minute without swearing?" Angeletti said, like a father scolding his teenage son. I almost laughed, but caught myself.

Earl's face reddened. He didn't appreciate being called out in front of company, but even a man with an empty skull wouldn't air those grievances to Angeletti. "Sorry, boss. Where was I? Oh – so we run it by Franco, and he gives the OK. Alders says he can't get to Boston, but he'll drop the price even more if I meet him down in Raynham. So I head down there."

"Did you see him?" I said. "Did he have a young boy with him?"

"Cool yourself," Earl said, proud to display any bit of dominance. "He was alone. No kid."

"Fuck," I said. Angeletti's eyebrows rose. "Sorry, Franco."

He waved off the notion that I had anything to apologize for. "I'd swear too if I were in your position." He saw Earl's objection before it materialized and preempted it. "He's got a good reason to swear, you dummy. You just want to sound like a hard-ass. Finish the story."

Earl shook his head and pressed on. "He has me park at a gas station. He hops in, hands me a bank bag chock full of rings, bracelets, necklaces – anything you could want. I give him the money."

"This is the good part," Angeletti said.

"When he gets out, I watch him. You know, to see what he's driving in case he's fucking us." He paused and looked at Angeletti, then back to me. "In case he's *screwing* us. But he doesn't get into a car. He goes across the street to a house."

Angeletti saw the hope in my eyes. "Good stuff, right? We haven't heard from Alders since, not that we want to. Fugitives are bad for business. So we don't know if he's still in that house, but you're gonna find out. Earl and Vincent will take you."

And there it was: a reason to not go back to prison.

"This is a lot to take," I said. I turned, took a few steps, turned again, and retraced my path. "I have to think this over, Franco."

He looked at Earl, who took the hint and left. The floor shook again as he waddled up the stairs.

Angeletti exhaled a cloud of smoke away from me before leaning in, but a small wisp lingered between us. "I know you want to go back. You're a good kid. You're trying to do the honest thing. I get it, I do. And you don't have to accept my help. I'll tell you one thing though – if you're ever going to try to find them and handle this situation of yours, you'll never get a better opportunity. They have no idea you're free, or that you got backup."

He walked across the room to a table. "Remember what I told you on that bus? About fate? Let me put that discussion in the context of our present standing." He pressed the head of his cigar into a glass ashtray and walked back. The cigar still burned through his return trip, sending ribbons of smoke to the ceiling behind him. "Of all the prisons I could have gone to, I landed in the one that held you. The place mysteriously crumbled." He smirked at this. "Then, of all the busses they filled this morning, I ended up on yours. Three empty seats. I picked the one beside you. You told me your story, about how your wife ran away with a man I've dealt with. A man I have a lead on. And to top it all off, there was an unfortunate riot that left us free men." He patted my arm and headed for the stairs. "You'd have to be a stubborn you-know-what to write that all off as coincidence. Think about it, kid. Let me know."

○ ○ ○

I sat in the cedar chair with my head in my hands when Benny came out of the bathroom.

"I never knew crime bosses were so hospitable," he said. "There's fresh toothbrushes in there, unopened deodorant, even face wash. Shit, I'm surprised there's no mints on our pillows." He noticed my mood. "What's up?"

I told him about Angeletti's proposal. "I don't know what to do. Marcus isn't safe with Lincoln. What the fuck kind of father would I be if I didn't try to find him?"

"I can't help you with that decision," Benny said. "But if you go, you know I got your back."

"Thanks, Benny. Means a lot. Do I even have to ask what you'd do in my position?"

"Not if you're packing an IQ over 30."

It's clear now that free will played no role in my decision. I pictured myself back behind bars, hearing the terrible news that something had happened to Marcus – some terrible fate that I had the chance to avert but didn't. I couldn't abandon him. I did the only thing I could do. I did what I'd do a million times over.

"I'm going," I said.

Benny smiled. "Then so am I."

TWELVE

"I don't need that," I said to Vincent, who held a gun by the barrel, waiting for me to grab the handle.

"Take it," Earl said in a salty tone, bringing a Twizzler to his mouth and tearing a piece off. "Franco's orders."

The backseat of the Cadillac was hot and unventilated, trapping the pungent colonge-mixed-with-sweat scent drifting off of Earl from the front. AC/DC played low in the speaker behind my ear.

I looked across the street at the house that I hoped held Marcus. "Fine, but if my son's in there, I want all guns away."

"Yes, sir," Earl taunted. Being forced to help me ate at him, and he'd spent the entire trip from Boston making sure I knew it. Vincent didn't seem to mind the task. He was a "go with the flow" kind of guy – a welcomed contrast to his partner.

I took the gun and put it on my lap. I couldn't relax with its weight on me. My muscles tensed up. *Please don't make me use this fucking thing*, I thought to no one in particular. All the knowledge I had about guns came from a visit to a range with my grandfather when I was sixteen. I wasn't sure I could do more than aim and pull the trigger. Benny sat beside me with a gun of his own. If he shared my inexperience and unease, he hid it well.

Vincent turned off the music. "All right, how do you wanna handle this?" His seldom-heard voice was mellow and raspy, like he kept a constant stream of smoke circulating through his lungs.

Angeletti had given me the command of our outing. The responsibility, which held no weight with Earl, put me out of my league. "I don't know," I said. "I've never done this kind of thing before. What would you do?"

"Glad you asked," Earl said, before Vincent could give his opinion. He continued chewing on the Twizzler as he talked, and each word sloshed through red, sugary saliva before hitting our ears. "We pull up in the driveway" – he pointed like no one knew which driveway he meant – "and the second the car stops, me and Vince flank to the back of the house. They won't recognize Benny, so he'll ring the bell while you hide off to the side. By the time they open the door, me and Vince'll be inside, ready to jump 'em."

"And if no one's home?" Benny asked, taking the words from my mouth.

"Then you get the car outta here while we wait inside for them."

"Benny stays with me," I said.

Earl exaggerated his grunt of irritation. "Fine, whatever. Then Vince will take the car. That work for you?"

I ignored his attitude, which irked him more than if I would've retaliated. "Let's do it."

"Ready?" Vincent asked.

Everybody grabbed their gun as if that was the universal sign for readiness. Earl pulled out of the gas station and crossed the street into the empty driveway. The pavement was level and smooth; our approach made no noise.

"Go," Earl said when the Cadillac stopped. "Don't shut the doors behind. They'll hear it."

We exited and dispersed. Vincent went around the right side of the house while Earl took the left. Benny and I jogged to the front door, where I veered right and squatted against the house.

Benny put his index finger on the doorbell, then looked down at me for the go-ahead. I waited a few seconds to let the others get into place, then gave it to him.

As the bell rang, I put my ear to the vinyl and listened for movement inside. The torturous stillness stretched long enough to convince me that we'd found nothing. Then footsteps tapped tile. The deadbolt clicked, the knob turned, and the door opened.

"Hello there." The familiar voice, so close to Julie's, gave me a second of hope before the truth sank in. The voice belonged to her mother.

Maureen? What the fuck is she doing here?

"Hello, ma'am," Benny answered, "I'm looking for Julie Deslar, please."

The inquiry caught her off-guard. "Oh, I… I'm sorry, but I haven't seen Julie in a long time."

The pounding of feet filled the foyer as Earl closed in like an overeager captain of a SWAT team. Maureen screamed as his voice boomed loud enough for the whole neighborhood to hear.

"Get the fuck on the ground! Who else is in the house?"

"Oh God, please don't hurt me!" Maureen begged. "I swear she's not here."

I leapt out of hiding, pushing Benny aside. The visual waiting for me made me regret the trip. Maureen lay face-down on the tiles while Earl towered over her, gun drawn, with the triumphant pose of a man who'd single-handedly captured Hitler.

"Put the fucking gun away!" I commanded with a vicious bite. Once my mouth started, my remaining fear of Earl shriveled. "You fucking imbecile. She's unarmed." Earl put away the gun, but not his sour face.

Maureen kept her head down until she realized whose voice she'd heard. "William?"

"Yeah, Maureen, it's me." I bent down to help her up. "Don't worry, you're not in danger." She lifted herself stiffly to her hands and knees, wary of making any sudden movements. "This is all a misunderstanding."

"House is clear," Vincent announced, popping out of a room to the right of the entryway.

When Maureen got to her feet, I waved the men toward the driveway. "Go. Let me talk to her."

"Sorry about that, ma'am," Benny said as he turned and walked away. Vincent put his head down, silent but apologetic. Earl strode by her without any acknowledgment.

I put my hand on her shaky arm to steady her. "If I knew you were here, I never would've come like this." I glanced inside the house, trying to remember if I'd ever been there. "What is this place?"

She didn't catch my question, still petrified, staring at the others. She snapped out of her shock in a spasm of blinks and head shakes.

"What is this about, William?" She put her hand over her mouth, mortified by the thoughts running wild in her head. "You're here for Julie," she said, then added with extra horror, "with guns. What do you want with her?"

"I just want to talk to her." I knew that wouldn't get me anywhere. "Listen to me. The guns are for protection. She's with someone very dangerous. Where are they?"

"Dangerous? *He's* dangerous? *He* didn't almost shoot me."

Frustration hardened my voice. "Where are they, Maureen?"

"I don't know, dammit! I haven't seen her in months." She spoke the truth, and that truth had been chipping away at her for too long. "She called me after you were arrested. She knew the police were watching my home, so she met me here."

"Where is here?"

"This? It's my mother's house. You've met her, remember? At the nursing home in Easton."

"Yeah, I remember."

"I've been staying here as much as I can ever since, hoping Julie will come back."

"Did you see Marcus? Please tell me he was all right."

"He was fine."

"Ah fuck, thank God."

"As fine as a kid can be in that situation, at least. I wanted her to leave him here. I told her, I said, 'You can get yourself into any mess you please, but you have no right to drag that poor thing into it.' How could she screw up so badly? And you, too. You deserve a share of the blame. When I think of what my grandson's been through…"

"I'm going to make it right, Maureen. You have my word."

"Your word, huh? Julie told me the same thing, and I haven't seen either of them since. Just an empty promise to shut an old woman up." A thought made her eyes lock onto mine with suspicion. "How did you get out of prison?"

"It's a long story. I'm going back as soon as I find Julie and Marcus."

"So you're not supposed to be out?"

"It's not important, Maureen. Right now, all that matters is that I find them. I can't do that without you."

"I won't let you harm my daughter."

"You know I would never do that. Even after what she did to me."

Her face became defensive. "You can't blame her for running. She's frightened."

I realized then that she had no clue what had happened the night of the robbery. And why would she? Her understanding of our crime came only from news reports and Julie's telling of it.

This isn't the time for the truth.

"You're right," I said. "I can't blame her for running, but I can convince her to stop. Marcus can't have a life with a fugitive mother. She needs to turn herself in. The two of us can do our time, and until we get out, you can give Marcus a real childhood."

"Yeah, some childhood that'll be, talking to his parents through glass." Her body rocked as she stared into nothingness, wanting to believe me. Her eyes showcased the fatigue and worry that had hounded her in the months since she last saw her daughter. Helping me was her only hope for escape from that. A little push would do it.

I put a hand on her shoulder. "Please. Neither of them are safe with that man. I know things about him that would keep you up at night. Help me."

Maureen closed her eyes and held them shut while she thought it through. Then she gave in. "Julie said that she'd talked to Keith." Her body loosened with the decision to spill the information, but that relief of shedding the burden came with the guilt of betraying her daughter. "She said he would be able to help her."

"Is there anything else you can tell me?" I asked.

"They were driving a truck. Maroon. Maybe a Ford, but I don't know. I almost called the cops, Will. I almost reported it, but I just couldn't. What kind of mother would I be?" Her voice cracked, and she took a deep breath to fight her emotions. "I just couldn't."

"It's OK," I said.

"Not if something happens to my grandbaby, it isn't. I'll never forgive myself."

"I promise you, I'll get him. He's my son, and I'll die before I give up on him."

She smiled through glazed eyes. "You were always so good to—"

A ruckus broke out in the driveway behind me. When I turned, a short, bald man in a sweater vest had his finger in Vincent's face.

"Oh, Lord," Maureen said. "That's Dick Mainard. He lives two doors down. Nosey like you wouldn't believe. You better get out of here. I wouldn't put it past him to call the police."

"Thank you," I said. "For everything."

"Make it worth it, William."

When I reached my group, they had Dick surrounded. He seemed immune to intimidation, yelling and flailing his arms around, causing a scene. He either had no idea who he was mouthing off to, or he didn't give a shit.

"Don't you try to bully me, motherfucker!" he said, his finger close to stabbing Vincent's nose. "I saw the whole thing."

"You didn't see squat, old man," Earl said with his best mafioso impression.

"I didn't? I didn't?" Mainard pointed to the shape under Vincent's shirt. "I saw that gun. You assholes better get outta here." The guy had a serious set of balls, I have to admit. Unfortunately, balls tend to get you in trouble if you can't back them up.

Earl pulled his pistol from his jacket and pressed it to the man's temple. "You saw a gun, huh? You see this one, cocksucker?"

"Hey, hey, hey!" Benny said. "Put that fucking thing away, man." He looked at me to back him up.

"Put it down," I said, standing straight to appear more solid than I felt.

Earl looked at me with zero respect, then back at Mainard. He lowered his gun, grabbed Mainard by the back of his shirt collar, and forced him to the end of the driveway. "Go home, you prick," he said as he shoved the puny man into the street. "You're lucky you don't have a chunk of metal behind your fucking eyes."

"We have to leave," I said when Earl returned. "He might call the cops."

He threw his hands up. "Then why the fuck ain't I blasting him?"

"Is that a real fucking question?" I said.

Benny got between us as Earl stepped forward. "Will's right. Let's get outta here."

THIRTEEN

"I think they're in New Hampshire," I said, looking out the Cadillac's rear window at Dick Mainard, who flipped us off as we drove away. "Her brother Keith lives up there, in North Conway. She's not dumb enough to be with him, but he'll know where she is."

"Well, you're on your own," Earl said. "I'm done with you."

I laughed at him. "You're done with *me*? You just pulled a gun on my mother-in-law. What in the flying fuck makes you think I want anything to do with you?"

"Fuck you."

"No, fuck *you*, you dim-witted bag of testosterone. What the fuck were you thinking? Never mind, I know – you get off on terrorizing defenseless women and old men. Is that about the gist of it?"

"Keep up the attitude and see what happens." He sprayed a mist of saliva on the dashboard as he spoke. "Franco might have a hard-on for you, but you're nothing to me."

"Cut it out," Vincent said, breaking his usual silence to keep the peace. "Deslar saved my ass yesterday, and Franco's too. We'd be in fucking jumpsuits if it wasn't for him."

Vincent's intervention only pushed Earl further into the red. "If I was there, Franco never would've needed saving in the first place." He looked me in the eyes through the rear-view mirror. "You wanna sit there and talk shit? You wanna judge me? You don't know a thing about me, you little cunt."

As the word "cunt" left his lips, a jolt zipped through my head.

Earl's tirade continued. "You think you know what made me this way?"

Another jolt hit me. This time, as it buzzed inside my forehead, images flashed in my mind. They came fast, rushing into me like pictures downloading to a computer.

A child sits on a faded, torn couch. Four years old. Maybe five. Blonde. Cute. He's surrounded by empty, dirty walls, littered with fist-sized holes.

He clutches a teddy bear twice as mangled as the couch.

His parents yell at each other. I can't hear their words, but I see the acid fly.

An open-hand slap hits the father's face.

His fist rams the mother's side.

She spits in his eye.

He drives his forehead into her nose.

She goes down. Her blood adds to the collection of muddy purple stains on the sky blue carpet.

He turns his back, waves her off like this is no big deal. Just another afternoon with the wife. His stance gives away his intoxication.

The mother stands up.

She grasps for something on the coffee table. A porcelain vase.

She trips, but catches herself. She's as drunk as he is. Maybe more. She catches up with him.

She raises the vase high. He's either too shit-faced to notice her approach, or too cocky to think it means danger.

Her arms come down hard.

The vase shatters on his skull.

He drops, face-first.

She's on his back, frantic, clawing like an animal.

She reaches for the largest shard from the broken vase.

She latches onto it.

Her grip is tight. Veins bulge on top of her hand. She ignores the damage the razor edges are inflicting on her palm. No regard for her own body.

Streaks of blood run down her forearm as she plunges the jagged point into the father's neck.

Blood sprays sideways. More muddy purple carpet.

The child cries.

The file of snapshots finished, replaced by the real world. I found myself staring at the back of the Cadillac's headrest through the after-image of the scene. It had all played out in the span of a second; Earl hadn't even had the chance to get his next statement off of his chest.

"Let me tell you a little something about me." His hand shook on the steering wheel. I already knew what was coming.

You were five years old.

"I was five years old when my psycho bitch mother cut my dad's throat. Killed him right in front of me. You'd be a violent prick too."

Please don't tell me any more, I thought. I'd already seen it, I didn't need to hear it too.

"But you don't wanna hear about that," he said, as if he had heard me. "That's too real for a delicate fucking dandelion like you."

What's happening to me? My head spun. I felt sick, confused, and crazy all at the same time. Vomit sat at the back of my throat, threatening to come up.

"You all right, brother?" Benny said, leaning in with concern. I shook my head, not able to manage anything else. Even if I could have spoken, no explanation would do.

Without warning, Earl jerked the car to the side of the road.

"Jesus!" Vincent said. "What, you gotta piss or something?"

"I'm gonna hurl," Earl said, then threw the door open and

hopped out. He made it around the car and to the grass just before it came up.

"Nice timing," Vincent said under his breath, then rolled down his window to tease Earl. "This is what happens when you get all riled up, you maniac."

Benny looked at Earl, then at me. He saw the connection, however vague and strange it seemed to him. "What the hell's going on, Will?" he whispered.

"I wish I knew." I reeled in a gag that made Benny back up. "I saw Earl. As a kid."

"What?"

"I saw…" I stopped, knowing that any further speech could lead to vomit.

"All right, brother, take it easy."

Earl finished throwing up and dry heaving, and approached Benny's door. "You two – get out."

"Is he serious?" Benny said.

"Get outta the fucking car."

"Franco won't like this," Vincent said, poking his head out the window.

"Fuck F—" Earl stopped as he looked past Vincent to the street ahead.

The three of us followed his gaze to a police cruiser rocketing toward us with its lights flashing.

FOURTEEN

Half a day. I only managed to make it a half a fucking day.

The blue and white flashes highlighted how pathetic my search for Marcus had been; they promised to end it right then and there.

"What the fuck are you waiting for?" Earl yelled at us. He pulled his gun from beneath his jacket and walked to the front of the car. "Get out here and shoot these cocksuckers."

"That fucking neighbor," Vincent whispered to himself before he opened his door.

"These crazy motherfuckers are gonna trade shots with police," Benny said. "This is madness. They're gonna get us all killed."

I watched Angeletti's men as they stood side by side with pistols raised, and waited for the first shot. I jumped when it came. Earl initiated the rapid clapping, then Vincent fed into it. I lowered my head in preparation for the inevitable retaliation. The cruiser screeched to a stop across the street. A young officer in the passenger seat got out and ducked behind the fender. The middle-aged driver climbed over the console to exit on the covered side of the vehicle. The two assumed an offensive position as Earl and Vincent's guns clicked empty. The gangsters hid to reload. The cops fired back. Benny lowered himself to my level as two shots hit the window beside me. The glass didn't smash; it only vibrated with a thud.

"It's bulletproof," I said with my heart in my throat.

Benny raised his head. "Does that surprise you?"

Vincent popped up long enough to fire four shots. The first hit the young cop in the shoulder. He barely flinched, soaring on adrenaline. A dark circle appeared in the cloth of his uniform and spread outward. He returned fire. His first and second shots hit the Cadillac's windshield. The third shot landed in the center of Vincent's forehead. The impact spun Vincent to his left as he fell with a blank stare to the sky.

With the upper-hand gained, the officers unloaded in unison, sending a wall of bullets in Earl's direction. The bangs gave way to clicks, and the officers dropped back behind the cruiser to recuperate. Benny and I waited for Earl to empty his reloaded clip, but he didn't. Instead, he moved to Benny's door and ripped it open. Benny recoiled, pressing me up against my own door. Earl grabbed his ankle and yanked him. Benny kicked with his free leg, slamming Earl's head against the car's ceiling.

Thud.

Bang.

All movement stopped, except for the shaky metal barrel aimed at our faces. The only sound came from Earl's heavy breathing. A tiny thread of smoke rose from a hole in the leather between Benny's legs.

"Get..." Earl started before needing to suck in more air. "The fuck" – another inhale – "out of the car. Or I'll put a bullet right through your fucking eye."

Benny put his hands up, followed the orders, and climbed right into a chokehold with a gun to his ear. The officers stood, refreshed and ready to resume firing, but stopped when they saw Earl's hostage. They fixed their sights on the pair.

Earl shuffled toward the front of the car. "Put 'em down or he's dead." He flexed his fingers on the handle of the pistol and pressed it to Benny's head.

Terrified as I was, I knew couldn't sit idle. *You have a gun*, I told myself. *And whether you like it or not, you're gonna use it.* I moved to the passenger side and climbed out. Then I raised my pistol at the officers.

"Someone grew a pair," Earl said without looking at me.

I sidestepped closer to him. *That's right, I'm on your side. Keep looking at them.*

"Let go of him," the older officer called. "No one else needs to get hurt."

"Fuck yourself," Earl responded.

I stepped over Vincent's body, only a couple feet from Earl and Benny. *Almost.*

The young officer redirected his aim to me. We stared at each other over our barrels. He was more afraid than he'd ever been in his life. No rookie would expect a shootout on their sixth day with the force, especially in Raynham, where he'd grown up and never considered dangerous. This young man, Phillip Steadman, had worked for years, supported financially by his fiancée, to get his badge. And now that he'd earned his position, they were trying for a child. He wanted a girl. She wanted a boy.

And then he ran into us.

I didn't imagine this backstory. I didn't learn it afterward. Phillip Steadman's history poured through me as my gun shook in his direction, and his shook in mine.

Please, God, he begged inside, *please don't let me die. Please, God. Not yet.*

I wondered if the transmission of information ran both ways. Did he know my name? My past? Thoughts? Beliefs? *Does he know what I'm going to do next*? I suspected he did, and as I made the final determination to follow through with my plan, his face left no question.

I swung my arm to the right, hoping my sudden movement

wouldn't provoke any gunfire. When the arc was complete, my pistol hovered an inch from Earl's ear. He didn't notice. I looked toward the officers. What I saw chilled me.

Phillip stood sideways, a mirror image of myself, with his gun raised to his partner's head. He looked back at me with fear and desperation in his eyes. He didn't understand what he was doing. He didn't understand why.

But I did, at least enough to know that if I pulled the trigger, Earl wouldn't be the only casualty. I would shoot. Phillip would shoot. Earl would die, and two officers would pay – one with his life, the other with everything else.

But Benny would live.

The sound of backup wailed close by. I didn't have the luxury of weighing the pros and cons of my decision. I broke my stare-down with Phillip, spotted my mark on Earl's head, gritted my teeth, and pulled the trigger.

Two shots rang out. Earl's head popped. He fell with Benny still trapped in his arms. I followed them down and pried the massive dead weight off of my friend. We rose, then looked across the street.

Phillip stood alone, one arm still raised, trembling. He stared down in horror at the body I knew hid behind the Crown Victoria. He shivered and dropped his arm to his side. The pressure of tears pushed against the corners of my eyes, and I hated that I didn't know if the urge to cry was my own. It didn't matter. Phillip and I both felt the tragedy.

I raised my gun, and like a puppet on a string, Phillip did the same. I opened my hand. He opened his. Both guns fell to the ground. Benny watched, speechless. The backup I'd heard rounded the corner a quarter-mile away.

"We need to jump," Benny said, hurrying away.

Jump? The statement confused me until I followed him and saw a river under the road. We reached the stone wall and looked over. The fifteen-foot drop didn't worry me, but the possibility of shallow water did. I looked back as a second squad car parked. Two more followed. Phillip stood among them, still reeling from what he'd done.

"Now." Benny plunged feet-first over the side. I watched him hit the water and go under. He surfaced two seconds later, which was all I needed to see.

The current took us a hundred yards before the police saw us floating away.

FIFTEEN

The tree branch came quick. I timed my leap from the water and grabbed it. Hours of swimming and treading water left every muscle weak, but I managed to keep my grip on the wet wood. Benny had already made it up the bank, and lay there on his back, catching his breath. He lifted his head over his rising and falling chest to make sure I didn't miss the mark.

"You need a hand?" he yelled with significant effort. I don't think he could have helped me if I did.

I didn't answer him, just shimmied over to the shore, where I used the limb to pull myself over a four-foot dirt wall. That final obstacle drained what little energy I had left, and I collapsed to my forearms and knees beside Benny. The night brought a strong wind, and the constant gusts pressed my cold, wet shirt to my skin. We both shivered like engines idled inside of us.

I rested my head in the mud. "I killed an innocent man, Benny."

He sat up. "That man wasn't innocent."

"I don't mean Earl." I tucked my face in my arms. "You saw it – what I made that cop do. Jesus Christ, he's just a kid. His life's ruined, and it's not even his fault. He had no control. What *am* I? What's happening to me?"

"You tried to tell me," he said. "You fucking tried, and I didn't believe you." He waited for me to look up at him. When I did, he said, "I'm ready to listen now."

I began my five-minute exposition with the night of my arrest at The Perfect Cut. I described (for the second time) what I saw when Julie hit me, how I watched her betrayal from her own eyes. I moved to the ceiling collapse, and the way my emotions turned in an instant to match his. Then the riot, the officer I attacked, what made me do it.

"When I shot Earl," I said, "I knew that officer would die. I knew it, and I pulled the trigger anyway."

"I don't know what to say."

"There's more." I reached into my pocket and pulled out Robert's water-logged note. I squeezed the river from it, then took care in unfolding it. The ink had suffered, but the words were still legible.

"What's that?" Benny asked.

"The letter. You remember? The one I found a week or so after I got locked up."

"The one you acted a fool over? What about it?"

I held it out. "Read it."

"I already did."

"Read it again. And when you get to the important part, read it aloud."

He took the paper. "What's the important part?"

"You'll know."

His lips moved with no sound as he skimmed the words. I saw his expression change with the subject matter, and waited for the passage that would wipe away those expressions altogether. His face dropped when he reached it.

"Holy shit."

"Go ahead. Read it out loud."

He coughed, then held his chin as he read Robert's message. "'Something happened. Something. Something in my head it burns like…' He struggled here. The writing's all scratchy, like he couldn't finish a thought."

"Go on."

He looked back down at the sheet. "'I saw something now, something. I didn't see it, I felt it like… You shoot. He shoots. Two drop.'" Benny rubbed his forehead. "Fuck, Will."

"I thought I was crazy," I said. "I thought it was all in my head, but it's not. Something's happening to me. And this man, this *Robert*, is real, and he's connected to me. Connected to all this crazy shit. He's out there somewhere, in trouble, hoping I'll come for him."

"Will you?"

"It doesn't matter."

"What do you mean?"

"He knew about me. He knew I was locked up, in no position to help him. He wrote this letter, not knowing how or why it would reach me. And it did. Three months later, I'm free. He knew about the towels, about what happened in the jewelry store, about Earl and the cop. If he thinks I'll find him, then… He's been right so far."

"I thought you didn't believe in fate."

"This isn't fate." The statement had an air of finality to it, and succeeded in sealing the conversation. I took the letter from Benny's lap, folded it back up, and moved to the next topic that needed attention. "Look, Benny – I understand if you need to get the fuck away from me. I wouldn't blame you. I don't want anything to happen to you because of me."

"I ain't leaving, brother," he said, stunned that I thought he could ever do such a thing. "You'd be lost without me." Then, with a grin, he added, "Plus, I can't resist a good mystery."

"I needed that answer," I said. "What do we do now?"

He pointed to his stomach. "I need food. And a dry place to sleep. And a beer would do wonders."

"Angeletti left cash in my jeans," I said, digging around for the soaked bills. "A hundred bucks."

"He did the same for me. A hundred bucks."

"It won't get us far, but it'll take care of us tonight." I put the money and the letter back in my pocket. "Do you still have your gun?"

He tapped his waist. "Mm–hmm. Not sure how reliable it'll be after taking a swim."

"Should we get rid of it?"

"I'm not a fan of carrying it," he said, "but we should keep it for now. Never know."

"Fair enough. I say we get a motel room and order some delivery. We can figure out how to get north tomorrow, when we're dry and rested."

"Sounds like a plan." He stood and looked into the darkness. "Where do you think we are?"

I rose after him, grunting in pain on the way up. "I couldn't even give a guess. Let's find out."

SIXTEEN

Benny and I walked a mile before we found a main road. We learned from a stoned liquor store cashier that we'd floated south to Fall River. We grabbed some snacks, water, and beers, then used the store's pay phone to call a cab. Any more walking seemed impossible. Twenty minutes and thirty dollars later, we stepped out of the yellow Corolla in the parking lot of The Sunshine Inn. High above us on a pole, a giant yellow sphere beamed, casting an obnoxious golden light on the property.

"Is that supposed to be a sun?" Benny asked.

"I assume so. I think that smiley face on it is supposed to be cute."

"Whoever made that thing has a twisted idea of cute. It looks like a pedophile ping-pong ball."

The lobby smelled like a gas station and had the atmosphere to match. Plain white floor tiles, bright lights, neglected walls, a bored overnight worker behind the counter. We used fake names, and the clerk wasn't attentive enough to ask for IDs. He didn't even seem to notice our damp clothes. All he cared about was getting our first night in advance and shooing us out of his quiet lobby. He took our money and handed us a mangled keycard that didn't look like it could open a water balloon.

Our room was as subpar as the rest of the place, but I didn't expect much for 60 a night.

"At least we each have our own bed," Benny said. "I know you were hoping to share one, but…"

"Yeah, I'm heartbroken." I walked to an ancient television set that sat high on a wall-mounted shelf. "Look at this thing." I pressed the power button. Nothing happened. "I bet it's older than me. How the hell is this shelf even supporting it?"

I checked out the bathroom, expecting to be horrified. And I was; it's enough to say that I never entered that bathroom without shoes. One pleasant surprise among all the motel's shortcomings came in the form of a small laundry room at the end of the hall. After settling in, we took turns drying each other's clothes.

"One of us has to stay dressed to make the trip," Benny explained when I questioned the logic of doing two loads. "People will notice a couple half-naked guys doing laundry. We don't need the attention."

"I guess," I said. "But I'd just as soon run down the hallway in a towel to get it all in one shot."

Later, comfortable in dry clothes, I tried to remember Angeletti's number. He made us memorize it before leaving his cabin, but I could only recall the last four digits.

"I still got it," Benny said when I gave up and asked him. He tore open the top of a Chinese food container. "What are you gonna tell him?"

"The truth. But, you know, without all the psychotic-sounding details."

"Good luck with that." He twirled his fork in the lo mein as he recited the number.

My nervous fingers misdialed twice. I'd been dreading the call since the river. "Let's just hope he's not a 'shoot the messenger' kind of guy."

Angeletti's voice came through after two rings, loud enough for

Benny to hear. "Yeah?"

"Franco, it's Will."

Without missing a beat, as if he'd expected my call at that exact moment, he said, "Where the hell you been, kid? Something went wrong, didn't it?"

"I don't know how to say this, so I won't beat around the bush – Vincent and Earl are dead. The cops caught up to us, and those two started shooting. I'm sorry. Benny and I got away. We're in a motel." I tried to keep the scene from my head, afraid that I'd transmit the whole truth to him.

"Fucking hotheads," he said. "Excuse my language." He seemed more annoyed than upset with the loss. "I take it you didn't find your wife and kid."

"No, but we got a solid lead."

"Good, good. Where are you? I'll send someone." I had expected the question with the hope that it wouldn't come. I hadn't told Benny, but during our trip down the river, I had decided to go on without Angeletti's help. I had enough to worry about without the trouble that he came with.

"About that, Franco..." Benny let the fork stand on its own in his noodles and looked at me. I looked down and tugged on the phone cord. "I don't know if that's a good idea."

"You saying what I think you're saying?" He sounded disappointed, which was a relief, considering the alternatives.

"I appreciate what you're doing for me, Franco, but I could have died today. On multiple occasions. I'm not cut out for this."

"No one's cut out for this, kid. Not even me." He pulled his mouth from the phone to let out a painful-sounding cough. When he came back, his voice was rough. "Fine, fine, fine. You're off the hook. I gotta tell ya, it's not every day someone tells me to screw off."

"That's not what this is. I don't mean any disrespect."

Another cough came, this time brought on by a subtle chuckle.

"I'm pulling your leg, kid. Don't worry, I'm not Capone, for Christ's sake. You still gonna look for them?"

"Julie and Marcus? I haven't decided."

"Bull," he said. "Of course you are, and I hope to hell you find them. My offer stands, by the way, if you need a little help. You got my number."

"Thanks, Franco." As I began my farewell, he interrupted me.

"Before you go, answer a question for me: Did you have anything to do with Earl's death? Directly, I mean." The question hit me like a taser to my ribs. Benny heard it too, and shared my momentary panic. Angeletti laughed at the silence. "I knew it. Something told me. Well, don't lose any sleep over it – Earl's had it coming for years. Take care of yourself. Tell Benny the same."

Then the phone went dead.

SEVENTEEN

I placed a hot cup of coffee on the nightstand beside Benny. "Wake up." He didn't respond, not that I expected him to. Nobody slept like Benny. Up by eight every day, but before that he was comatose. "Hey Benny, the Fugees are getting back together." Nothing. At least I made myself smile; I needed it. I grabbed a pillow from my bed. "If words won't wake the beast…" I gave him a good whack in the head.

"Son of a bitch," he said, and shielded himself with his blanket, preparing for another hit.

"I got you coffee." I reached into my pocket for some sugar packets and tossed them at him.

He sat up and rubbed his eyes. "What time is it?"

"Almost seven. Drink up, I need you alert. Got something to run by you." I put a piece of paper in front of him on the bed.

He ignored it as he ripped two of the packets at once, dumped them into his coffee, closed the lid, swirled the cup, and took a sip. Only after savoring that first taste did he acknowledge the sheet. "What's this?"

"It's a satellite image I printed from the computer in the lobby. It's a neighborhood outside of Boston."

He looked a bit frightnened. "You can do that? Get into satellites and shit?"

I laughed at him. "You've been locked up waaaaay too long, Ben. It's called Google Maps. Anyway, I was thinking about our situation. We have 67 bucks left. We're gonna need more, right?"

"Yeah, I thought about that last night."

I jabbed the printout with two fingers. "This is our ticket."

"Please tell me you're not thinking of robbing one of these houses." My lack of response confirmed his fear. "You have to be joking."

"No joke. I know, I know – I don't like it either."

"Oh, really? You seem pretty fucking excited about it."

It took that accusation for me to notice my own giddiness. "OK, maybe a little, but only because it's the perfect solution. It's practically victimless."

"A victimless burglary? I can't wait for this reasoning."

"Hear me out before you go shutting this down, all right? The guy who owns this house" – I pointed to the white roof in the north corner of the cul de sac – "he's a world-class douchebag. And he's loaded. *Loaded*, Benny. See that? That's a Ferrari in the driveway. We'd only need to take a little something from the house. He wouldn't even notice." I saw Benny's disapproval. "Look, we have no legitimate way to get money. If we want to keep going, we're gonna have to break the law, plain and simple. We're too suspicious to pull off a scam, and too decent to rob someone at gunpoint. And no, I'm not calling Angeletti for more cash. That leaves burglary, and trust me, this asshole deserves much worse."

"Who is he?" The question encouraged me. It meant he couldn't argue with any of my points.

"Ted Cole. He owns the company I used to work for."

"Meaning he'll recognize you if he's home."

"First of all, who gives a fuck? We're already fugitives. On top of that, the guy owned the company – he didn't sip tea and roast s'mores with the employees. He has no friggin' clue who I am. And best of all, I know his schedule. He won't be home."

"Wife or kids?"

"A wife," I said. "Not sure about kids."

"You don't see a problem with that?"

"The wife's a wild card, I'll give you that, but if he has kids, they'll be in school." I pushed forward with my pitch before he could attack the fact that it was August. "Look at that patch of woods." I circled the deep green with my finger. "It's a quarter-mile deep, and it's thick. All pine trees. We could take a cab to some place close, walk there, and take a look. If it seems safe, we go in. If not, we leave."

"It's gonna take all the cash we have left just to get up there. What happens if we can't pull it off? We'll be broke."

"One more day of doing nothing will leave us in the same position. We need cash, there's no way around it. If you have an alternative, I'm all ears, but we can be in and out of this place in minutes with enough to get by until we figure things out."

"I don't like it," he said, ending on a note that suggested the addition of, "but it looks like we have no other choice."

"It's for my son, Benny."

"Why do I feel like you're gonna use that argument a whole lot in the coming days?" He sighed and sipped his coffee. "Fine." I stood up with an urge to celebrate, but kept my victory modest. Benny aimed his index finger at my heart. "But this shit better not become a habit, let me tell you. We're not thieves."

"Did you forget what got me locked up? I'm the definition of a thief."

"Yeah, the definition of a *shitty* thief. You'd probably get caught stealing a fucking Snickers bar from a blind man."

"Exactly, and that's why I need you. Of course, if you'd rather let me go alone…"

"Shut up and let me finish my goddamn coffee in peace."

EIGHTEEN

We checked out of our room at ten that morning. From there, we stopped by a hardware store, and by noon we were crouched in thick foliage, scanning the windows of Ted's house for movement. Twenty minutes of careful observation revealed none. As impressive as Ted's house was, it ranked below the others in that neighborhood. Every house seemed to be pulled from someone's dream. Every garage likely held vehicles worth more than I'd earned in years.

The perfect stillness in the area gave my plan extra support. Benny tried, but couldn't find a reason to back out, and so the job began. At the left side of the house, fifteen yards away, a concrete stairway led to the basement. A quick sprint would get us there, out of view of the neighbors and anyone inside. Benny put up three fingers and started a countdown. When the last finger retreated into his fist, we moved. We reached the door seconds later and tucked against it to stay hidden. Benny raised our shiny new hammer and prepared to put it through the small window in the door. I stopped him on the backswing and checked the knob. My last-second common sense paid off.

Benny sighed and slapped his forehead with his palm. *Dumbass,* he thought to himself. I heard the word in his voice, clear as if he'd said it aloud, like I'd eavesdropped on his internal monologue. It felt wrong, but I pushed the guilt aside, opened the door, and entered.

Benny tapped my shoulder as I shut the door behind us. I turned, followed the direction of his pointed finger, and saw the death of my plan. An alarm control panel hung on the wall, staring back at us like an extension of Ted's middle finger. Benny rushed to it. I followed. The display woke as we approached it. The interface on the LCD screen (or LED, maybe – they changed so often back then, and it's been so long) looked like an inexperienced UX designer's idea of the future. Benny turned when he read it, then walked away, laughing silently. I took a look, then I laughed too. In the bottom-right corner, set in fluorescent blue, capitalized Futura type, flashed the word "UNARMED." I turned to see Benny miming relief, running the back of his hand across his forehead.

"Fuck," I said. "I think I need new pants."

We scoured the basement, which doubled as Ted's man cave. Sports memorabilia lined the far wall, surrounding a giant, wall-mounted, flatscreen TV. A bar large enough to serve a night club stretched along the left wall, complete with stools, glasses, tons of liquor, and neon signs in the shapes of beer logos. I searched behind the counter for any place that might hold money. No luck. I accepted the fact that we were likely going to have to pawn jewelry at the end of the theft, but I still hoped for simpler, safer cash.

Nothing on that level seemed like efficient loot. I walked to the doorway that led upstairs and opened it an inch. Benny followed. We listened for any sign of life. After a minute of hearing only our own breaths, we ventured up.

If the basement was proof of a man's presence, the main floor was that of a woman's. The décor was feminine. Obsessively tidy. The majority of the space was stark white, including the carpet (a dangerous choice that always gave me anxiety). Vases of fresh flowers broke up the white by adding spots of muted spring colors every few feet.

We checked the entire floor. Still no sign of life. Still no sign of valuables.

I stopped at a photo of Ted and his wife at a company outing. I recalled that day. Julie and I were there somewhere, just outside of the camera's lens, with the rest of the people Ted didn't give a shit about. His wife's name escaped me. *Carol? Clarissa?* She was far too lovely and charming for Ted. I wondered how she didn't see right through him, down to that slimy core. *Maybe she does,* I figured. *Marriages aren't always based in love.*

We moved up to the second floor, where I had faith that we'd find our treasure. We inspected the rooms, starting at one end of the long hall and working our way to the master bedroom at the other. The first door we opened revealed a guest room, unused and forgotten. Next came an office with a large, mahogany desk in the center and bookshelves lining the walls. An ornate leather throne loomed behind the desk, while two smaller seats cowered in front for visitors. Only a pompous prick could feel comfortable in that setting. The scent of tobacco made it easy to imagine Ted's smug face puffing away at a cigar with an aged scotch in his hand.

A predictably impressive bathroom followed, then a child's bedroom. It belonged to a boy old enough to read novels (*Alice's Adventures in Wonderland*, the entire *Harry Potter* series, *Goosebumps*), but not too old to display superhero posters. Expensive electronics filled the room; the kid had a better TV than I'd had before prison, a newer computer, video game systems I hoped to buy for Marcus one day, and at least a half-dozen other gadgets I couldn't even identify. An odd atmosphere hung over that room. Its tidiness reminded me of a display at a furniture store, as if the OCD that designed the first floor had bled into it. We pressed on, neither of us considering a child's belongings to be an acceptable payday.

A closet and another guest room later, we reached Ted's bedroom. It covered at least half of the second floor, with enough square footage to host a tennis match. A king-sized bed stood five feet tall in the center, with plush steps on each side. All the other furniture (solid wood that made my back ache at the thought of moving it) hugged the outside walls.

"We got a jewelry box and a walk-in closet," I said. "Those are our potential goldmines. You choose."

Benny walked toward his choice. "Jewelry box."

"Great minds think alike. Let's just grab a few pieces and be out."

We opened the wooden box like a couple of eager archeologists cracking into a long-buried sarcophagus, then shared a triumphant grin. Gold and stones screamed from every inch of the interior, which was split in half – one side for Ted's jewelry, the other for his wife's.

"Leave his wife's stuff alone," I said. "A couple of Ted's watches should be more than enough." I grabbed a Movado watch while Benny picked a Rolex. A gaudy, gold "look at me" ring with a ruby the size of a quarter caught my attention. I snatched it, knowing he'd notice it right away. I wished I could see his face when he did.

Deja vu whacked me so hard that I gave in to the urge to look behind me to make sure I didn't get slugged and left for the police. *Ironic*, I thought, *I can trust a felon more than my wife.*

Benny reached back into the box.

"No," I said. "This is plenty. Let's get out of here." He withdrew his arm in agreement and closed the lid.

As we made our exit from the bedroom, good and bad luck struck us in tandem.

The bad: someone was in the house, climbing the stairs, likely en route to the bedroom.

The good: not only were those stairs hardwood, giving us ample warning, but the bedroom was carpeted, letting us slip into the walk-in closet without a sound.

NINETEEN

The footsteps closed in on us until they vanished on the bedroom's carpet. Benny slipped the gun from his waist in case we needed to exit behind its barrel.

"We should have gone to my place," a man's voice said. "We wouldn't have to worry about your husband coming home." The angle of the slits in the closet door prevented us from seeing out, but let us hear the dialogue as if there were no barrier at all.

"Your place is so far away." I recognized this second voice as Ted's wife. "Plus, Ted's at the office until five, at which point he'll unwind by fucking Tina, the office dick depository."

Benny cracked a contagious smile and thought, *We stumbled into a damn soap opera.*

"Don't worry," she continued, "you can always hide in the closet if he shows up."

With a confidence that I doubt even he believed, the man said, "I'm not afraid of your husband. I can handle myself. I'm looking out for you."

"My knight in shining armor," she said sarcastically. "All right, hero, take your clothes off. Even the chain mail."

Benny's eyebrows raised, along with his cheeks. He wondered what she looked like. I pointed toward her through the door and put up ten fingers to satisfy his curiosity.

"How did I get so fucking lucky?" the man said, lending credibility to my score.

"No need for flattery, hun – I'm already in the bed. You gonna take advantage of that, or just let me lie here by myself?"

Cameron, I remembered. *Her name is Cameron.*

The nameless lucky man wasted no more time. I won't include all the details of the fucking that followed, but some are worth mentioning, if only to add some much-needed levity to my story. The man couldn't stop himself from spewing these deep, monotonous grunts and hums which, while embarrassing enough in and of themselves, were risen to absurdity by their even pacing. He seemed like he was trying to keep them on beat with some music track only he could hear.

"Mm. Mm. Uh." *Squeak.* "Mm. Mm. Uh. Uh." *Squeak.*

Benny and I almost blew our cover, fighting to contain ourselves during one of the funniest things either of us had ever heard. Cameron must have had impeccable self-control to be underneath the guy (or on top of him) and not laugh him out of the house.

It's been way too long, I thought, trying to calculate the last time I'd been laid. *Five months.* Benny did his own math and arrived at a much longer time.

When the lovers (lusters?) finished (it took four, maybe five minutes for the groaner to let out his last, climactic roar), I worried about the possibility of Cameron coming to the closet for fresh clothes. I tapped Benny and held my hands together in the shape of a pistol, with my index fingers extended. He readied the gun.

"Sorry to be so rude," Cameron said, seconds after the stud came, before he'd caught his breath, "but you should go."

"That's it?"

"That's it."

He sounded hurt. "So this is what you do? You bring strangers home, then show them the door ten seconds after they pull out?"

"Listen, Eric—"

"It's Derek!"

"Sure, OK. Listen, Derek – I put my cards on the table before I finished my first julep. What did I tell you?"

Derek answered like a child reciting a lesson in school. "You hate your husband. You wouldn't fuck him with *my* dick."

"And what did I say next?"

"You satisfy your needs elsewhere."

"Ding, ding, ding. I satisfy my needs elsewhere. And by 'needs,' I don't mean anything that lasts more than an hour. Or five minutes in this case."

"Fucked and tossed aside," he said over the jingling of his belt buckle. "Fine, have it your way."

"Spare me the guilt trip, kiddo," she said. "You weren't in that bar looking for Juliet. You wanted a pair of spread legs, and you got it. And all before three o'clock! Most men would consider your day a success, don't you think?"

I wavered in a dizzy spell that hit me like an airstrike. A rage filled me, too random and intense to be my own.

Must be Derek. No. Fuck. It's Ted.

"Whore!"

My former boss stormed into the room, and even the thick carpet couldn't muffle his approach.

"You fucking whore!"

A noticeable amount of the brass attitude drained from Cameron's voice. "Ted? Shit, what are you doing home?"

"I'm catching my slut wife naked with another man, that's what the fuck I'm doing."

"Sir," Derek said, "I had no idea she was married."

I thought you could handle her husband, I thought.

"Shut up," Ted said. "I didn't drop from my father's nuts yesterday. Zip up your pants and get the fuck out of my house before I grab the forty-five from the closet. If I ever see you again, you'll never fuck another woman in your life. You hear me?"

"Yes sir, loud and clear. Thank you."

"Don't thank me you spineless little— Get the fuck out!"

The married couple stood silent while Derek stumbled out of the room and down the stairs.

"It was a one-time thing," Cameron said when the distant click of the front door reached the bedroom.

"'You hate your husband,'" Ted said, imitating Derek. "'You wouldn't fuck him with *my* dick. You get it elsewhere.'"

I could feel Cameron digging for an explanation. She remained silent.

"I knew you were a two-timing bitch. For how long, huh? You're lucky I don't…" The sentence fell to a growl before its end. "I work my ass off so you can live like a queen, and this is the fucking thanks I get?"

"Oh, right," Cameron said, regaining her edge, "I forgot I was talking to the virtuous and faithful Theodore Cole. What a fucking joke. You roll in here at all hours of the night smelling like liquor and stale bitches, and you expect *me* to be celibate?"

"If you'd fuck me every once in a while, maybe I'd be more faithful."

"If I fucked you, I'd probably have syphilis."

"Don't test me," he warned.

"Or what? Big, bad Ted's gonna hit me like the fucking coward he is? I dare you."

"You dare me? You dare me?"

He rushed her, leaving us no choice but to intervene. Benny knew my intent. Without a single word between us, he ripped the door open and stepped out, gun drawn.

Our entrance paused the violence. Ted straddled Cameron, who lay on her back, still naked. His hands clamped her throat. The two looked up at us, frozen and confused. Ted's grip weakened, but his hand remained glued to Cameron's skin. She sucked in air and coughed.

"Get off her," Benny said, locking onto Ted. "Now."

Ted raised his hands, keeping his movements slow and deliberate. He looked at his wife in disgust. "How many guys did you have in line?" He wanted to spit at her. "Unbelievable."

"We're not with her," I said. The bag in my hand explained the rest.

"Look fellas, if it's money you want, I got plenty. There's uh – there's a fortune in jewelry over there. Take it all."

"We have what we came for," I said, raising the bag. "Now let's try this one more time: get off of her."

He obeyed and pivoted on his knees over Cameron to face us. She shuffled backward until she reached the leg of her bed. She sat up against it and hugged herself, doing her best to cover her bare body. A small blanket sat on the foot of the mattress, somehow still neat and folded after Derek and Cameron's romp. I walked over, snatched it from the bed, opened it, and draped it over her. Her eyes thanked me.

Ted began worrying when Benny didn't lower the gun. "You guys saw the whole thing," he said from his knees, trying to recruit us to his side. "She cheated on me in my own bed. I was aggravated. I overreacted, that's all. I wasn't going to do anything crazy, I swear. You understand." He looked so pathetic. So desperate. The Ted before us was the Ted I always knew existed outside of the office. The Ted stripped of his title, his position of power. Nothing to hide behind.

You walked past me every day, nose in the air, never noticing me enough to remember my face when I burst from your closet with a gun. Always thinking about your next million. Those millions mean nothing now. All you have is your true self and the hope that we'll excuse it.

"Don't leave me alone with him," Cameron begged, clutching the blanket and looking to me for help. "Please. He'll try to kill me."

Ted shook his head. "Full of shit. You see that, right? She's completely full of shit."

"Fuck you," she said. "You'd never lay a finger on me, right? Right. Why don't you tell them why my wrist hurts every time I close my left hand."

My head pounded.

Please, no. Not now.

The familiar shock ignored my plea, and as it scorched the inside of my forehead, Cameron's hate trickled into me. Then her fear. Then her pain. My wrist throbbed; I felt Ted's claws twisting and pulling it. Memories came in surges, like I was an amnesiac remembering a past that wasn't my own.

Cameron walks through the front door, tipsy from cocktails, high from the music and the dance floor.

Ted confronts her before she makes it three steps into the foyer. "Where have you been?"

"Dancing. With Liz and the girls."

"Don't fucking lie to me. Who is he?"

She ignores him and walks toward the kitchen.

He cuts her off.

She pushes him.

His nostrils flare, he slaps her, he snatches her wrist in his vice grip. Her struggle worsens it.

"What's the plan, brother?" Benny said, pulling me from the couple's scuffle. His left hand trembled.

"What's happening?" Ted cried, holding his wrist and grimacing.

They felt it, too. Cameron's experience that night was pumping through me, amplifying before being beamed into everyone in that room. Cameron rocked back and forth, writhing, reliving the abuse, strengthening the transmission. I gritted my teeth, fought the agony. She wanted Ted dead. That meant I wanted Ted dead. Benny's left hand clenched and shook. His right tightened around the gun as Cameron's bloodthirst made its way to him.

"Who is he?"

"Let go of me. Fucking asshole, let go!"

She throws a sloppy, drunk punch with her free hand, but only succeeds in getting it caught as well.

Ted pulls both arms and thrusts his knee into her stomach.

She moans and dry heaves.

He pulls one last time.

Everyone in the bedroom wailed from the mutual sensation of Cameron's snapping bones. A second later, a gunshot tore through our screams.

I fell to my hands and knees. My vision clouded. I didn't know which way was up. I struggled through the internal ringing to regain my composure. When I looked up, my watery eyes went to Cameron, who covered her mouth with both hands and stared at something to my right. I traced her gaze to Ted, who lay still on the floor in front of a blood-spattered wall. Benny's aim remained on the lifeless body. A tear ran down his cheek.

"What did I do?" Cameron asked from a trillion miles away. She studied her hands like she would study an alien object, not understanding what happened, but knowing she caused it.

"Nothing," I said in a low voice, rising from my knees, my eyes on Ted.

"How can you say that? My wrist. You felt it. All of you. I wanted you to shoot him." She ran a hand through her hair, forgetting her nakedness, and looked at Benny. "I wanted you to shoot him, and you did. How did I do that?"

"It wasn't you," I stressed. "You should get up. Get dressed."

She recoiled when she remembered her nudity, then rose and rushed to the closet.

"Don't do anything stupid," I called after her. I don't know what kind of stupid thing I expected.

"I killed him," Benny said, his pose still frozen in the moment he pulled the trigger. I put a hand on his shoulder. He lowered the gun, sniffled, and wiped a tear away. "Why? I didn't even know him, then… then I just hated him so much."

"Benny, listen to me. That wasn't you. You had no control over what just happened."

He looked at me as if I'd missed the point. "Is that any better?"

"Yes," I said. "It's much better." When I heard Cameron emerge from the closet, I turned to face her. She clutched a gun. "Whoa!" I jumped back. Benny saw it too, but his own weapon remained pointed at the ground. He only turned away like nothing besides himself existed.

"No!" she yelled. "Shit, no, I didn't mean to scare you." She raised her hands and the gun above her head in surrender. "I'm not using it, I'm giving it to you."

I stepped forward and snatched it from her hand. "Why would we want this?"

"Is yours registered?"

"No."

"Good. Wipe it down and leave it. Take my husband's, it's not registered either."

"What's your angle?"

"My husband was just shot in the head, not ten minutes after Eric—"

"Derek."

"Whatever. Not ten minutes after he left us ready to tear each other apart. What's the first thing the cops are gonna think?" She saw that I understood. "Yeah. They're gonna figure Ted and I got into a hell of a brawl after Derek left, and that I shot him. If you leave your gun, I can tell them it was a hit. Hitmen leave their guns behind."

"Kind of a stretch, don't you think?" I said.

"Not if you knew what Ted kept locked in his desk. There's a reason he has an unregistered gun in his closet. You don't want to take your gun with you anyway."

"It'll connect us to the bullet," Benny mumbled in the opposite direction of us, then wiped the gun down with his shirt and dropped it.

"See?" Cameron said, pointing to him. "He's smart." She crossed the room to a bookshelf. She pulled a vase from it, removed some fake daffodils, and reached in. After some rummaging, she pulled something out. The flowers returned to the vase, the vase returned to the shelf, and Cameron returned to us.

"My jewelry," she demanded with one hand out, palm up. The other offered a stack of cash as a trade.

"Why are you doing all this?" I asked. "Giving us a gun, and now cash?"

"You two saved my life." Those five words carried a long-awaited relief, and an unguarded sincerity that she hadn't seemed capable of. Then, returning her attitude to its status quo, she said, "And because I'd rather you take my cash than my jewelry."

"We only took Ted's watches."

"Give 'em here," she said. "Come on, I don't have all day. I need to call the police and get ahead of this thing."

This thing.

I accepted her trade, and as we swapped items, our hands touched. A spark jumped between us on the spots where our skin met. It startled me, but no more than a static shock. Her reaction was much more dramatic; she retracted her hand and backed up. Her eyes studied me with a blend of awe and sympathy.

She walked to her nightstand while I looked on, confused. She grabbed a notepad and pen, scribbled something, ripped out the sheet, and folded it. Then, instead of handing it to me, she pushed it into my jeans pocket. "Go."

TWENTY

"There's over eight thousand dollars in here," I said, capping off another thousand-dollar stack with a fifty-dollar bill. Rain thumped against the roof and pinged on the metal awning above our motel room's door. The lightbulbs buzzed, and each flicker threatened to kill them for good. A five-second darkness halted my accounting duties, and when the light returned, I finished in a hurry before another came. "Eight thousand, one hundred, and fifty bucks. Hey, Benny, you listening? We're set. Thank you, Cameron Cole."

Benny didn't respond, but instead continued the silence he'd kept up since we left the Cole home. Our jog to a payphone and the subsequent cab ride consisted of zipped lips, punctuated by my awkward attempts to keep our focus away from what we'd left behind in that bedroom. These attempts only bounced off of Benny. By the time I finished counting the money, an hour had passed since he'd spoken. I couldn't ignore it any longer.

"You have to talk to me, Ben."

The lights blinked three times.

He twisted a paper towel in his hands. "Nothing to say."

"That's not true. Come on."

"Why not just reach in my head and pull out what I'm thinking?" he said. "Go ahead, take a look."

"You know that's not how—"

"I don't know shit!" he hissed with an abrupt shift from melancholy to anger. The paper towel dropped in pieces as he stood up and turned to me. After four more blinks, the light gave up altogether. Benny's tense face disappeared, but he persisted, unfazed. "Whatever you have going on inside you just made me kill a man. A father. In his own fucking bedroom. I just…" My eyes couldn't find him in the lightless room, but I heard him pacing somewhere in front of me. "I need to understand why I pulled that trigger."

"I wish I could give you an answer," I said, not knowing exactly where to aim my voice. "Trust me, I know how you feel."

"No," he said, suddenly much closer. "You don't know the half of what the fuck I feel."

"No? You can't trust your own thoughts. You're wondering which decisions you've made in the past two days were your own. Which emotions. You're constantly paranoid in your own head, hoping I'm not looking in there. You're afraid. Spot on, right?" I still couldn't see him, but I felt the fire in his eyes two feet away.

"That's just scratching the surface of the shit that's pumping through me right now," he said. My eyes finally adjusted enough to see the shape of his head. "But it doesn't matter whether or not you know how I feel. It makes no difference whatsoever. It ain't gonna change what happened. It won't undo what I did, and I'll still have to live with it."

"Christ, Benny, grow a pair."

"Excuse me?" He cut the distance between us in half. I felt his warm breath on the bridge of my nose.

"Look at you," I said, hoping he felt mine. "Sulking. Sorry for yourself. How the fuck do you think I feel? My whole world's upside down. I have to live with this fucked up shit, too. I can't even pay for a fucking hammer at a hardware store without worrying if some schmuck in the next aisle is gonna get a glimpse of the cop I beat with a baton. You killed one wife-beating, attempted murderer – involuntarily – and you want me to feel sorry for you? News bulletin: it's not happening. At least you have the luxury of being able to leave. I'm stuck with this shit."

"You're right," he said. "I *can* leave, and I'd be a whole lot better off." A few short-lived flashes lit up the room before the bulbs faded again.

"Go on then, leave. I need this like a knife in my nuts, you know that? Fuck you, guilt-tripping me over shit I can't control. Take your half of the cash and get the hell out of my room."

He felt his way to the bed and his money. "Gladly." The light returned after his hand found the first stack.

As he gathered his cut, I gave in to the temptation to deliver the last barb. I could have let him go in peace. I could have been civil. But I didn't. And I wasn't. This is what I pierced him with:

"You're acting like you've never murdered anyone before."

I didn't know the full weight of the statement when I said it, since I didn't know the details of Benny's crime. Now I know. I know that those words were cruel beyond belief. I still feel like a bastard, after all these years. But I said it, and I can't change that. Benny made me pay for it, though, and I'm glad he got that satisfaction.

A quick right hook put me down. I deserved worse.

The door slammed behind me. I crawled to the bed and pulled myself onto it. Below me, even through watery eyes, I saw dots of blood hit the forest green comforter and saturate the threads of the fabric.

Great.

I forced myself up and into the shower, thinking I could wash the quarrel off of me. I couldn't. Afterward, I swept the cash off of the bed and fell into the mattress. As my eyes began to sag and my mind had almost quit for the night, I remembered the note that Cameron Cole had slipped into my pocket. Without getting out of the bed, I reached down to the floor for my pants and reeled them in. I dug for the folded paper, opened it, and read it, still half off the mattress. I heard her voice as I read the purple, almost calligraphic message.

You'll need help finding Marcus.
Call me when you do.
774-406-7145
P.S. Your secrets are safe with me.
All of them.

The spark, I thought. I saw then that the split second of contact had opened me like a book with all its stories leaping from the page. A chill ran through me, adding to the cold I already felt from the ceiling fan blowing down at my still-damp skin. My first instinct told me to run out of the room, to find Benny and tell him all about it. But my stubbornness wouldn't let me do it. Even so, I wished he would come back.

Maybe he's in a room nearby, I thought.

It turned out he *was* in a nearby room, with plans to take off the next morning. The clerk put him only one wall away from me, in an arbitrary decision that would save my life. From any other room, Benny wouldn't have been able to hear my screams the next morning.

TWENTY-ONE

This is how I met Lincoln Alders:

Julie and I stepped into the vestibule of an apartment building that probably charged more per day than the Waldorf Astoria. Even with no one in sight, I felt underdressed in my t-shirt and jeans. Julie hit the call button for apartment 23. The circle lit up blue, then white when Lincoln's voice came through the speaker.

"Jules?"

"Hi, Lincoln," she said.

Without another word from our host, the door unlocked with a hum.

"Jules?" I said with a raised eyebrow as I held the door for her. "Really?"

She shrugged. "That's what he calls me. Never had the heart to tell him I didn't care for it."

We entered the lobby. I let Julie lead me to the elevator, too entranced by the sea of tan marble, dark wood, and gold accents to make my own way. The *ding* of the opening elevator door broke my admiration. When we reached the second floor and exited the lift, I saw the half-open door at the end of the hall. A James Bond look-alike leaned out of it, lacking the suit, but fittingly dressed in all black and white. He waved to us.

"Jules," he said as we approached him, "gorgeous as ever." I held back an eye roll as he hugged her and kissed each cheek. "And this must be the lucky husband."

"It is," Julie said. "Lincoln, this is Will. Will, Lincoln." We shook hands and gave each other a smiling nod.

He was middle-aged; his black hair had traces of grays, his face had traces of wrinkles. He had a sure manner, like he knew he surpassed all expectations simply by existing. Nothing about him suggested mediocrity.

He opened the door wide and gestured for us to enter. "Please, come in."

His apartment was plucked from my own unrealistic ambitions. Modern styling graced every inch. Black, white, or red covered everything, without exception, from the light fixtures to a fountain pen and the table it rested on. If Lincoln owned a yellow cereal box or a green pack of gum, he kept it hidden. I felt as if my own clothing threw off the balance of the space.

"Can I offer either of you a drink?" he said, opening the freezer for ice as if we'd already answered. "A friend of mine just sent me what he describes as 'the greatest rum the world's ever tasted.' I've been waiting for an excuse to pour myself a glass."

I looked at my watch. Two o'clock.

"I'd love some," Julie said. "Not too much, please."

Lincoln held up the glass decanter. "Will?"

"None for me, thanks."

"A beer, perhaps? Or water?"

"A beer sounds good."

After serving our drinks, Lincoln led us to the living room. The décor followed the rest of the apartment, but with an added punch: the room held an intimidating collection of weaponry. No less than a hundred pieces adorned the walls. The calculated placement of each item led my eye smoothly through the display, up and down over swords, daggers, crossbows, axes, knives, guns, and other tools of death I couldn't name. And true to the rest of the apartment, black, white, and red covered every handle, stand, sheath, and blade.

The visual journey ended at the far wall, where a fireplace stood surrounded by black and white tiles. The deep, red flame inside reflected off of them to give the structure its one missing color. Above it hung the focal point of the room, the obvious pride of the collection: a magnificent, entirely black katana. The handle took the shape of a snake, knotted and coiled around its own body. From its open jaw came the blade, a dark strip of metal without a single blemish. The sword levitated on the wall, with no visible shelf or brackets.

Lincoln noticed me taking it all in. "What's the verdict?"

"It's amazing," I said.

"I think we'll get along just fine." He sat on a black leather chair, leaned back, crossed his legs, and took a sip of his clear rum. "I apologize for being blunt, but I assume the two of you didn't come here for drinks by the fire. Please, sit down." Julie and I sat on the couch. "What can I do for you?"

Julie shuffled in her seat and sat straight. "Do you remember what I asked you when I found out what you do for a living? What you told me?"

"Yes," he said. "I told you that if you didn't have that foolish spending habit hovering over you, you'd make an excellent partner." He looked at me. "I don't know how much Julie has told you about me, Will. About what I do."

I didn't know how to respond. How much was I supposed to know about this man? What was appropriate to say? I turned to Julie, who gave me a silent go-ahead. Seconds passed as I tried to find an eloquent way to put it. None came to me, so I resorted to simplicity. "You're a thief."

Lincoln half-laughed. "Not a flattering label, but true nonetheless. Has she told you how we became acquainted?"

"No," I said.

"I met your wife – long before she held that title, of course – at the bar she used to tend. Are you still working there, Jules?"

"I quit a while back," she said. "I'm at a pub a few miles away now."

"Hm. Anyway, I'm not proud to say that I was drunker than I should have been that night, and I filled poor Julie's ears with my pent-up aggravation. You see, I can't go around venting the stresses of my career, for obvious reasons. But she seemed trustworthy. Kind, caring. So I spilled my story, and in return, she told me hers. The maxed-out credit cards and the debt collectors. We became each other's confession booth. It wasn't long before she pictured herself in my line of work, which must have seemed so exciting and cinematic coming from my drunken accounts. She wanted in on the action. But even after a dozen drinks, I knew enough to see the danger in working with a shopping addict." Julie looked down into her glass of rum. "I'm sorry, Jules, but that's what you were."

"No need to apologize."

"I did, however, value our conversation, and we kept in touch. For a while. We haven't spoken in some time." He addressed Julie now. "I visited the bar a year or so ago. You weren't working, but I spoke with Melissa. I was glad to hear that you bettered yourself. And that you were married." He lifted his glass in a silent toast. "I admit I was shocked, maybe even a bit worried, by your call yesterday."

"I'm sorry that I don't have an innocent motive for getting back in touch," she said.

"Go on."

"Will and I are going through a tough time. He was laid off a few months back. He's done everything to find another job, but you know how it is out there."

"I'm sorry to hear that," he said to me.

"I send out resumes every damn day," I said. "I can't catch a break. The few bites I get tell me I'm overqualified. I'd work at McDonald's right now if" – my speech twitched and my chest shuddered – "if I could. We have a kid to feed."

Lincoln sipped his rum. "That's terrible." We sat in silence for a few seconds before he said, "Forgive me if I come across as cold or unfeeling, but again I must be blunt with you. What is it you want from me?"

"I hoped you'd give us a job that could buy us some time," Julie said.

"A job?"

"You know…doing what you do. We'd make it worth your while. You plan it with us, then we'll do all the field work. We'll give you fifty percent. You won't need to step foot on the site or risk yourself in any way."

"Sixty percent," he countered without hesitation.

"Done," she said.

He took down the rest of his drink and set it on the glass table. "You finally caught that break, Will. I happen to have something on my radar that would bring your forty percent to at least a quarter million. I assume that's enough to pay your bills until you get back on your feet?"

I nearly spit out my beer. I swallowed hard, then coughed as it went down the wrong pipe.

Lincoln chuckled at my reaction. "I'll take that as a yes. And who knows? Julie may even get some new jewelry out of the deal."

TWENTY-TWO

Thud. Thud-thud.

"Will?" *Thud.*

Thud-thud-thud.

"Will!" *Thud.*

I emerged from sleep in time for the knocking to stop. When I shifted in the bed, my upper body exploded in agony.

From the door I heard, "I'm coming in." A key slid into the lock of my door. I raised my head as Benny barged in, frantic. "What's going on?" said the silhouette in the rays of the morning light. "You were screaming." He froze at the sight of me, his stare both terrified and terrifying.

I clenched something in my hand that bit into my skin. I raised my arm to see the mystery item. Blood ran from the edges of a mirror shard embedded in my palm. My arm was an abstract composition of reds and maroons. I lifted my head further. More blood. The bed looked like a set piece from *A Nightmare on Elm Street*.

Too much blood to have come from just my hand, I thought. I dropped the shard and bolted to the bathroom. Every movement ripped me apart. A gruesome reflection filled what remained of the shattered bathroom mirror. At least a dozen slashes (seventeen, I would later count) crossed my upper body and face, running downward from my right to my left. Even the smallest of them looked worthy of stitches. The largest were windows to the muscle underneath. I couldn't breathe. My body shook.

Benny stood behind me, looking at me like I'd been marked with stigmata. "Why? Why would you do this?"

I tried to speak, to tell him I didn't know, but my voice failed. My shakes grew more violent until I couldn't stand. Benny caught me as my legs melted and led me to the edge of the bathtub.

"Lay in there," he said, easing me backward into the tub. I followed his orders, gripping his arm until I was in place. "Good God," he said, assessing the mutilated mess. He motioned the sign of the cross. "OK, don't worry, brother. You're gonna be fine. We just gotta get you cleaned up." He grabbed a towel, looked at me again, and decided that it couldn't handle the job. "Fuck." He ran to the other room and back. "It's eight o'clock. The pharmacy up the street should be open. I'll be back in a few. Don't move, all right?" I tried to agree as he disappeared.

I waited in perfect silence, staring up at the scowling shower faucet that loomed overhead.

Darkness.

A hand presses a kitchen knife against my chest, waits as if to taunt me, then rips it away. Blood flies, then flows. I scream in a pitch higher than I thought I was capable of.

"Why?" I yell. I try to budge, try to escape, but coils around my waist and wrists hold me in place. "What do you want with me?"

A distorted laugh answers me. It sounds familiar.

My vision cleared. The shower head eyed me once again, like it wanted nothing more than to rain down on me. The reprieve didn't last; I fell back to confinement. Back to the blade.

My torturer calculates each slice. The edge of the steel rests on my forehead. He laughs again and yanks downward to my left. Blood drapes over my eyes.

The crimson curtain fades.

I returned to the real world, to the motel's bathroom. Benny stood over me, panting. I felt safe from the nightmare's clutches. He dropped four heavy plastic shopping bags on the floor. From one he produced a bottle of ibuprofen. From another, a gallon of water.

"Take these," he said, holding the pills over my mouth. I opened and let them drop in, swallowing them without the water. "Drink." I took the gallon, barely able to support it, and poured the cold spring water in and around my mouth. It tasted like heaven. Benny went to work emptying the bags and scattering pharmaceutical products across the sink counter. When he finished, the lineup contained three gallons of water, aspirin, ibuprofen, sterile cloths, antibacterial ointment and soap, medical tape, gauze, wound closure strips, and a bucket of ice from the motel's lobby.

Benny focused on one wound at a time, from the largest to the smallest, each one getting the same multi-step treatment.

Step 1: he numbed the area with the ice.

Step 2: he gave the slice a gentle scrub with the bottled water and antibacterial soap.

Step 3: he patted it dry, fighting the constant rush of fresh blood, and applied ointment.

Step 4: he placed the closure strips over the couple gashes that they could reach across.

Step 5: he wrapped me with gauze and medical tape.

Neither of us spoke a single word during this process. I wanted to. I tried to thank him, to apologize to him, to tell him that how I acted the night before was disgusting and wrong, but the thoughts wouldn't turn to words.

With all the damage dressed, Benny cleaned the remaining dried blood off of me. We managed to get me out of the tub and to the main room, a feat I couldn't have accomplished alone. I saw the bed and the mess I'd made of it. The white sheets were now covered in red-brown patches, like giant used Band-Aid pads. Benny set me on the bed that had been his before our argument, then replaced my bloody boxers with a towel.

"I appreciate it, brother," I said, my voice a low croak that only reached him by chance. "All of it." It was all I could say. No apology would do. No amount of thanks.

"Yeah, you better," he said. "Now shut up and sleep."

"What if I do it again?"

"You won't. I'll watch you."

I closed my eyes and slept.

TWENTY-THREE

When I returned to the waking world, Benny sat cross-legged on the floor, studying the notepad from the room's nightstand. I knew any significant movement would mean self-torture. I turned my head toward him like a long-neglected tin man. "What are you reading?"

"You should be sleeping," he said without looking up. "It's barely been an hour."

"I slept all – ah, fuck that hurts – I slept all night, in between mauling myself. Come on, what is it?"

He looked up at me, not knowing how to answer. After a second or two of hesitation, he said, "A letter."

"From him?" I asked with sudden surge of anxiety. "From Robert?" He nodded. "Read it to me."

He stood and held out the pad. "I think he expects you to read it yourself."

I gave a slight effort to sit up. The shift made my chest feel like it was under attack from a squad of circular saws. "Fuck, fuck, fuck. God-fucking-dammit!"

"I told you," Benny said, "you need rest. Need to stay still."

I took the notepad. "I'm gonna to go out on a limb and say that this letter is more important than a nap." I held it above my face, and even in that stiff, conservative pose, I could feel each and every gash burn like lava bubbled beneath them. I held still with a clenched jaw until the pain passed, until I could focus on the letter. Traces of my own penmanship hid behind the tiny, sloppy, manic writing. "Is it bad?" I asked.

He turned away from me. "It sure as hell ain't good."

Will
You're in danger. Somethings going to happen to you - I don't know what it
No.
It happened It did, didn't it? I was too late. What was it? What happened to you? I can't see it but I feel blood. My chest hurts. Burns. But you're alive Thats good, really good. You'll recover I know you will. You have to, you're meant to find me. You have to.

I saw your escape. The busses and the inmates running in every direction and Angeletti's voice in your head and

No, there are more important things I need to tell you while I can. I'm still trapped, but I know more now. Still not enough. The woman in the next room spoke to me. It took time. She's paranoid, I understand. Paranoia may save her here. Our conversation was bad, will. I didn't—she has no answers. She's the same as me. She knows nothing, same as me, just a nameless bird in a cage. And I had so much hope.

She knows NOTHING. A cruel fucking joke.

Do we have families? Does anybody miss us?

Heather. We call her Heather. For now, until our real names come back to us. Then—no more Robert & Heather.

She's thin. Blonde. By her own description, she told me that, I haven't seen her. Her face is bruised. Her cheek is split. She doesn't know how either happened, but it doesn't take much of an imagination. Something knots up inside me when she speaks. We knew each other before this, Her voice is comforting in a way that only familiarity breeds.

And she's seen him. Our captor. He's tall, she says. Handsome, but cold. 50-55. Black hair with bits of gray. He visited her for something. He's looking for something—something he thinks we know about. She told him what I've told you. The truth.

She cant remember anything. He thinks shes lying. He asked again & again and he hit her and asked again. But you cant pull water from stone. Hes still not convinced. He stopped feeding her. Its been 2 days. I feel guilty about eating while she goes hungry. It makes the meals taste like greed.

These terrible gashes across my body and face — the ones I told you about — must be from him. He must have interrogated me. Before I lost my memory. How did I hold out? Maybe I had no choice. Maybe its better that I cant remember the encounter.

Now his moved on to Heather. Will she face the same brutality when the starvation fails to produce an answer? Is this man capable of hacking away at a defenseless woman? I know the answer. Still — I hope Im wrong.

So many things so many

You're afraid, and with good reason, but you're not the only one experiencing these things, Will. The strange visions, the images like photos speeding by, the unexplainable emotions, the emotions you know can't be your own. The thoughts you would never think dropping into your head like I don't know what, like oil dropping into water and rising to the top, just sitting there impossible to ignore.

You're not alone in this. Remember that. And you blame yourself. For the deaths, the officer, your boss. None of them are your fault. Remember that too.

It's horrifying, this thing inside us, yet I, I don't know how to explain it. Amazing? Phenomenal? Neither seems right. When I first wrote you it seemed impossible that an incarcerated man could ever help me with my predicament but I knew it somehow I knew it and look at you now. A free man. Is there any stronger proof that your path is connected to mine?

We need you, Heather and I.

I'll try to hm

It happened again that shock the fucking shok charging through my head it hurts like a bitch. You know it. I saw you I have to write fast can't lose it you in the back seat of a cop car in the back seat of a your concentrating Bennys concentrating youre in cuffs no youre not in cuffs or I don't know I see both I

It's been hours since I wrote the gibberish above, Im better now. It hurts still, but Im better. Less pain. I would elaborate on what I wrote, but as I read it now, it means nothing to me. I don't remember seeing anything involving a cop or a back seat or cuffs. My mind is splintered I need to rest.

One last thing.
Whatever happened to you whatever I was
too late to warn you of - pull through
it. We need you.

Robert

I dropped the pad on the bed beside me and looked at Benny. "Am I still in the real world, Ben?"

"Funny," he said, "I asked myself the same thing when I finished it."

TWENTY-FOUR

I only ventured from the bed once the next day, and only to use the bathroom. That painful trip took over twenty minutes and left me wary of eating or drinking anything that would usher in the next one sooner. My upper body burned so much that I half expected to see smoke rise from it. Every movement required a plan, and even a small cough had rippling effects that made me desperate for Percocet. Benny took care of me, all the while showing commendable restraint by not prodding too much into what had happened.

"I know what you know," I told him when that restraint finally caved. "I woke up mangled. That's all I got." That was a small lie; I could've told him about the visions I had in the bathtub, of those hands reaching from the dark, pressing the blade to my flesh and jerking it away. But they had been unclear at best. *Just confusion from blood loss*, I told myself. *Hallucinations.* I wonder if I knew, somewhere deep inside, that I was bullshitting myself.

We refused housekeeping. We had to. The sight of those bed-sheets would have sent the poor cleaning lady (a sweet, thick-accented, Portuguese senior citizen named Maria) running to the cops. Washing them ourselves wouldn't work; the maroon splotches would never be white again. So we decided that when the time came to leave, we'd flee before anyone discovered the mess. That's not to say we left the room looking like a massacre during our stay. Benny cleaned the best he could and covered the bed in case any curious eyes peeked in.

Our newfound bankroll made my recovery possible. I hate to think about what the hell I would have done if we didn't have the cash to keep that room. I could barely get to the toilet to take a leak, let alone survive out on the streets. The cash also allowed us (Benny) to go shopping for supplies to get us through our stay. He left at ten o'clock on the morning after the incident and returned six hours later with enough bags to require a second trip to the cab.

"You weren't supposed to spend it all," I said as he came in with the second round of bags and closed the door with his foot.

He plopped the bags on the ground. "That damn laptop you wanted cost more than all the rest of this stuff combined."

"It'll make our lives easier, trust me. Now, let's see the atrocious clothes you picked out for me." He put two bags on my bed. I rummaged through them, stiff as if I'd been encased in a cast. "I doubted you, but these ain't bad. What about boxers and socks?"

"They're in there somewhere," he said. "Let me tell ya, eight years of lockup makes you appreciate buying your own stuff. I never thought of freedom as being able to grab a magazine from a store shelf. And I saw the craziest shit – the guy in front of me in line had the cashier scan his phone as a coupon. Did you know they could do that?"

"Technology's come a long way since you've seen the outside. Expect a serious culture shock. What else did you get?"

"Let's see." He knelt down before the pile and took an inventory of his purchases. "We got some food, water, a few beers, deodorant, toothbrushes, toothpaste, a *Sports Illustrated*. Oh, and a book for you."

"Sweet. I thought about that after you left. What'd you get me?"

"I asked the guy at the bookstore what a hipster would like, and he gave me…" He pulled out a book and read the cover. "*Sirens of Titan.*"

"Perfect." He frisbeed the book to me, and I flipped through the crisp pages, spotting and trying to pronounce in my head the phrase, "chronosynclastic infundibulum."

"I also grabbed a couple duffle bags for when we get moving again."

"Good thinking."

"Some string and sewing needles…"

"Come again," I said, then realized what they were for. "Oh, hell no."

"Those strips will be fine for some of your smaller cuts, but the big ones need to be closed up."

"Fuck, man."

"Gotta be done."

"Jesus, this is gonna suck so fucking much."

"Sure will," he said. I threw him an evil eye. He put his palms up as if to push the glare back at me. "Hey, I ain't gonna sugarcoat it. There's a bright side, though – I got something for you when it's done."

"Nothing is worth being stitched up without an anesthetic by a guy who can't even sew a button."

"Preventing an infection is worth it, asshole. But if that's not enough of an incentive for you, I got this." He reached into the pocket of his new jeans and pulled out a sandwich bag, then tossed it to me. Three joints, rolled so well that they resembled filterless cigarettes, sat inside. I laughed and grimaced from the pain it caused. "It gets better," he said, holding up a blue package. "I got Oreos, too."

I resisted a chuckle to spare myself more pain. "What makes you think I wanna get high?"

"What the hell else are you gonna do sitting in that bed?"

o   o   o

Two and a half hours later, my body looked like an amateur

seamstress's practice run.

"How bad was it?" Benny said, putting a flame to the tip of a joint. "On a scale of one to ten." The sweet aroma hit my nose and brought me back to my teenage summers.

"How would you rank being fucked with a fork?"

He took a puff and answered, holding his breath. "Nine."

"Well, there you go."

I'll skip the two hours it took Benny to sew up the thirteen worst wounds. The "improvised stitching" scene has been done in every storytelling medium you can name, although I've never seen any character do it guided by an internet video in which the host (a doctor, allegedly) stitched a hunk of pork. The only thing I'll note is the most obvious but obligatory – the process was brutal. Afterward, we sat on the floor, drinking beer and passing the weed back and forth. I don't know why we sat on the floor, but we did.

"If you so much as get a paper cut," I told my surgeon, "I'm returning the favor."

"Well," he said, passing the joint to me, "the way things happen around you, you might get your wish."

I took a hit. "Knock on wood." The pull struck the back of my throat like steel wool. After a short, painful coughing fit, I asked, "How long's it been for you?"

"Since I smoked? Shit. Nine, ten years. You?"

"Six months, but before that it was probably three years or so. You realize how high we're gonna get?"

"The higher, the better, brother. We need a break from reality right about now." He walked to the mini fridge and came back with two beers. He handed one to me and said, "Hey, I got a joke for ya."

"I've heard every joke in your arsenal."

"Nah, I read this one at the store when I bought your book. Check it out: Three sick guys go to a doctor. One is an alcoholic, one's a chain smoker, and the last dude's gay. Doctor tells them that if they indulge in their habit one more time, they'll die."

"Are you calling homosexuality a habit? One that makes you sick?"

"Man, it's a joke – shut up and listen to it. So the three guys leave the doctor. The alcoholic, he sees a bar and hears the music, the people dancing. Shit's too tempting. He starts partying, and before you know it, he takes a shot of tequila. Right when it hits his throat, he drops dead, just like the doctor said he would." Benny paused to take a quick hit, nearly blowing into the joint from laughing at the untold climax of the joke. "So the other two walk away, talking about how serious the shit is. Then the chain smoker sees a half a cigarette on the ground, still burning. The tobacco smell is too much for him. He can't resist. He goes to grab it, and the gay guy says to him, 'If you bend over and pick that up, we're both dead.'"

We cracked up at that dumb joke like only a couple blazed nitwits could. It hurt. A lot.

"One more, one more," he said. "Why are black people so tall?" I shrugged. "Because their knee grows!"

I laughed. "All right, my turn," I said, remembering a joke that Riley had told me back in prison. "What's the difference between Batman and a black man? Batman can go into a store without Robin!" I delivered the punchline with all the confidence in the world, expecting hysterics. Instead, Benny's face hardened. His eyes grabbed mine with a stare that would've intimidated Bruce Lee.

"Will," he said, "don't you ever say some racist shit like that to me again."

"Benny, c'mon. You know me. I didn't mean nothing by it. Riley was just talking shit one day and—" I stopped at the sight of his lip straining to keep straight. "Motherfucker," I said as he broke the act.

"Should'a seen your face, man. Trembling like you said 'nigger' in the fucking projects."

We laughed for five minutes straight, taking turns starting back up again as the other calmed down. My cheek muscles hurt almost as much as my chest did. I still smile when I think about it. I'm smiling as I write this. That was the best I'd felt since getting locked up. My upper body was a war zone, and the laughing made sure I didn't forget it, but my spirits were high.

A somber silence followed the end of the exchange. We each sipped our beer.

"My girls and I used to laugh like that all the time," Benny said. "I miss them like crazy, man."

"I know you do. I can feel it. Tell me about them. You know everything about Marcus, but I feel like I know nothing about your family."

"Well, Tammy's the smart one. Not that Destiny's stupid by any means, but she don't care about books and art and all that. Tammy wants to be a physicist when she grows up. Imagine that – a thirteen-year-old girl who wants to be a physicist."

"I don't even know what a physicist does," I said.

"Neither do I, but Tammy does. Then there's Destiny." He scratched his head as if he was thinking through an impossible puzzle. "She's a hard worker. Passionate. But she don't know what the hell she likes. She's done ballet, baseball, painting, and every other extracurricular activity you can think of. And she excels at them all, too. The problem is she hates them." He sipped his beer through a smile. "All in all, though, I got a couple of angels."

"You should be thankful your twins are girls. They're easier. Two boys would drive the Dalai Lama mad. Marcus is always looking for trouble, always karate-chopping something." I thought of him kicking pillows, pretending to be a ninja.

"Neither is easier," Benny said. "Just different, that's all. I came up in a big family. Had a hand in raising over a dozen kids. Brothers and sisters, nieces and nephews. You know what that showed me? Boys are tougher when they're young. Too goddamn energetic. They all love to fight, and they throw tantrums in stores when you don't buy them that new *Transformers* toy. But when they get to be teenagers, they chill out. They do their own thing, hang out with their friends, and don't bother anybody for the most part. There's exceptions, no doubt, but that's my experience.

"Girls on the other hand…" He paused. I saw his daughters as he pictured them, their identical faces glowing as they blew out four candles on a cake. "Girls are sweet when they're young. They play with their dolls, they have tea parties. Shit like that. No fuss. Then they turn thirteen, fourteen." He shook his head. "When they hit that age, you better wear a fucking helmet, 'cause you're in for a bumpy ride. They start dating, and you spend all your time worrying about where they are, who they're with, what they're doing. You want them to keep their innocence, but all they wanna do is get rid of it. I dread the day mine start showing up with boys." He shuddered.

"Did you and your wife want girls?" I asked.

"We wanted one of each," he said. "Then the twins came. We decided to keep trying for a boy." A rock hit his stomach. "And we got one. Isaiah. He, uh…he only lived six months, God bless his soul. My wife died right after."

Benny had never told me any of this. His daughters were the only family he ever talked about in any detail, and up to that point I'd assumed his wife was raising them. "I'm sorry, Ben. If I knew, I wouldn't have brought it up."

"Don't sweat it. I don't mind thinking of them. I think about them every day. Plus, it's about time you knew."

"You should go see your girls. I know you want to."

"I will, when the time is right. The law will be watching them, hoping I'll turn up. I gotta let things cool down. For the time being, I belong here."

TWENTY-FIVE

"They need to stay in longer," Benny said from the other room as I evaluated my healing progress in the demolished bathroom mirror. "The website says seven to fourteen days."

"And it's been nine," I called back. I put my face closer to the mirror and scowled at myself. I had grown accustomed to the sight of my soon-to-be-scarred chest, but the matching face above it still twisted my mood. I looked like Wolverine or Freddy Krueger had taken a swing at me. I'd been thinking of a believable story to tell people about how my face came to look that way. To this day I don't have one. Don't need. I never go out. "Look at these things, Ben," I said, walking out of the bathroom, pointing to my chest. "They're healing over the stitches. If we wait any longer, we're gonna have to dig the strings out."

"I'm telling you, brother, you gotta keep 'em in. Give it one more day. One more friggin' day."

"Tomorrow morning, then. And if you still refuse, I'm ripping them out myself."

The nine days since the incident were uneventful. I regained my ability to move like a human, and most of the pain became tolerable. The only wince-worthy sensations came from direct contact with the wounds.

Morning number ten saw our hasty exit from that motel. The

catalyst snuck up on us as Benny finished plucking his sloppy stitches from my flesh. I don't remember what day of the week it was, but my memory makes it feel like a Sunday. It had that calm that only Sundays seem to have. I returned to the bed after my routine reflection inspection and sipped at the crap coffee we brewed in the flimsy four-cup maker.

"And now we go to Lily for the follow-up on a story we first brought to you nearly two weeks ago," the television news anchor said, grabbing hold of our attention. We had watched the news the previous four mornings, expecting details of the prison break, but this was the first mention we'd seen. The camera cut to the very attractive Lily, who stood roadside at a familiar location.

"Thanks Gene," Lily said. "Some of you may recognize the road behind me in Bridgewater where, less than two weeks ago, a caravan transporting sixty-seven inmates erupted into a brutal riot. Nineteen of those inmates escaped, including known organized crime leader Franco Angeletti. Initially, we reported fourteen fatalities – six police officers and eight prisoners. The police now tell us that the total has risen to seventeen, with one officer and two prisoners succumbing to their injuries since. We spoke to Police Chief Nick Chesen earlier, and here's what he had to say."

A prerecorded clip played, in which a red-faced, overweight police chief spoke into a microphone shoved into his face. "Obviously our biggest concern is for the safety of the residents in the Bridgewater area. We've tracked down most of the escapees, but six of them are still out there. If anyone sees them, we urge you not to approach them, and to call the police immediately."

Benny approached the TV like he could intimidate it. "You better not show our faces." Six mugshots filled the screen, ours among them. "Fuck. This is bad, Will."

"Take a look at your screen," Lily continued. "Again, if you see any of these men, do not approach them, and call Bridgewater police right away. Details on the funeral ceremonies for the deceased officers can be found on our website."

"This isn't anything new, right?" I said. "I mean, they've probably been showing these pictures all along and we've been—"

My lips, tongue and throat locked up. My head tingled like a housefly was buzzing inside, trying to get out. "I can't believe it," I said without knowing why. "That's them. I just saw that one last night."

"What did you say?" Benny asked with scrunched eyebrows. I just looked ahead with a deadpan stare I couldn't break.

"Hello," I continued after a short silence. "Yeah, uh, my name's Harold Kinney. I work over at the Rolling Meadow on Bristol Ave. Yup. Yessir. Well, I'm watching Fox 25, and they're showing those six inmates that are still on the loose. Yeah, from the prison break. Right."

I stopped as the absent other side of the conversation had their turn. I didn't hear them start or stop, but I knew when they were done. I continued with Benny at my side at full alert, waiting for the axe to drop. We both knew it would.

"Yeah, I do," I said. "Two of 'em are here right now." Another pause. "Yeah, they got a room here." Pause. "Benjamin Short and, uh, William Deslar. Those aren't the names they gave me, but that's them. Been here 'bout a week and a half."

Benny snapped into action and shot around the room, gathering everything we owned. I remained trapped, unable to help him.

"It's Room 12. Sure will. No, thank you."

My self control returned, but I didn't use it until Benny bumped into me during his race to pack our duffel bags. I took a few seconds, then joined him.

"The cash and the gun," Benny said when he realized I'd returned.

I put the gun in my belt, and the cash in a bag. After that, I swept up all the clothes that dotted the carpet. With our belongings bagged and in our arms, we gave the room one last survey. When we were satisfied, Benny opened the door and peeked out.

"We should make our way to the woods in the back," he said. "We'll hit a road in no more than a half-mile. They'll search the room and the rest of the property before fanning out, which might give us time to stop a driver and hitch a ride." He looked at me as if about to break some bad news. "We might need to use the gun to get through this. You want me to take it?"

I put my hand on the grip, ready to give it over to him. Then I changed my mind. "No. You shouldn't be the only one with that burden."

"Fair enough," he said, then scanned both directions. We moved out toward the rear of the building. I looked back for witnesses, as if spotting one would've prompted any action on my part. As we clawed past the treeline, the thick brush did its best to resist us. The duffel bags made movement sluggish and irritating, catching every thorn and stray branch we passed. Despite the opposition, desperation kept our pace consistent.

The sirens came shortly after, as expected. They started in front of us, on the road we'd soon reach, then travelled far away to our left, and back around behind us.

"The road to the motel circles this patch," I yelled to Benny. "We're running straight for their route."

"We can't go back," he said from ahead. "Keep moving." He rammed his shoulder into a tree, but persisted. "We just gotta be careful when we get there."

He reached our destination about twenty yards ahead of me and stopped at the opening. The way he looked down told me that the treeline sat above the road. The way he ducked told me that police were near.

My foot caught a root, and I fell to a push-up position. My chest slammed a rough, twig- and stone-covered patch of ground. The sharp sting reminded me of my fragility, and I worried about how much of my healing the fall had reversed. I began to rise, but a finger snap stopped me. I looked up to see Benny signaling for me to stay down. With the message sent, his eyes returned to the street. He held still as a mountain. His heart punched his ribcage.

Our elevation hid the approaching car from me, but didn't mask the sound of its breaks. A door opened, introducing the sound of boots on pavement, then closed. I concentrated on Benny, focusing every bit of mental energy I had on what he saw. I remember thinking, *I can do this. I can control it*, but the lack of results humbled my confidence. Still I tried, imagining being in his head, hearing his thoughts. Nothing. I had to wait for the situation to play out. I crawled behind a large fallen tree to my right, then lifted my head to peek over it.

"Hey," a non-authoritative voice said with attempted authority. "What're you doing in there? I see you. Come on out."

Benny stood, turned, and sprinted to my left. A few moments later, a uniformed officer broke through the bushes in pursuit. I dropped down and watched the chase unfold.

Benny tripped and fell face-first into a stump. Even if he hadn't fallen, he wouldn't have stood a chance; the cop ran like a track champion caught in a swarm of hornets. Benny writhed on the ground and held his face as the officer approached him with his stun gun ready.

This is what I get for taking the pistol, I thought, realizing what I had to do.

I pulled it from my belt and aimed at the officer. He didn't hear me rise, too high from the action scene he was starring in. I stepped forward, broke a branch, and caught his attention. *Idiot*. He turned. His training sent his already full hand to the butt of his pistol.

"I swear to God," I told him, "if you touch that fucking thing, you're a dead man." I made a radical decision just then, and I only let the weight and questionability of it stall me for a second. "Get up, Benny," I said. "We just found ourselves a chauffeur."

○ ○ ○

Thump. Thump-thump.

The three doors of the new, blue Dodge Charger shut, making that satisfying sound you only hear in a car fresh off the showroom floor. The officer – Richard "Richie" Collins, as I figured out – started the vehicle under my orders. Benny sat beside him, holding Richie's own service weapon.

"If you so much as look at your radio or reach for a button that I don't recognize," I said from the backseat, talking through the metal mesh divider, "Benny's putting a bullet through your palm."

"Sure, OK, I'll do whatever you want," he said, and stiffened his neck to keep his eyes off of the radio. "I swear. Just calm down."

"I *am* calm," I said in the flattest note I could hit, hoping to capture the sociopathic criminal vibe that I knew would keep his courage to a minimum. "Drive north."

In the present – that is, as I write this – I've lived forty-one years with my ability. My disease. I know how it works in general. Its broad tendencies; its vague patterns. The intricacies of it, however, remain elusive. For example, I've discovered no concrete rule to explain why certain people are impossible to read while others open up like an unlocked vault. Emotions and moods play a role, that much I know, but there's more to it than that. Something I may never understand.

Richie was one of those unsecured vaults. No guard. No lock. His life became a catalog of data for me to pick through. The access was thrilling. Family history hung in one corner of his mind, his favorite drink in another. Beliefs, opinions, tastes, secrets – all available. In seconds I knew him like an old college buddy.

Thirty-one years old. One daughter, one son. Married. Faithful. Miserable. Daydreams of divorce. Weights four times a week, cardio two. Likes nothing more than to smoke a joint and play his guitar in the garage. It gets him away from the family. Cocky. The cockiness offsets his inferiority complex. Thinks Benny and I—

"You think that uniform puts you above us, don't you, Richie?" I said. To Benny, the question came from nowhere. To Richie, it came straight from his brain. "Yeah, you're a community hero and we're just dirtbags. What's your favorite saying about felons? 'Hang 'em all and save the taxpayers some green,' right?"

He swallowed hard. "How?"

"Don't worry how." I wanted to leave it at that, I really did, but I couldn't let this guy go unchecked, thinking he was any better than us. I had to make him know that we were humans, not some irredeemable candidates for the chair. Maybe I just needed to appease my own conscience.

I tapped the wire mesh. Richie jumped. "Why do you go to work every day, Richie?"

"I…"

"You come out here every day and bust your ass to feed your family, correct? Janet, Tim, and Wendy."

"Don't you fucking dare," he said, pretending he had any power at the moment.

"Don't threaten me unless you want to feel the burn of your own bullets, Richie. Now, picture this: one day your job vanishes." I leaned forward, my nose touching the cool metal divider. "You search for months for a new one, but nothing comes of it. Can't even get a job scooping ice cream. You've got your college education and your eight years of experience in the field, but – keep your eyes on the road – but no one gives a flying fuck. Dozens of resumes, zero bites.

"Meanwhile, you got a wife working slave hours and only coming up with half the money you need to pay the bills, plus a six-year-old growing out of his clothes and living on mac 'n cheese and ramen noodles. You hate yourself. You hate your life. But you're too much of a pussy to end it, so you're stuck in the cycle. Then, after so long in that pit, you meet a man. This man tells you he's got a job that'll earn you more money in one night than you've made in your entire career. You don't wanna do anything illegal, Richie, but you think of that crying kid with his crummy clothes and his crap food. You think of the woman you love, breaking her fucking back to stay out of the red, but drowning in it anyway."

I stopped at the realization of how tense my body and attitude had become during the one-sided conversation. The contracted muscles in my chest throbbed. I sat back in the seat and relaxed with a deep breath.

"We're the same, you and me," I said with an orchestrated calm.

No, we're not, he thought.

"Yes," I said, to his surprise, "we are. You just haven't had the rug pulled out from under you. Ask yourself this question when you deposit your next paycheck: How would you feed Tim and Wendy with no job? I found an answer to that question. I did what I had to do. And believe me, you would too."

"I'm sorry," he said with the humble sincerity of someone who has seen the error of their ways. I wanted to think that my words and not my own projected emotions were what turned him.

We drove twenty or thirty miles north before I began looking for a dead-end street to pull into. I spotted one and gave the order. A short distance in, the narrow suburban road turned from pavement to dirt, from houses to trees. A couple dozen yards later, a row of boulders blocked the path. Richie stopped. Dense woods filled every direction, removing us from civilization.

Richie cried as he followed my instructions to cut the engine. "Please don't kill me," he said. "I'll tell them you had masks. That I didn't see your faces. Honest to God."

His fear made it hard for me to speak. "We're not monsters," I told him, expecting it to alleviate his terror. It didn't. He needed more assurance. "Look, I *promise* we won't kill you." His relief felt like ointment on a rash. "Unless you cause trouble for us. Now listen, and listen good – I assume you know who Franco Angeletti is?" He did. Every cop did. "Franco's a personal friend of mine. Not just a friend, but a friend who owes me a favor." I held up Richie's wallet. "And I know where you live."

"Please don't."

"Don't make us," Benny said. "It's the last thing we want to do."

"He's right," I said. "We don't want to, but one phone call…" I let his imagination fill in the blanks. "I'm telling you this because I want you to follow my instructions down to the finest detail. Do that, and nothing will happen. You have my word. Agreed?" He gave a panicked string of nods. "Good. I'm going to cuff you to one of your car's rims. Once we're gone, I'll give your colleagues a call and tell them where you are. You'll tell them we were wearing green shirts and said something about heading west. Don't try to escape, you hear me?"

"Yes sir."

"All right. Get out."

○　○　○

"Were you channelling John McClane back there?" Benny asked when we emerged from the dirt road. "Or have you just lost your mind?"

I laughed. "Would you believe it if I told you I'm getting used to this shit?"

"Brother, I'm right there with you. So, what now?"

"I have a plan, but brace yourself – you won't like it."

TWENTY-SIX

"This is a bad idea," Benny said, stirring his coffee. He studied the poorly-lit restaurant for customers on cell phones. He eyed one, but unless she was talking to police about her newborn nephew, she posed no threat. Benny's mug shook in his hands, and black waves swished back and forth as he sipped from it. "We shouldn't be here."

"You've made that clear," I said. The words came laced with aggravation. I couldn't help it; the sweat from our two-mile hike stung my chest and face; the two families and three early drinkers threatened my freedom; the anticipation of Cameron's arrival made my neck muscles tense. I felt like the universe's punching bag.

The only payphone we could find hid in the corner of a closed sports pub. Even after we spotted it through the window, we had to wait for eleven o'clock to roll around to use it. I made two calls, then tried to force-feed myself a club sandwich. I quit after two bites.

"I guess I haven't made it clear enough," Benny said.

"We need her."

"Like hell we do. We have money. Plenty enough to reach North Conway and get to Julie's brother. Explain to me why we need to bring someone else into this. Her, of all people."

"We're fuck—" I stopped after getting the attention of a couple patrons. I leaned in, and at a lower volume said, "We're fugitives. We're using fake names, taking cabs everywhere, and worrying about every trip to the damn store. Three hours ago, you were on the ground with a cop standing over you. Think about that for a second. It's only a matter of time before this shit catches up to us. Cameron knows about everything. She knows about *me*. And she wants to help."

"You're assuming she's just gonna drop everything and join our little adventure. She's got a kid. She's got a life." He raised his mug to take another sip, but stopped before it reached his lips. "Shit, there's a hell of a chance that she's a suspect after what happened. A person of interest at the very least. You think she's gonna jump at the chance to do something suspicious?"

"We're not going across the damn country, Ben. Christ, we're talking about a two-hour drive, tops. I just want to talk to her and see if she can help. Can you please bear with me on this? Have some fucking faith."

"Do what you want, brother – you're steering the boat. I'm just trying to make the motherfucker sail smoother, that's all."

The door opened, piercing the dim dining room with daylight and exposing the thick cloud of dust that cloaked us. The three sad souls nursing their liquor alone looked at the newcomer. They never expected the gem that strutted in. Cameron Cole: slick, confident, gorgeous. Every man in the pub, including a father with his wife and kids, thought of what they would do to her if given a free pass. I saw a compilation of male fantasies I wish I could forget.

"Boys," Cameron said when she reached us, the same way she would greet old friends. She didn't sit, only stood beside our table. "What kind of trouble have you gotten into?" She stopped and put a palm on the top of my head, then turned it to the light. "Jeez, Will. What the hell happened to you?"

"You didn't see it the moment you touched me?" The levity of the question was a thin cover for my curiosity.

"Not this time. You'll have to tell me the old-fashioned way. You get in a brawl with a panther?"

"This isn't the place for that conversation," Benny said, squashing her humor. "We should leave."

"Cheery as ever, I see," she said. "So… That serious, huh?"

I nodded. "That serious."

For the next half-hour, Cameron's massive Mercedes sedan served as our briefing room. As I recapped recent events, I learned how much info I had passed to her during our split-second of contact eleven days earlier. An alarming amount, it turned out.

"I've had a batshit crazy week-and-a-half, boys," she said when I finished, "but you've got me topped. And now you're heading to New Hampshire to keep the insanity going."

"No choice," I said.

"Whatever gets you peaceful sleep. But let's get down to why I'm here. You don't want to ask, but you're hoping I'll be your ride."

"*He's* hoping," Benny chimed in from the backseat.

"Oh, Benny," Cameron said in mock disappointment, "stop being so grumpy. You and I both know there's a cuddly teddy bear somewhere inside you, trying to get out. Anywho, I'd love to be your driver."

"You would?" Benny said.

"Really?" I said.

"Did you hear your own story? You guys suck at being fugitives. And *you*," she said, gesturing to me, "you suck at being a psychic."

"I'm not a psychic."

"You suck at being *whatever* you are. Be honest – if you were the betting type, your money would be on your own failure."

"Odds aren't important with my son on the line."

"Great quote for a movie trailer, but if you're ever going to find Marcus, your plan needs some finesse. It needs me. And given your desperation, I should make you beg for my help. Lucky for you, I'm not that kind of girl."

"So, you're in?" I asked. "Just like that?"

"There's nothing in Mass that can't get by without me for a day. We can leave right now if you're ready."

What about your son? I thought.

"What about your son?" Benny asked.

"My son?"

"When we were in your house," I said, "we saw a boy's bedroom."

"Oh." She looked away from us, out her window. "Marshall's room. He passed. Eight months ago."

"I'm sorry to hear that," Benny said. "It's terrible."

"There's nothing worse," she said.

Benny's stance on Cameron evolved with that revelation. A few unexpected words moved him from seeing a liability to seeing himself. They shared knowledge of life's greatest loss. I saw the two innocent faces. Isaiah. Marshall. Then I saw Marcus.

Cameron sniffled. "Why don't we change the subject?" She waited, but no one said anything. "Come on. Tell me how you're planning to approach your brother-in-law."

"The same way I approached his mother," I said. "I'll tell him that Marcus and Julie aren't safe, and try to convince him that it's in everyone's best interest to get Julie to prison."

"But you don't really believe that," she said. "And he'll see it."

"You don't know what I believe."

"I don't? OK, then explain it to me. What do you really want to come out of all this?"

"Safety for my son."

"Thanks for the obvious answer. What about Julie? What about when you come face to face with her? Will your intentions hold up then?"

"Fuck if I know," I said. "But I'll tell you one thing: I sure as hell won't let her walk free while I do my time. Not after what she did to me, and not after what she's doing to Marcus."

"Keith's not going to give up his sister," she said. "Their mother was vulnerable. She was worried about her daughter. You don't have that on your side this time."

"I assume you have a solution."

"Wouldn't be much of an asset if I didn't. Angeletti owes you a favor, right? I'm sure he has no problem prying information from tight lips."

"We're not torturing the guy," Benny said, leaning through the opening in the front seats to emphasize his statement. "I don't want to hear you suggest it again."

"If that's what you're getting at," I said, "Benny's right. I've done enough damage. I can't support something like that."

"Sure," she said. "Sorry I mentioned it. I'm sure Keith will jump in joy at the chance to betray his sister to a man with a motive for revenge."

"I might get lucky," I said, ignoring her sarcasm. "I might be able to read him."

She laughed. "Your mind reading is about as dependable as a car in a river."

o   o   o

We drove a bit over two hours to North Conway, then spent another hour finding a suitable place to stay. We settled on the Cliffside Manor, a hundred-and-sixty-four-year-old hotel that looked like an English Queen's wet dream. Benny and I shared a room while Cameron stayed in the next.

I set my laptop high up on our room's oak wardrobe with its screen open, angled toward my bed.

"Care to explain?" Benny said, flipping through the hotel's welcome brochure.

"I'm doing something I should've done a long time ago. I'm recording myself."

"You knew you could do that, and you're just thinking of it now?" He tossed the brochure on the bed and reached for his week-old, twice-read-through *Sports Illustrated*. "If only we had that thing when you hacked yourself up."

"Better late than never, right?" I set the camera to record. "We're wasting time, you know. Keith's house is right there." I pointed in an arbitrary direction. "We could've gone already." I sprawled out on my bed and clicked the TV remote. Roger Rabbit's face appeared on the screen for a moment before Bob Hoskins pushed his head under sink water.

"You don't want to hear this," Benny said, "and I hate to admit it, but Cameron's right. Going straight there would've been a mistake. We've had enough action for one day. We need to rest. Besides, look at this room. This is the nicest place I've slept in God knows how long. Enjoy it. We'll go to Keith's first thing tomorrow."

TWENTY-SEVEN

This is how I learned of Lincoln's true nature:

Julie and I stood on the porch of a secluded house, miles outside of my geographic comfort zone, two days prior to the robbery. We waited for Lincoln, who had arranged the meeting to brief us on our jobs for the big night.

"I don't think he's here," I said, peering through a window. The glass fogged as I spoke.

"We're half an hour early," Julie said. "I told you we'd have plenty of time."

I paced. I looked around. I tapped my foot. I peered through the window again. "You sure this is the place?"

"He told us to turn into the driveway before the bear carving. Did you see any other bears out there?"

"I guess we wait, then."

"What was that?" she asked.

"I said, 'I guess we wait, then.'"

"No, not you. I heard something." She hopped down the porch steps and disappeared around the left side of the house. I rushed to catch up with her. As I rounded the corner, an enormous backyard stole my attention. From the front of the house, the football-field-sized lawn would've seemed impossible. Pine trees towered over both sides, giving it a tunnel-like quality. A pickup truck sat against the right edge of the yard, a couple hundred feet from us, about halfway to the back. The tailgate and the driver's door both hung open, but the truck's owner was absent.

"Think he's out there?" I said.

"Most likely," Julie said, then started walking in the truck's direction. I grabbed her shoulder and pulled her back. She slapped my hand. "What the hell?" Her pitch was that of a woman violated.

"Let's just go back out front," I said. "We're not supposed to be here for another thirty minutes. I doubt he wants us snooping."

She headed to the front with a strut that said, "Fuck it, whatever."

I tried to bring some light back between us as I followed her. "This place is gorgeous, huh?"

"Mm-hmm."

"I'd love to get something like this one day. Perfect yard for Marcus to play in. Woodsy and private." Julie didn't share my daydream; she seemed lost in her own. I took a few hurried steps to catch up to her. "Not feeling that idea?"

"No, no. It's nice," she said. "I could see myself living here." This agreement was meant to shut me up, of course.

"Our luck will change," I said, not taking the hint. "When we get through this job, we'll have plenty to fall back on. I'll get my ass back to work, and things'll be how they were."

She gave an empty nod, clipped at the end by the clanking sound of struck metal. We spun and looked to where it originated, at the truck. Lincoln stood beside it, his clothes covered in dirt, a shovel in his hand. He drove the spade into the ground, wiped sweat off of his brow, and climbed into the truck's bed. Once inside, he squatted and grabbed something. Something heavy, judging by his struggle to pull it to the rear.

"What's he doing?" I whispered, as if my normal volume would have reached him. He dropped from the tailgate and pulled the object, a large black bag, hard to the ground. The sound of its impact travelled far in the quiet, walled-in yard. "Is that what I think it is?"

"Don't jump to conclusions," Julie said, thinking the same.

"It's not a big jump. Shovel. Dirty clothes. Big black bag."

"Could be anything."

Lincoln plucked the shovel from the ground and propped it up on his shoulder. He wiped the sweat from his face again, then dragged the bag out of sight.

"Fuck," I said, turning and power walking to the front of the house. "Why did I have to see that?"

"Don't overreact," Julie said, far too calm for my liking. "You don't know what it is you saw."

"I can't do this shit, Julie. I can't."

"Man the fuck up, will you?" The stab was uncharacteristically brutal, as was her grip as she grabbed my arm and spun me around to face her. "We're beyond the point of backing out. We started this, and we need to finish it. What do we have, Will? Nothing. We have nothing. This will save our lives."

"If it doesn't end them first."

"Don't be so dramatic. Even if that was what you think it was, you don't know the circumstance."

"Are you serious?" I said. "If Lincoln's out there dumping a body, the circumstance doesn't mean shit."

"Drop it," she said. "Get it out of your head."

"So I'm just supposed to act like I didn't see that? For Christ's sake, Julie, how are you fine with this?"

"I'm fine with it because my son needs me to be."

"I knew you'd go there."

"Listen to me – we're gonna sit on the porch and wait for Lincoln to come back. You're gonna do whatever it takes to keep your goddamn nerves in check."

My will to fight laid down and died. Julie had a way of squashing debates like grapes under a brick, regardless of my argument's validity. That talent wouldn't erase the black bag from my mind, but it managed to keep me there despite my anxiety.

We waited for twenty minutes in silence before we heard the turn of a stiff doorknob behind us. Lincoln stood in the doorway.

"Jules, Will. I hope you haven't waited long."

"A few minutes," Julie said. "We tried knocking, but you must not have heard us."

"Yes, I apologize. I was in the middle of something."

"Rolling around in the mud?" she asked, pointing to his dirt-smeared clothes. Her tone carried no trace of suspicion, only that of a playful tease.

"A neighbor to the west won a land dispute," Lincoln said. "Turns out I had a stone wall on his property. I've spent the morning taking it down. Still have a bit of work to do." He withdrew into the house. "Please, come in."

"What is this place?" Julie asked.

"It belonged to my parents. My mother left it to me when she passed. I hate the country atmosphere, but selling it would feel like a betrayal. I visit from time to time. It has its uses."

"It's beautiful," she said.

"You're too kind." He lifted his chin as he glanced at me. "Why so quiet, Will? I know – you need a drink to take the edge off."

"Anything you got," I said.

We tailed him to the kitchen, where he poured a round of drinks. I didn't ask what he put in my glass, and only learned it was scotch when it set my tongue and throat on fire. I took the pain like a seasoned lush, gulping the caramel-colored gasoline while Lincoln began his overview of the plan. I struggled to keep a grip on his words, too distracted by thoughts of body bags and the burn of the scotch. He carried on as if he didn't have the dirt of a grave spread across his clothes. When I finished my drink, he paused his presentation to pour me another. I sipped at the second drink, holding the glass like it contained a precious medicine. Lincoln continued, explaining that an associate of his worked for the security agency that installed The Perfect Cut's alarm system. This associate would be on call to cut the system remotely. Further details slipped by me, and I banked on the assumption that Julie would fill me in later, when I was level-headed.

As Lincoln demonstrated how to work with plastic explosives (much to my surprise), I spotted a patch of dark dots on his shoulder. Was it blood? Dirt? I couldn't tell, and in my tipsy state, I failed to hide my investigation.

"What is it, Will?" he asked, mistaking the direction of my gaze and looking behind him.

"Nothing, sorry. Just lost in thought." I took down the last of my drink.

"Another?" he offered.

"I think two drinks in twenty minutes is more than enough," Julie answered for me.

"I'll take another," I said.

Lincoln looked to Julie for permission. She shrugged and rolled her eyes.

Fuck you, I thought. *You're gonna put me in the same room with a murderer, then roll your fucking eyes when I need a drink?* With a bit more alcohol in my blood, the words may have reached my mouth.

Lincoln filled my glass, and everything after that was background noise. I got by with a few nods and yeses, each timed to hide the soup of conflicts churning inside me. I looked at Lincoln now and saw him for what he was. *How many has he killed?* I hated myself for sitting there, pretending everything was straight. For planning to work with that animal. For putting money in the pocket of a killer. What did that make me?

It's for Marcus, I thought. *Remember that. Bullshit. You're kidding yourself. Justifying it any way you can. There are other ways to get money. Honest ways.*

Lincoln finished, and after we assured him that we understood the plan, Julie excused herself to use the bathroom.

She left me alone with him.

"Good scotch, isn't it," he said, twirling his own and sipping it to the soundtrack of clicking ice cubes.

"Tell ya the truth," I said, trying to keep the world from rocking back and forth, "I wouldn't know good scotch if it pissed on my foot." I expected a laugh, or a smirk at least, but got no such reaction. Instead, he shot me a flat, cold look, like a villain sizing up his enemy.

"You seem distracted," he said. "Why is that?"

I sipped my liquor, and through the liquid and ice chunk in my mouth said, "Because I saw you." I didn't run the response through any kind of filter or judgment process. Maybe it was the liquor. The courage a good buzz gives you. It could have been my nerves, sick of trying to keep themselves below the surface. Who knows? But I said it, and letting it out felt like a successful exorcism.

"Saw me?" He tilted his head in confusion. "Saw me do what?"

"We saw you out back. With the shovel and the black bag."

He smiled, once again nailing the sinister appearance. "Good. I'm glad you saw. I assume you know what that bag held."

"A body."

"Indeed." He turned to look at the backyard through the window. "George Evans. An arrogant little shit who decided that he deserved more money from our last job, and that his compensation would come from me. Now I have both of our shares, and he has dirt in his mouth." He allowed the words to sink in, pleased with himself. "Do you know why I'm being so forward with you, Will? I could just deny what you saw. We both know you don't have the spine to push your accusation. But I want you to know who I am. I'm not your friend. I'm not your accomplice. I'm your boss, and unless you do your job, you'll receive the same payout as Mr. Evans. Do you understand me?"

I stood up, fueled by intoxicated bravery, and muttered a sloppy threat. I stepped toward him, and a blurry moment later, he had a grip on my throat and a knife pressed to my stomach.

"Be smart," he whispered in my ear. The tip of the cold steel poked through my shirt to my skin, promising to draw blood with any added pressure. "Don't do anything that will make Julie a widow. I'd rather not find someone new for this job, but if you become more trouble than you're worth, I'll slit your throat while your family watches." He pulled the knife away at the sound of Julie's clicking steps, and pushed me back in my seat.

"We all set?" Julie asked as she entered the kitchen, just in time to miss the blade retreat into the handle and into Lincoln's pocket.

"I believe so," he replied. "But before you go…" He grabbed the bottle of scotch and poured three shots. He raised his. "To my new team."

Julie smiled and raised her shot. I lagged behind.

Our glassed collided.

TWENTY-EIGHT

I woke to the laptop's glow in the darkness of the night. The computer rested on my lap. The webcam application I had set to record showed me my own face. I blinked and rubbed my eyes. The face in the window did the same. I stopped the recording.

"Benny?"

"You awake?" he asked from my right.

"Yeah. What am I doing?"

"You've been talking," he said. "Eyes closed, sporadic as hell."

"What did I say?"

He pointed to the screen. "See for yourself."

I dragged the progress bar back a few minutes and hit the play button. I watched my shadowy self grab the laptop from the dresser and bring it to the bed. My eyes never opened. I sat on the mattress and began dictating Robert's third message to the camera.

○ ○ ○

"I'm weak, Will. I can't write anymore, but you hear me, don't you? I haven't eaten in days. I don't know how many. Two. Three. No water. Nothing. Heather, too. And she's hurt badly, she needs a doctor. Without a miracle, we'll both die in this basement.

"He came to her again. He… He cut her. I felt it. All of it. Saw it through her eyes. Every slice. He must have drugged her food. The vegetables. She passed out. She was talking to me when it happened, when she fell. She came to, strapped, duct-taped to a chair, trapped, and he stood before her, no sympathy, no humanity. He showed her the knife. Twisted it in front of her. He said, 'You know what I want,' and 'You know what I'll do to you if you don't tell me.' She begged. She told him she knew nothing. He pushed the edge of the blade against her forehead and ripped it away. I felt the bite in my own skin. She screamed and I screamed and she yelled, 'Why? What do you want with me?' He laughed. Then he slapped her. I felt that too. 'You know what I want, you know where you hid them. Tell me.' 'Please,' she said, but he just waved the knife in her face. Dragged it across her chest. No pressure, just let it glide over her shirt. Taunting her, Will. Playing with her. Trying to frighten her. She cried and begged but he only became impatient. 'Tell me. Tell me where they are or I'll open you up.' That voice. I can't place it. 'I don't know,' she said. 'She doesn't know,' I yelled. 'Next time you talk,' he called to me – I heard it through the vent, through the wall – 'next time you talk, I'll cut her throat and move on to you. Tell me, you fucking bitch.' 'Please, I swear I don't know anything.' He slashed at her and she screamed and I screamed and he slashed again. 'Tell me.' 'I don't know.' He slashed again and again and each time she cried louder and begged harder. The pain hit me with every swing he took and that's fine, I'll take it, but she…

"It was the worst thing I've ever heard and felt and seen in my life. She's had no treatment. Infection is inevitable.

"I've given up trying to figure any of this out. Why we're here, who we are, what this thing is between you and I. I just want to sleep.

"If souls exist, that man lacks one."

At this point in the recording, I saw Benny sit beside me on the bed. The recorded version of me didn't seem to notice.

"There are things I need to tell you before it's too late. I've confirmed my suspicions of a child in the house. Think of his life, Will. It's not right. I spend every moment daydreaming of escaping, of killing that bastard, of taking Heather and Marcus to safety, it's a tragedy that… Wait. That name. Marcus. You know it. You do, I felt your heart spike as I said it, he's— My God. He's your son. It's no coincidence, don't you see that? I've told you we're connected, I told you that, and it's getting stronger. You're coming for him, and you'll find us, too."

Five seconds of silence passed before Robert came back with a flash of hope. His voice had a new energy; a second wind.

"Sixteen. Marcus told Heather that the mailbox has the number sixteen on it. Of course, sorry, yes, you want to know how he is. He's unharmed. I haven't spoken to him, but Heather has. She tells me that he's a sweet kid. A healthy kid, but he's scared. He's… He's been through a lot. He's not safe, not safe with that man. None of us are, but you're close. I don't know if I'll last long enough to see you, but I'd die happy knowing they got out of this mess, no fucking question. I'd die happy, even though I'd die not knowing my own name or my family or if I draw or write or play golf or why I see what you see and feel what you feel and whether or not I'm cared about or if there's anyone to notice I'm gone."

Another pause followed, this one long enough to make me think Robert was finished. Then: "Will. My last request…

"Everything that's happened. The unexplainable things, the thing between us, the things you've seen and known. Everything you've done and will do, even the things you wish you didn't do, the things that you regret that give me a lump in my throat when you dwell on them. The hell of it all. Make it mean something."

○   ○   ○

"That's the end of it," Benny said. I stopped the video. "I don't know how these messages are getting to you, brother, but if they're real – if Robert and Heather are real – we need to find him. Real fucking soon."

TWENTY-NINE

"I'm telling you," I said to Benny, "it's Lincoln. He's got Robert and Heather locked up, for God knows why – take this left, Cameron, where that truck's pulling out – and he has Marcus."

"I don't doubt it," Benny said from the backseat. "I'm just considering the possibilities. Think about it – Robert never mentioned Julie. She'd be in that house with them, right?"

The thought had already eaten at me. "Maybe she's there, and Robert just hasn't seen or heard her." I didn't believe that. Julie wouldn't sit by and let two people be kidnapped and tortured. She wouldn't let Marcus live around that. "Maybe she's…" Silence finished the sentence better than words could've. I wondered if I'd care if it were true, and if I'd have any tears for her. *Not a drop*, I decided. *She can burn in hell.* Grudges make it so easy to harbor hate. So easy to lie to yourself.

"Are you sure you want to do this alone?" Cameron said, eager to change the subject.

"I'll get further with Keith if it's one-on-one. I can't strong-arm my way to an answer." My stomach wobbled the same way it would back in high school, during those walks to the front of the class to deliver a presentation. Everything depended on that meeting, on Keith's cooperation. If he refused to tell me where they were, my quest would ram face-first into a brick wall. I wasn't sure I could make it past that failure. "All right," I said to Cameron, "the house is about a quarter-mile past those lights. Drop me off after the intersection. I'll walk the rest of the way."

"Why would you do that?" she asked.

Benny answered for me. "He doesn't want Keith to see him coming. If Will catches him off guard, he might get a read."

"Nothing gets by you," I said.

Cameron pulled over. "We won't be far," she said, turning on one of the two CB radios she insisted we buy. "We're on channel one."

"How am I supposed to remember that?" I said, trying to suffocate my nervousness with half-assed humor. She saw through my attempt with sympathetic eyes. I got out of the car and looked around. Fields flanked the road, all empty except for a few lonely houses.

"You got this, brother," Benny said, slapping my arm on the way to the front seat. I nodded and walked, wishing I shared his faith.

Their departure left me with a silence that gave way every few seconds to the sound of wind blowing through trees. I inhaled the mountain air. It tasted pure and smelled like fresh-cut grass. I wanted to bottle that combination of sensations so I could experience it every day.

Reality broke my calm. I had a meeting to get to.

I first met Keith, along with most of Julie's family, on our first Thanksgiving as a couple. We got along well enough, Keith and I, but we may as well have been different species. In his testosterone-dominated brain, a real man didn't sit at a computer for a living. A real man invited hard labor. Lived on steak and protein shakes. Keith had spent four years in the Army before leaving to start a construction company. That's what he considered masculine, and he had subtle ways of making me feel inadequate for not fitting the mold. I don't mean to paint him as a bad guy. On the contrary, he was an honest, decent guy. He had an unbreakable loyalty to his family. The latter trait was the hurdle I worried about clearing.

Keith's house crept up on me. When I pulled myself out of my own head, I'd passed his driveway. I backed up and looked at my destination. I'd been there once before, when Julie and I helped him move in, but the place was different then. He had purchased a beat-up, hoarder-owned relic and shaped it into something from a Thomas Kincaid painting. It even seemed to sparkle when the sun hit its emerald green paint. A well-kept lawn lay before it, a reflection of Keith's OCD, which began as military-taught discipline, but later twisted into a handicap. It worsened over time until it forced him to quit working alongside his company's grunts in favor of managing from home. *He's probably in there right now, scrubbing something*, I thought.

I took a deep breath, held it for ten seconds, exhaled, then scaled the porch steps. The door opened before I reached it and presented Keith's football-player silhouette. He opened his mouth to speak, but before the words hit the space between us, I fell away from the moment.

Keith opens the door for Julie before she knocks. The relief feels wonderful; knocks irritate him almost as much as a raised toilet seat or dandruff on the shoulders of the guy in front of him in line. Julie holds Marcus by the hand. Millions of germs fester between the two palms. Billions, maybe. Keith wants to gag just thinking about it. Marcus holds his favorite toy, a sci-fi laser pistol. His eyes never leave the ground. Can't even look at your Uncle? Keith thinks. Kid hates me. Always has, always will. Julie looks tired. Keith wonders who the hell this guy in his driveway is, standing beside the maroon Dodge. The mystery man's presence influences Julie's temperament; even the way she stands, with that stiff stance, seems off. "What are you doing here?" Keith asks. He doesn't want to scold her, but he has to point out her foolishness. "Are you trying to get yourself caught?" He raises his water bottle and takes three quick, even sips.

"I know what you want, Will," Keith said, pulling me back to myself.

I wanted the vision back. I wanted to see Marcus for one more second. Just one more. The space inside me that he used to fill felt wider and emptier than ever.

Keith opened the storm door. "You want to know where they are. I can't help you. I haven't seen them."

"Don't lie to me, you fuck," I said, trying to gain a position of power like a chihuahua barking at a grizzly.

"Easy with the hostility," he said. "I'm on your side." He motioned for me to enter. "Let's talk."

I followed him in. The inside of his house was an oxymoron – a sanitized, comically, yet somehow tragically neat country-style home. Tasteless decorations littered the whole place. Wagon wheels. Clay planters. Horse paintings. An American flag. Every other country western cliché known to man. The collection would have looked so natural with a layer of dust coating it, but not a speck escaped Keith's rabid cleaning. The carpet in the living room still had lines from a recent vacuuming. He led me to the kitchen and opened the fridge.

"I don't want a drink," I said. "I want my son. I know they were here."

"I haven't seen my sister since before your arrest," he said, closing the fridge with a water bottle in his hand. "She knows better than to come here." He put the bottle to his lips.

"You were drinking water when they showed up," I said. "Just like you are now. Three sips at a time. Julie wore a purple peacoat. Marcus wore his Spiderman sweatshirt. They came in a Dodge pickup, with a man you'd never seen before."

He tried to hide his astonishment, but I could almost see his brain fumbling as he tried to catch my words. "How did you know that?"

"Where are they?"

He dropped the denial. "Somewhere safe."

"They're not safe. That man they're with – I need to get them far away from him."

"Thomas? He seemed all right. Julie said he was helping her."

"His name is Lincoln, and he's not 'all right.' He's a kidnapper and a murderer."

"I don't believe that for a second."

"Do you want to take that chance? With your sister? With your nephew? Tell me where they're staying."

"I can't do that," he said, shaking his head. "I know what she did to you. It wasn't right, and I'm sorry you had to pay for it, but she's my sister. I can't know you won't hurt her."

"You have my word. I just want Marcus. I talked to your mother."

"She told you Julie came here?"

"Yes, because she understands the severity of the situation. Your sister and nephew are on the run with a killer. Is that what you want for them? What if Marcus was your son?"

"Julie has more of a right than you do to decide what's best for him. I can't give her up."

"You *will*."

"I'm done with this conversation. Please leave."

"You're not even close to done."

"Get out of here," he said, stepping toward me to apply pressure. "Now."

I pushed him backward and caught him in his cheek with a right hook born from panic. He backed up and paused a moment, holding his face. He looked at his hand, expecting blood. There was none. *Don't do it, Keith*, he thought to himself. *Give him one more chance to—*

I charged him and swung again. What did I hope to achieve by assaulting a retired soldier? Satisfaction. Stress relief. Did I think a man with one drunken bar squabble under his belt could contend with a trained fighter? Definitely not. All I can say to defend my actions is that I needed to hit him. I needed to inflict just a fraction of the pain

I felt as I watched my chance of success wither. But I failed at that too. He dodged my punch with enough ease to convince me that the one I'd landed had been charity. I didn't see his counterattack, but it pounded me to the kitchen's tile. I rolled over and rose to my knees, just in time to catch a boot in my stomach.

"You come into my house," Keith yelled, kicking me again, "expecting me to hand over my sister" – another kick landed – "and you attack me when I don't?" I blocked the fourth kick, but that didn't save me much pain. "You got a giant set of balls on you, you piece of shit."

I scrapped my way to a standing position, but he still owned the fight. He jabbed my left eye. I stumbled back into a counter. Three more jabs landed in my abdomen, followed by an uppercut to my jaw. I tasted my blood as it dribbled from my lip onto his clean countertop. Even in the midst of fucking me up, the mess caught his obsession's attention, but not enough to give me a break. He kneed me in the stomach and pulled my bent body to the foyer, where he opened the storm door with my head. He whipped me out onto the porch. I stumbled down the steps and landed on my side at the edge of his driveway. He followed and crouched beside me.

"You're my brother-in-law," he said, clamping my throat. "That's gonna buy you two minutes to get the fuck off my property. If you come back, the cops will have to take you out of here on a stretcher."

"They have my son, goddammit," I said through bloody coughs when he let go of me.

He stood and walked to the house without looking back. "Two minutes." The door closed, and with it, my hope.

THIRTY

Cameron's Mercedes stopped in front of me. I looked down in a failed attempt at hiding my beaten face, just as I heard her reaction to it from inside the car. I knew pity would follow. Cameron leapt out and ran to meet me.

"Let me see," she said, holding my face and lifting my chin to the sky. A hint of a grimace escaped her. I didn't know what kind of damage I'd taken; I only felt the dried, caked-on blood that covered my face and neck. "You caught a good one," she said with a blend of ridicule and consolation that only she could whip up. "I don't think you'll need stitches, though." I'd forgotten the effect of a woman's concern; the comfort it carried.

"I still have a bunch of first aid stuff back in the room," Benny said, his head poking out the passenger window.

"Get me away from here," I said.

○ ○ ○

I reclined on the hotel bed, unable to refuse treatment. I knew Cameron would shut down any fuss I made, so I sulked and let the two of them repair my busted lip and cheek.

"You're lucky," Benny said, swabbing the gash on my left cheek.

"If the hit that caused this would've landed on your nose, you'd be in rough shape."

"Lucky? I got nothing from Keith. Nothing. How am I lucky?"

"It's only a setback," Cameron said. "We knew this was a possibility. We'll find another way."

"I've already found it," I said, siding with my darker half on a decision that I'd opposed whole-heartedly a day before. "Keith's going to tell me what he knows, whether he volunteers it or not."

"Use your head, Will," Benny said, dropping bloody gauze pads into the trash. He knew my resolution, and he hated it. But his disapproval wouldn't stop me. Nothing would.

"I am using my head," I said. "I'm done letting morals stand between me and Marcus. I won't find him with diplomacy. Give me Angeletti's number."

He sighed. "No. If you want it, remember it yourself."

"I could reach into your head and get it."

"We both know that's a crock of shit."

"Give it to me."

"You know what Angeletti will do to him. Think about it."

"Now, Benny."

"Fuck you."

"You're gonna stand in the way of finding my son? After all we've been through to get this far?"

"You got a lot of fucking nerve," he said, backing up to keep from opening my other cheek. "How dare you say some shit like that, after all I've done for you. You stopped yourself from getting to your son. You did it, when you decided to attack the only lead you had. And now you think I'm sabotaging you, you ignorant motherfucker? I'm saving you." Something happened inside him then – a debate and a concession, visible in his eyes. "You know what? Fuck it." He ripped the nightstand drawer open and pulled out a pad and pen. He scribbled the ten digits and threw the pad at me. It hit my chest and landed on the bed. "There it is, Will." Then he threw the pen. It did the same. "The key to your problems. The magical solution that's gonna make it all better. Go ahead, pick it up." I stood still, waiting for the punchline. "But if you go through with it, you're crossing into a territory that doesn't suit you. Don't come crying to me when it haunts you in your sleep." With that final warning, Benny left the room.

Cameron caught me by the arm as I began to follow. "Let him go," she said. "He'll be back when the smoke clears. He just needs to keep his clean conscience."

"I gotta tell you, Cameron, I'm worried about my own conscience. This isn't right. What makes it worse is that I know it's wrong and I'm still going to go through with it. What does that say about me?"

"I'm not the best person to judge morals, or even give my two cents on the topic," she said, "but you tried the peaceful route. Morals didn't get you this far, and they're only holding you back now. Do what's right for you and Marcus, not what's right by some made-up code of ethics."

Her validation gave me the push I'd been fishing for. I picked up the phone and dialed the number.

One ring, then, "Hold on, don't tell me… Will. It's Will, isn't it?"

"Yeah, it's me."

"I swear, it's like the phone rings different for you. I always know. How the hell are ya, kid? Where are you staying?"

"Doing good," I said. "I'm in North Conway."

"New Hampshire, huh? Nice place. I don't have to ask if you're still on the their trail."

"I'm close, Franco. That's uh – that's actually why I'm calling."

"You need help."

"I do."

"I've been waiting to hear that. Unpaid debts bite my ass, you know that? My own debts especially."

Cameron smiled, able to hear Angeletti from her spot at the foot of the bed. I walked him through the situation, and as the story spilled, I could sense the gears working in his head, like those of a mastermind winning a game before he even knows the rules. He had decided the best course of action before my narrative even reached the present.

"Go back there in four hours," he told me, jotting down Keith's address. "The lights will be off. The door will be unlocked. Don't knock, just walk in. You'll find one of my guys there. His name's Lou. He'll get you what you need."

"Thank you."

"We're even now, kid. Good luck. Take care of yourself."

"You too, Franco." I hung up and looked at Cameron. "Tell me one more time that I'm not a scumbag for making that call."

"If my son disappeared," she said, grabbing the rest of the first aid items from the bed and placing them on the dresser, "I'd do a whole lot worse than Angeletti ever could."

"Just what I needed to hear."

"We have some time to pass," she said. "You should get some rest."

"I probably should." I sprawled out on the bed, wondering if she would follow, hoping she would. She did. The aches from the scuffle dissipated with her beside me. I turned to her, but she didn't look back at me. "Can I ask you something?"

Her eyes stuck to the ceiling. "You can ask, but I won't guarantee an answer."

"Do you feel guilty for what happened to Ted?"

"I have nothing to feel guilty about," she said with perfect resolve. "I didn't kill him."

"But you wanted him dead," I said. "I felt it. You hated him."

"Yes, I did hate him. And at that moment, with my emotions built up, I did wish he was dead. But wishes aren't actions. I'm no murderer."

"You don't miss him at all, do you?"

"I miss the man I married. The man who gave me Marshall. But those early years, when we acted like a real family – they're like a movie I saw a long time ago and can barely remember. Ted burned those memories. His attitude, his ego, his cheating. The abuse. It all wore me down. Love has limits."

"Why did you stay with him?"

"Digging a little deep, don't you think?"

"Come on. A single touch told you my whole story. I'm just trying to balance out our knowledge of each other."

"Fair enough," she said, eyes still staring up, through the roof and into the sky. "Why did I stay with Ted?" She closed her eyes and exhaled through her nose as she found her next words. "His money. But it's not what you're thinking."

"What am I thinking?"

"That I'm a gold-digger. I'm not. It wasn't about luxury. I grew up with poor parents. I don't need nice things. The truth is, Ted's money was security for me and Marshall. I wanted a divorce, but by the time our relationship soured, I'd been jobless for years, taking care of our son. No college education, no real work experience. And I wouldn't get a dime from Ted. How would I support Marshall? And would I even win custody? I'd have nothing, going up against a spiteful millionaire. So I lived with it for a long time. Then, when Marshall passed…" She broke her stare-down with the sky, but not to look at me. She turned away. My eyes watered, and I assumed it was because hers had done the same. "When he passed, I gave up on the marriage. Gave up trying to repair it, gave up trying to get out of it. I just pretended it didn't exist."

"Cameron," I said, then waited. She looked at me for the first time during the conversation, over her shoulder, with glossy eyes. "I have to ask…"

"A drunk driver," she said, turning back around. "He was only twelve. Ted was driving him to a friend's house." She didn't want me to see the picture she'd constructed in her imagination of the events, but

I did. The image came to me so clear, so fully-realized – the product of too many nightmares. I can't bring myself to describe it here. It hurts too much; when I think of it, I can't help but transpose Marcus into the frame. "The other driver got on the wrong side of the highway. Ted made it out with broken ribs, some fractures." She opened her mouth to say something else, but she held it in.

"No one should know that pain," I said to her.

"No," she said, sniffling. "And we'll make sure you won't ever have to." She turned her body and put her head on my pillow. "We'll get Marcus back."

"I hope so."

"I know so."

Then we slept.

THIRTY-ONE

I broke out of my slumber, fearful that I'd missed my appointment. My eyes darted to the alarm clock. Plenty of time.

Cameron shuffled out of the bathroom, eyes closed, yawning. "Good, you're up. We should get going."

"Any sign of Benny?" I said, echoing her yawn.

She shook her head. "He won't be back until this business with Keith is over. Come on, get up."

When we pulled into Keith's driveway, the sun was well into its retreat behind the mountains. The bright, sparkling house I'd visited earlier now lacked life. No light inside. No movement. Cameron parked in front of the porch, beside Keith's green Crown Victoria. A black Cadillac Escalade, with windows so dark they seemed painted, towered over both vehicles from the other side. The SUV reminded me of Earl, and I worried that this "Lou" would come with the same baggage and shitty attitude. I opened my door. Cameron opened hers.

"No," I said. "I don't want you here for this."

"I'm not a porcelain doll," she said, prepared for my objection. "I can handle whatever's in there."

"That's not the issue," I said. "I'm dangerous in stressful situations, you know that. They trigger…" *They trigger whatever the fuck you call this thing inside me.* "I don't want you anywhere near me if something crazy happens."

"I'll wait here, then."

"Dammit, Cameron. No. I don't know how far it can reach."

"I'm not leaving, so stop wasting time. You won't win."

"Why are you so difficult?"

"Because someone has to play the part. Now get in there, and don't come back out until you know where your son is." With that command, she won the debate.

I followed Angeletti's instructions and entered without notice. All the blinds were closed, and when I shut the door behind me, I cut off the only helpful light source. I paused and listened while my eyes adjusted. Faint voices came from some indistinguishable corner of the house. When the path in front of me materialized through the blackness, I searched the first floor. Every light switch I walked past tempted me, but I resisted. The voices amplified in the hallway, and as I made my way through it, I found their origin: the basement. The door leading down hung open an inch. A dim orange glow leaked through. I put my ear to the opening.

"You can end this," a rough voice said.

"You can suck my dick," Keith said, then grunted as a clap echoed through the basement.

I descended the stairs with light footsteps to meet the horror I had set in motion. When I rounded the corner into the open, unfinished basement, I found what I expected: Keith in a chair, tied and bloody. A tall, thin man stood in front of him, his back to me. A table beside them held a weak lamp and an open briefcase. Its contents hid in shadow.

Keith's eyes widened when he saw me. They plagued me with pity – not just because of his predicament, but because he thought help had arrived. The truth would crush him. The man who could only have been Lou followed Keith's gaze and turned to me.

"Deslar?" His tone caught me by surprise. I'd never heard my name bundled with such resentment. He didn't want to be there (and who could blame him?), but that wasn't the source of his animosity. Something else had him ornery. Then, with no patience, he said, "Let's get this over with."

"You know each other?" Keith said. Hope evaporated as reality drove a stake through his heart. The shadows of the basement hid most of his face, but the orange light illuminated enough to see that he had already taken plenty of abuse. "Please, Will. You gotta help me."

"He's not here to help," Lou told him, beheading what little optimism still lived inside him. "Tell the man what he wants to know."

"Will, for Christ's sake, we're brothers."

Lou punched him in the face. I felt a twitch in my jaw. Lou punched him again. Another twitch, stronger this time. Keith moaned and drooled blood.

I looked down, unable to watch. "Just tell us where they are. Then it's over. I promise."

"I'll die before I hand my sister over to you," he said.

"I won't let you die," Lou said. He reached into the black hole on the table and pulled out a taser. He held it up for both of us to see, then pressed the button. As Keith watched the small spark dance between the metal prongs, his mind returned to some point in his twenties, to the muddy yard of boot camp.

"*Do it, you big pussy,*" *says Miller, holding out a taser.* "*Shit, even Pond did it, and that faggot can barely fire a fucking forty-four without dislocating his shoulder.*"

"*Call me a faggot again,*" *Pond says.*

"*Shut it, Pond, the adults are talking,*" *Miller says, entertained by the backtalk. He laughs like the prick he is, thinking he's hot shit because the sergeant complimented his run through the obstacle course.*

His focus returns to Keith. He begins a chant. "*Do it. Do it.*"

Other men join in. "*Do it. Do it. Do it.*"

"*Fine,*" *Keith says.* "*You want me to do it? Give me the fucking* thing." He grabs it and flicks the switch. *The faint vibration trickles through his palm and down his forearm before it fades around his elbow. The blue and white stream taunts him almost as much as Miller had. He gives himself a mental countdown. One. Deep breath. Two. Deep breath. Three.*

The lightning stream bites into his bicep.

A blink is all it took for the memory to plow through Keith's consciousness. He eyed the taser in Lou's hand like an old enemy. *Nothing you haven't felt before,* he told himself, but the pep talk didn't work. It wouldn't be the same this time. No laughter would follow. No cheers or jeers. Only more jolts – or worse.

We both gritted our teeth as Lou jabbed him with electricity. Keith tried to keep his pain silent, but some oozed out of his mouth through closed lips. The pulse lasted three or four seconds before Lou retracted the taser.

Those few seconds injected me with the distant sensation of a static shock. *Why now? Of all times?*

Keith said nothing. *You'll need more than that to break me,* he thought. Lou hit him with another two seconds.

This time I felt the taser's full force. The volts that zipped through Keith reached every inch of my body. I roared and dropped to the floor.

Lou stopped and spun around. "What happened?"

"Nothing," I said. "Don't worry about it." I couldn't allow this to go on any longer. I wasn't built to take that kind of pain, and it would only get worse. I pulled myself to my feet, walked over to Keith with my muscles still convulsing, and bent down to meet his eyes. "End this." His answer came in the form of blood and saliva in my face.

Lou grabbed my shoulder and pulled me back, irritated by the interruption. He threw the taser back in the briefcase. "No more games. Tell us where they are, or you're gonna lose something precious." Keith held firm on the outside, but inside he dangled over the edge of submission. "Yeah," Lou said in response to the silence, "I expected as much." He reached into the case of terrible mysteries, and when his hand emerged, it brought a power drill with it. A grin spread across his face as he looked at it like a child with a new toy. He pressed the trigger and sent the inch-long forstner drill bit spinning with a whine.

That whine gave me the access I needed. Even the hardest men tend to soften when facing a threat so visceral. I heard Keith's internal panic; half of him pushed to confess while the other half demanded discipline. It didn't matter; the gates were open, and the information I needed floated somewhere inside his head. Somewhere among the mess. Sifting through the noise was like wading through quicksand. Yet between the unspoken pleas, empty threats, cries, regrets, and hopes, one word rose to the surface: "Corby." Corby held importance to him. He tried to keep it down, but over and over again it popped up to the top of the thought heap. Keith squirmed as Lou moved the twirling tip toward his pelvis. Again the word boomed above the riot in his brain. It had to be the answer. It had to be the secret he was trying to hold tight.

Corby. The person sheltering them? A town? A street? I braced myself as the drill hovered a foot from Keith's pants.

"This is it," Lou said over the whirring motor. "Give it up or I turn your dick to pudding."

Then I remembered Robert's words: *Marcus told Heather that the mailbox says 16.* And I understood. Corby was a street name. 16 Corby held my family.

"Stop," I said, then again, louder. The bit stopped a centimeter from its target. "I have what I need. You can stop."

Lou faced me, blood boiling. "What the fuck are you talking about? He didn't say shit."

"It's over."

He took two steps toward me. "Don't you fuck with me. This man didn't say a fucking word. It's *not* over. I didn't drive three hours to be played with, especially not by the little shit stain who got my brother killed."

I shook my head, not understanding the random comment.

"You probably didn't even know his goddamn name, did you, Deslar?"

Earl.

"His name was Earl. You might remember him. Big guy, built like a tank. Took a bullet from a cop trying to help you."

I was backed into a dangerous corner. If Lou knew the truth of what happened to Earl, I wouldn't make it off of Keith's property. A single thought could give it up.

And a single thought did.

I tried, but trying to keep your mind off an image goes against everything the brain does. Even the voluntary act of not thinking about it amounts to thinking about it. The shootout materialized in my mind's eye. I tried to tuck it away. Impossible. The more I tried to suppress the memory, the more it urged its way to the forefront, and the more stressed I became. The picture grew stronger, feeding off my nerves. My nerves grew frantic, feeding off the strengthening picture. The two volleyed back and forth as I relived the terrible moment. The pistol in my palm, aimed at Earl's head. The fear I felt. The hope that when I let that hammer go, his gun wouldn't fire and take Benny with him. The pull, the blast, the mist of blood. It all bubbled inside me until I couldn't stop it from overflowing. The scene broke free of my mind and hurled itself outward to anyone it could reach.

Every muscle in Lou's face tightened. He didn't understand what had just happened, but he knew what it showed him. A moment later, the barrel of his gun dug into the skin between my eyebrows.

Keith sat still, dumbfounded at the mental image of me murdering a man. He held his breath and waited for the situation to make sense.

"Motherfucker," Lou said through clenched teeth. Even in the dim light, I saw his skin deepen to a red. The anger brought forward the resemblance to his brother. "You didn't even have the balls to look him in the eye when you did it. You put him down like a fucking dog."

"You don't understand."

"Keep your fucking mouth shut. Turn around."

I did as he said. *It's over*, I thought. *Everything I've worked toward. Everything I've been through. All for nothing.* I closed my eyes. Five seconds passed as I waited for death. *I'm sorry, Marcus.*

Lou's gun fired. Even turned away with closed eyes, I saw the flash. The hot metal burned inside my chest.

THIRTY-TWO

I don't believe in God. Any god. And yet I prayed to Him, to Her, to It. It's all I had, the only chance of living long enough to accomplish the most important job of my life. Still the bullet sizzled inside me.

"Get moving," Lou commanded. "Up the stairs."

How could I make it up the stairs? I wouldn't make it another ten seconds. I opened my eyes. The burn faded. I wondered if that was the numbness of death. I looked down at my chest for an exit wound. I saw nothing. Felt nothing. I turned to discover the truth.

Keith slouched, limp in his chair, with a circle of blood soaked into his shirt. The burn had belonged to him. I'd shared his last seconds.

"Why?" I asked, unable to look away from the death I'd brought upon an innocent man. "You didn't have to kill— Why?"

"Go," Lou said. "Or would you rather stay down here and get the drill?" He pushed me with his free hand. "Go."

I scaled the staircase, pressured onward by the end of his pistol.

Twelve steps to the top.

I remembered playing horseshoes with Keith the day Julie and I announced our engagement to their family. He hid his disappointment well. I'd always appreciated that.

Nine steps.

I'd gotten drunk with him, laughed with him, argued with him.

Six steps left.

I imagined Julie and Maureen's reaction to the news of his death.

Five.

I imagined them learning that I'd delivered his murderer to his doorstep.

Three steps.

I deserve whatever happens to me.

One.

I deserve to die.

When we reached the first floor, Lou steered me to the front of the house. He spread the closed blinds with his fingers. "Who's in the car?"

"Please," I said, "she has nothing to do with any of this. Leave her alone."

He grabbed the back of my shirt and pushed me toward the kitchen. "Back of the house. Move." He shoved my face into the door that led to the backyard. "Open it." I struggled with the lock in the dark, but managed to get the door open. "Walk straight back. To the woods."

To my execution.

The wet grass soaked my shoes as we made our way through it. The closest neighbor was too far away to see my death march. Only the crickets would witness my last seconds. Chirps filled the air.

"Your brother…" I searched for the words to explain what Lou had seen of the shootout, but after starting, the impossibility of it shut me down. My thoughts failed to cooperate, too terrified and scattered to pull together a defense.

"Earl was a good man," Lou said, like a robot given a spark of humanity. "A good man who helped you because Angeletti told him to. He fought for you. And you repaid him with a bullet. You fucked up, Deslar. You took the only family I've ever had."

I remembered my vision of Earl's childhood. Lou wasn't there; he hadn't seen his mother jam a shard of porcelain into his father's throat.

"Earl raised me. He worked like a slave to scrape together every penny he could manage. All that struggle, all those long days with Franco, just for me. To fill my stomach. Now he's gone. You took the wrong man."

I felt cheated knowing that Lou's glimpse of his brother's death came with no context. Edited. Cut. Condensed to a single blast. His skewed perspective didn't matter, though. I could have shown him the whole thing: Earl taking the first shot at the police, using Benny as a shield, like a coward. The truth wouldn't change Earl's legacy as the victim. The fallen hero.

With every step I took toward the woods, a chunk of my life broke away. When you have so few seconds left, each one holds the weight of a year.

"What'll you tell Angeletti?" I asked.

"Don't concern yourself with that."

"He'll kill you if he finds out." My toe hit a stone. I stumbled. Lou grabbed me by my shirt before I fell, then pushed me forward.

"Franco won't hear a peep about any of this. As far as he'll know, the interrogation was a resounding success." He chuckled without humor. "Or is your ghost gonna pay him a visit and rat me out?"

"I'm not alone. Word will get back to him."

"All you got is that clueless broad out front. I'm terrified. Really, there's piss running down my leg."

"Not just her. There are others."

"Of course there are," he said. "Well, you better hope your army makes a move soon."

We reached the thick wall of trees. I stopped. The cover made the territory beyond that wall a cave of black. A cave I knew I'd never exit.

Lou dug the gun barrel into the space between my shoulder blades. "Did I tell you to stop?"

I broke the threshold. All light disappeared. Branches and pine needles thrashed at me as I forged a path. Stones and roots tripped me. *How long before he shoots? Will I know it's coming?*

What if he decides not to?

I could have slapped myself for not thinking of it earlier. I had a weapon that could top his – the power to pluck the strings of his mind, to influence his decisions. But could I? I'd tried and failed before. I wasn't the master of my ability. I was the slave.

I didn't have a choice. I had to try. *Please, for once, just work for me.* I pictured Lou's hand letting go of the gun. *Come on!* I pictured him changing his mind. I saw him suffering an anxiety attack. A heart attack. A coughing fit. A cramp. *Please.*

Nothing happened.

"Stop here," Lou said. I did. "Kneel." When I refused, he kicked the back of my knee. I dropped. The steel barrel parted my hair. "Any last words? An apology, maybe? An admission of guilt?"

You don't want to kill me. You don't want to kill me. You can't kill me. Every neuron in my brain, every synapse, every ounce of emotion and adrenaline and hope in my body – they all united in the fight against Lou. *Please work. Just this once, please work.*

"Nothing?" he said. He relished the power. Just like Earl.

Your hand is numb. It's cramped. Your chest hurts. You don't want to kill me. Your chest hurts. You can't do it. Fuck. Your hand is numb, dammit. You don't want to do it. Come on. Work, dammit! You can't pull the trigger!

My vision crumbled. The ground in front of me vanished into pitch black. My mind fizzed like someone had poured water and Alka-Seltzer into my skull. Then the blackness and fizz faded, replaced by clarity. I'd left my body, just like I had when Julie hit me so long ago in The Perfect Cut.

I saw myself, ten feet away, failing to fend off death with my thoughts. Lou stood behind me, face to the sky, savoring the moment. I felt like the target of a cruel joke. In the moment I needed my ability the most, it laughed and gave me a better view of my own death.

Lou looked down at me. "I hope Earl's waiting for you on the other side, you fucking worm."

Then, on the right side of my new perspective, an arm rose into sight. It continued to rise until its hand came into view. It held something, unrecognizable in the dark. Then it passed through a patch of moonlight, reflecting a rare ray that leaked through the tree cover. Metal. A gun. Its ascent stopped in alignment with Lou's head.

Fire. For fuck's sake, fire!

My mind went blank at the sound of the blast.

I opened my eyes. My own eyes. I felt my own head, turned my own body. I saw Lou on the ground behind me but couldn't make out anything past him.

Ten feet away, twigs crunched beneath feet.

THIRTY-THREE

My savior advanced with a pace of intentional suspense, like they wanted me to squirm before the reveal. I squinted and saw a shape form through the blackness. "Who's there?"

"You know who's there," Benny said. "It's the sucker who's always pulling you out of your own messes."

I leapt up and stumbled to him, emotionally whiplashed from the shift in my fortune. When I crashed into his chest, I hugged that big bastard like I meant to suffocate him. "You're a saint, Ben. A fucking saint."

"Oh, *now* I'm a saint," he said, not returning the embrace, but letting me go on squeezing. "That ain't the melody you sang earlier."

I let go. "I know. You told me. I was wrong. I was dumb. God, I can't believe I'm breathing right now. How long have you been here? What did you see?"

"Everything." The answer carried regret. He motioned to Lou's body with his pistol. "I came straight from the hotel. Got here before he did. I sat right outside that basement window. Watched the whole thing. This sick fuck tied up your brother-in-law and just beat him. He didn't even say what he wanted, or why he was there, for five minutes. I saw you show up. Saw the shot. I knew no good would come from this. Why couldn't you just listen to me?" I had no answer. He tried to look up at the moon, but the trees hid it. He looked back at me. "Two people are dead, Will."

"It's my fault," I said. "All of it. I should've listened to you."

"You're right," he said. "It *is* your fault. That's harsh, I know – but you need to hear it. I wish I could say some shit to wash off that guilt, brother, but I can't. I won't. This wasn't fair. Wasn't right. You can't keep going on like this." He sighed and put a hand on my shoulder to mark the end of his brutal truth. His voice softened. "Did you get what you needed?"

"I think so," I said.

"You think so?"

"Yes, I got it. I heard Keith think it. Before he…" I pulled back the urge to let tears fall, then cleared my throat. "Cameron's out front. She has no idea."

"She's gone," he said. "I told her to get out of here when this guy fired."

I looked down at Lou's body. I saw Earl's doppelganger in that lifeless heap. Same orcish face, same open skull. "Should we bury him?"

Benny put his gun in his belt. "Wouldn't be smart to stick around."

"Yeah. Fuck him. He can get picked clean by a pack of wolves for all I care. What about Keith? I don't want to leave him like that."

"I know you don't, but we have to. We can call it in when we're gone."

I nodded. "We should check the house, make sure there's nothing connected to me in there."

We walked. I felt better and better as the distance grew between us and Lou. Neither of us spoke on our trip back across the lawn. The silence forced me to face the deaths in my wake. I tried to convince myself not to dwell on them, that they were necessary sacrifices. All of them. But I didn't buy my own lies. Where would it all stop? When would the cost outweigh the reward? I had no response to my own questions, but I knew I couldn't file every lost life as just another stepping stone on my path. What if something happened to Benny? Or Cameron? And what would Marcus say when he became old enough to understand? Would I tell him about the lives I trampled to find him? How could I? I wanted to believe that I did everything in my power to get to that point in peace, but I couldn't.

My throat begged for hydration, as if the debate with myself had happened aloud, with each side screaming its key points. Upon reentering Keith's house, I made a beeline for the fridge and grabbed two bottles of water. I tossed one to Benny and sucked down half of mine. The gulp felt like a glorious bonus, a privilege I shouldn't have been alive to enjoy.

"Don't leave these behind," Benny said, holding up his bottle, then took a sip.

We made our way to the basement door. I opened it, but the frame stopped me like a force field. I didn't want to face what it led to. As I pulled together the courage for the descent, Benny saw my hesitation. He went in first, reaching the bottom as I took my first step.

"Where's Keith?" he asked, looking up at me, then around the open basement.

I halted on the top step. "Over to the left. In the chair."

"I know where he's *supposed* to be."

I threw myself down the staircase with two strides to see the empty chair for myself. A smear of blood and a limp rope inhabited the seat.

"Fuck me." I dropped the water bottle and darted around the basement, searching every nook he could fit into, and even some he couldn't. My hunt turned up nothing. "He's not down here." I rushed back to the stairs and found what I expected. A path of blood, almost invisible without light, stained every step on the way to the first floor. We had walked right over it. "We need to search the house."

"Stay together," Benny said. "He's hurt, but if the military taught him anything, he'll have a weapon, ready to fight."

"I'd bet my life he's got a gun somewhere in this place," I said.

"Let's hope he's too weak to reach it." Benny led the climb, gun ready. At the top of the staircase he said, "The trail's gone. He made it to his feet." He peeked in both directions of the hallway. "One room at a time. I'll lead, you watch our back."

We started our search in the kitchen, then moved to the living room, turning on lights as we progressed. With both of those rooms cleared, we entered the foyer. In the center of it, ready to greet anyone who walked through the front door, a puddle of blood sat so still it looked like a solid. A trail of red, streaked footprints stemmed from it, leading past the hallway to the dining room. Benny held up a palm as he inched closer to its arched doorway. I turned and scanned the foyer, fearing a trap. Benny reached the dining room and peered in. He looked back at me and shook his head, unable to see far past the entrance.

I opened my mouth to advise against entering, but before I could, he went in. The room swallowed him in a curtain of shadow. Five seconds later, the chandelier inside lit up.

"Jesus," Benny said to himself from inside. Then, calling to me, he said, "I found him." The drop in his voice gave more information than his words. I entered to find him lowering his gun, looking across the room. Both his gaze and the red trail led me to Keith's body. It sat against the wall, underneath a mirror that reflected my own mixed emotions back at me. His struggle still showed in his bent joints and twisted face. Dried blood formed a thick, red fountain that ran from his mouth to his chest.

I approached him and squatted. Somehow that second confrontation with his death affected me on a deeper level than the first. I knew the image would never leave me. "He didn't deserve this."

"He's holding something," Benny said.

I saw the item in Keith's grip. "It's his cell phone. It's open."

"Think he got the chance to use it?" Benny said.

"I'll check the recent calls. If he got to Julie, everything's ruined."

"That's the least of our worries," he said, hurrying to the window. I pried the phone from Keith's stiff, still-warm hand. I looked up to see Benny peek through the blinds, then stumble backward like Godzilla had peered back from the other side. He ran his hand over his stubbled head. "He called the cops."

"What?"

"The cops. They're here."

I dropped the phone and pushed past him to the window. Four cruisers came to a stop in front of the house. Two more entered the driveway behind them. A seizure-inducing overload of blue and white lights lit up the property.

"No," I said, as if I could make them vanish with disbelief. "No, no, no. What do we do? Run out the back?"

Benny didn't answer. He didn't move. He just stared past me. Outside, the two cars at the rear of the pack passed the others to take up positions in the backyard. From the remaining four, eight officers emerged, took cover behind their doors, and drew their weapons.

"Benny," I said, letting go of the blinds and leaving the window, "talk to me." He remained in his trance, refusing to acknowledge anything outside of his head. *Tell me you have a plan brewing in there*. He heard the thought. He smiled. That mental connection gave him confidence in whatever scheme he had pulled together.

A loud beep sounded from outside, then a voice blared through a megaphone. "William Deslar and Benjamin Short…" The voice paused to let our defeat register. "We have you surrounded. Exit the house via the front door with your hands on your head."

I wondered how they knew Benny was with me. Keith couldn't have told them that.

"They've known we were together since the motel clerk called them," he said, breaking his silence. His voice held a renewed vigor. He sounded motivated, ready to face our challenge like a warrior. Then, preempting my next question, he said, "We're going to turn ourselves in."

"To the police? That's your plan?"

"The beginning of it. Your ability gets stronger in tense situations, right? With high emotions? High stress?

"If you're gonna try to use that to get out of this, it won't work. I can't control it, Ben."

"Yes or no?"

"I don't know. Yeah, I guess, from what I can tell. But I don't really know – it's not that simple. There's no formula."

"This is your last chance, fellas," the officer said, following the megaphone's screech. "You've got 'til the count of twenty"

"When they cuff you," Benny said, "remember which one has the keys." He put his hands on my shoulders and looked me in the eyes like everything hinged on his next words. "Then you need to focus on me."

"Twenty."

"What are you going to do?" I said.

"Just focus with everything you have."

"Nineteen."

"Connect with my thoughts. If it doesn't work right away, keep trying. Don't stop for anything." He walked across the foyer to the front door and grabbed the doorknob. "Ready?"

"Eighteen."

I held the door shut. "No, hold up. You can't predict what will happen, Ben. My ability didn't help a fucking bit when Lou's gun was pressed against my head. We can't rely on it."

"Seventeen."

"I need you to trust me."

"I do trust you, but I—"

"Will. Trust me."

"Sixteen."

How could I argue? I owed Benny my life, my loyalty, and my trust.

"All right, brother," I said. "Let's get arrested."

THIRTY-FOUR

Benny turned the knob and pulled the door open an inch or two. A hard wall of white light, infused with a pulsing blue, broke through the slit. "Here we go."

The sliver of light grew to a deluge as he opened the door wider. We walked out onto the front porch with our hands on our heads. He stopped. I stepped beside him. We both looked down, away from the blinding spotlights. We shared a numbing fear of flying metal. All those guns aimed at us. One wrong move would seal our fate. One nervous finger. We waited for our orders.

Get the fuck on the ground before I put ten rounds in each of you. That's what the one with the megaphone thought – what he wanted to say but knew he couldn't. "On the ground," he said. "Arms out in front of you, palms open and down."

We obeyed.

Nice and slow, Benny thought. *Don't give them an excuse to pull those triggers.* We assumed the commanded position without incident. Benny turned to me. *Focus, brother.*

I tried to get deeper into his head. I failed. The commotion made me tense, and the anticipation of an officer's knee in my back didn't help. I heard footsteps scamper to the porch and scale the steps. The knee came as predicted, but heavier and sharper than I had expected. I suppressed a grunt as the weight pushed the marred muscle of my chest into the planks. The cop twisted my wrists back and cuffed them, then pulled me up and frisked me. Benny experienced the same sequence, including my chest pain. His own pat-down produced the gun and radio.

"Well, well, well," his officer said, then handed them off to an older man who would've killed for a Budweiser. "Take these, will ya?"

I ignored the recitation of my Miranda rights and took note of the man in control of me, the one with the keys to my cuffs. Short. Pudgy. Italian.

They dragged us down the steps. The spotlight cut off. Three officers (dark blobs in my spotty vision) raced by us, into the house in search for Keith, as two ambulances turned into the driveway. Our handlers split us up; the Italian pushed me to the back of his cruiser, while a lanky kid took Benny to another. The rest of the squad lowered their weapons, thinking my cuffs meant their safety.

"Good work, boys," the Italian announced. The closing door snipped the word "boys." I watched the smug dick make his rounds, congratulating everyone with high fives, hugs, and pats on the back. A big fucking celebration. I guess small towns like that don't get much crime drama outside of *Law and Order*. A pair of escaped convicts must have been a circus to them.

I looked to my right, into the car that held Benny. He looked back. With my attention captured, he stared ahead, closed his eyes, and meditated. I imitated him, trying again to connect. I wanted to believe in his plan, and I'd follow his lead to the death, but I didn't like our chances. He couldn't predict success with such an unreliable keystone. Without a miracle, I'd be back in a cell with years added on to my sentence.

The Italian climbed into the driver seat and started the engine. Another officer took the passenger side.

"New England's gonna breathe a sigh of relief when they learn that we caught you two assholes," the passenger said. He had a trail of short, stringy scars running from his ear to his jaw, like dozens of inchworms had made a home under the skin. His head missed the ceiling by less than an inch, and he couldn't have been older than 30, no more than 160 pounds. He turned his strange, leathery face to me. "You had a respectable run, but we always win in the end." Pride oozed out of him like he'd single-handedly caught Whitey Bulger.

"You're right to be proud," I told him. He turned his body further in my direction, a bit surprised that I had answered him. "Yup, you're a bonafide hero. Grade-A police work you did there, standing by while your fat, Mario-looking friend here cuffed me." He laughed off the insults and turned back around.

"I'd rather be fat than a prison bitch," the Italian said. "Tell the truth – all them boys fight over you at shower time, don't they?"

The skinny one loved that, and giggled like a fifth-grader. "Bet you thought you were the luckiest man on Earth," he said, "escaping like you did. Bet you thought you hit the jackpot. Franco fucking Angeletti busts out of prison, and you just happen to be on his bus. What are the fucking odds?" He laughed. "19 of you got out that day. Now 18 are right back in."

"Only one left is Angeletti himself," the Italian said. "Matter of time, that's all. You monkeys don't know how to live outside them walls. That's why we keep you in 'em."

I ignored the temptation to return shots, and kept all my mental faculties on the task at hand. I felt like a blind man reaching in the air for something that may or may not be there, but I had to trust that Benny had it all figured out. The Italian put the car in reverse and backed out of the driveway. Benny's car followed, along with another.

"So, what were you in for?" the skinny one asked, knowing the answer, but seeing an opportunity to break my balls. I ignored him. "Oh, he don't wanna talk now," he said to the Italian. He turned to me and pressed his nose against the divider. "You don't look like the drug-dealing type. Nah, I bet you're one of the sick ones." He laughed. The Italian gave him a light chuckle that only compelled him to continue. "Yeah, I bet you did something real messed up. You film little boys or something? Lure 'em into your van with candy?"

A zap struck me.

Benny. He's driving. He's nervous, but he keeps it in check. The windshield wipers fight to keep up with the rain. The car phone flashes through the dark interior. If it makes a noise, the beating water drowns it out. He recognizes the number. He answers.

"Hey Trish, what's up?" The other end doesn't respond. Benny raises the volume on the receiver. "Tricia? You there, babe?"

"Shh," Tricia says in a low, far-away tone. "The devil. He's here, Benjamin." Benny's twin girls cry and yell in the background. Their words are unintelligible.

"What do you—"

"I have to save Isaiah," she says. A baby squeals. "What kind of mother would I be if I didn't?"

"You'll be trading blowjobs for cigarettes in no time," the skinny cop said, disconnecting me from the vision. I forced myself to hold my tongue. He'd shut up if I didn't give him the ammo to work with. I needed to get back. Back to whatever Benny was leading me to. I replayed what I'd seen.

Benny. The car. The rain. The phone. Tricia's calm voice. Her words. A pulse in my forehead encouraged me. I focused on Tricia's voice. The dark road. The devil. The girls. Isaiah.

The pulse intensified.

The car rockets down the highway. Benny's car. The experience is richer now, more vivid. Closer to reality. I feel what Benny feels: the panic, the need to get home, the knowledge that something life-shattering waits for him there. Rain continues to batter the windshield. His speed makes it worse. The odometer reads 95 miles per hour. He's never driven that fast, not even as a young, dumb kid. A red icon blinks on the dash.

Low traction. The car hovers on water for a moment. Benny takes his foot off the gas. His heart pounds. The red light disappears as the car slows. Benny keeps it steady at 60.

The flooded road became a dry one. I opened my eyes, back in the cruiser. Back in cuffs. Trees flew by as I looked ahead for any indication of the station. I didn't know how much time I had; I needed something to happen.

I drew in shallow, rapid breaths to get worked up. Two for every second. I wanted my blood to jet through my veins at mach speed. I wanted my heart to pound like a swat team breaking through a door. The cops said something, but I didn't hear them over my own thoughts and rushed breathing. My head tingled. I kept breathing as fast as I could. In and out. In and out.

"Trish?" Benny says, throwing the apartment door open and scanning the living room. I sit behind his eyes, peering through them like a screen to his past. I know a twist waits around one of those corners, ready to spring from its trapdoor and pull us in. A darkness fills the place, like the home itself is dead and rotten. "Trish? You here?"

He enters the kitchen. Nothing. Then the hall. Nothing. The door of the kids' room is shut. He opens it. Inside, his little girls, Tammy and Destiny, sit huddled together on one of their matching purple beds. Seeing them eases his mind some, but there's still plenty to worry about. They flinch as he approaches.

"Thank God," he says. "Everything's all right, babies." He wraps one arm around each of them. They tuck their faces into his chest. "Everything's all right. Tell me what happened."

Destiny sniffles. "Ma told us to stay put."

Tammy nods in agreement and adds, "Isaiah was crying a lot." Something horrible sticks on the tip of their tongues – something they want to express but don't understand enough to do so. Tears run down their cheeks.

"OK, babies, OK. I want you to stay here. I'll be right back, I

promise."

He kisses their foreheads, then closes the door behind him. The bathroom across the hall is empty. Only his bedroom remains unchecked. The door is shut. No light leaks through the bottom of it. Benny puts his ear against the wood. Water runs on the other side, from the bedroom's bath. He turns the knob slowly, without a sound. When the door is opened a crack he hears sobs. Tricia's sobs. He pushes the door the rest of the way.

Tricia sits at the edge of the bed, with only the alarm clock's red glow defining her silhouette. She looks up as he enters. Her stare goes through him, past the hall behind him, past the walls of the building, straight to the sky, and up to the stars. The only sign of life on her vacant face comes from the satisfied smirk and a single tear dangling from her chin.

I returned to captivity and immediately began a desperate attempt to flee back to Benny's apartment. Tricia's blank stare filled my head as I zeroed in on it. I used it to keep an anchor in the vision. I'd seen pictures of her before; Benny kept family photos tucked in the back cover of his bible, which used to sit on his shelf in our cell. The way she smiled at the camera, you would think she had never known a moment of sadness in her life. I wondered if he still had that bible. I hadn't seen it since we left our cell the morning after the collapse.

"What did you do?" Benny says. "Where's the baby?" When she doesn't answer, he grabs her shoulders and shakes her. She blinks her eyes a few times, then opens them wide. His voice cracks as he shouts in her face, "Where's Isaiah?"

"Benjamin?" she says, realizing who is standing in front of her. "Oh, Benjamin."

"Answer me."

Her eyes dart to the hallway. "Shh," she whispers with her index finger over her lips. "It's not safe yet." She waits a few seconds, then looks at Benny. "I had to protect him. Our delicate boy. Evil's in this house. Evil like you ain't never seen. But it's a mother's job to protect her babies, no matter what. I did my job, Benjamin. You'd be proud if you saw it. Now God will take care of him."

Benny twitches.

"The girls, Benjamin," she says. "Go get the girls. We need to save them, too."

I snapped back to myself with a sudden stop. My body slammed into the cruiser's mesh divider.

"Oops," the Italian said, laughing. "Sorry about that." I licked my bottom lip and tasted blood. "We're here, Deslar. This is your kennel until they come and drag you back down to Mass.

The police station looked like a foreclosed house that they had bought from the bank for pennies and nailed a blue sign to. I wondered if they even had enough cells to separate me from Benny.

The other two cruisers stopped beside us. The driver of Benny's car climbed out and retrieved him from the back, then waited for my escorts to do the same with me. The Italian's clammy claws cut off my attempt to reenter Benny's memory. They pulled me out by my arm and neck, then threw me to the pavement. As I landed on my back, the rough ground shaved the skin of my cuffed hands. The Italian stood over me, and his name came to me – Randall Ricci – just before he drove his boot into my chest. Through the sting I felt fresh blood ooze from at least one of the wounds beneath my shirt.

"Seven officers died in that bus attack," Ricci said, twisting his boot, drawing a grunt from me. "Seven good men. I knew a couple of 'em. Sanders and Murray – good fucking men." He twisted in the opposite direction. His foot felt like it could push through me to the ground. "None of those guys deserved that – to be taken down by you fucking animals." He backed up a few steps. "This is for them." He sprinted forward and connected with an unrestrained kick to my side. The force rolled me to my stomach. My breath paused a couple seconds before I gulped more air.

"You gonna let your girlfriend get beat up like that?" Benny's handler said to him, shoving him toward me. Benny would've kept his balance if it weren't for a leg sweep that dropped him beside me. All six of the pricks laughed.

"I can't get back there, Ben," I said underneath their cackling. "I'm sorry."

"Don't give me that shit," he said. "You can and you will."

"I'm trying. I don't—" Another kick landed in my gut. They laughed louder.

"All right," Ricci said, "fun's over. Get the fuck up."

I sat up, but needed time before I could go any further. The last kick still rippled through me. Benny made no move to stand. He sat still, his mind back with Tricia in his bedroom.

Ricci took this as defiance. "Get up, you fucking shit stain." No response. "I swear to God, if you make me get nigger on my hands…"

On the outside, Benny didn't seem to notice the insults. I knew better, though. Inside, his pulse sped up. He used the abuse, harvested it into kindling. His apartment bedroom began to reappear in my mind. I saw a faint ghost of Tricia form over the dim parking lot.

"He don't wanna listen to me," Ricci said to the group. "He don't wanna stand. Should I make it so he can't?" He pulled a nightstick from his belt and slapped his palm with it. "Whaddya say, boys? Should I knock the fucker's head off?" I felt their silent, varied reactions, but their opinions didn't matter. No one would stop Ricci. And Benny didn't want them to. He welcomed the extra fuel for the fire he'd started. Ricci drew back both hands and twirled the weapon like a baseball bat. Benny prepared. The cop's arms snapped forward.

I'm no longer the audience of the memory, no longer a bystander. I'm Benny. His thoughts, his breaths, his blinks, his fear – it's all my own. I face the door to my bedroom's bathroom. Tricia sits behind me, weeping with a smile. Behind the bathroom door, the tub's faucet pours water. Under it, that water streams into the bedroom with a long tendril that follows a groove in the hardwood. I step into the river and grab the handle. I don't want to go in there, but I have to. I push the door open before I lose my nerve. The door hits the wall behind it. Water covers the tiles. The floor mat squishes as I step to the shower curtain and grip the edge of the plastic.

Just leave, I think. You know what's waiting for you. It won't do any good to see that. No. I'm his father. I have to see him.

I rip the curtain aside to the backdrop of metal rings screeching along the curtain rod and water splashing over the edge of the tub onto the floor.

I see Isaiah. I see my baby boy.

My world dies. My mind stops. Cohesive thoughts vanish.

I take two steps back and drop to my knees. I can't move, can't tear my eyes from the tiny body. My arms fall limp, my mouth hangs open, and I try to let out a sound that can express my misery. I only manage a dull moan. A voice fills my ears. A violent shake fills my body.

"Will!"

I lunge at Tricia. She took my son from me. A defenseless child. I force her to the ground and wrap my hands around her throat. It feels terrible, but it feels like justice. This is my duty as a father – to show her what Isaiah felt as he gasped for air under the running water. That wild panic that strikes when lungs flood.

"Stop," she says, choking.

"No," I say. "It's too late for redemption. You did this. You." I squeeze with all my strength.

"It's me, brother," she says, coughing and struggling with every word. "It's Benny." Her voice deepens. She looks at me, eyes red and bulging. "Snap out of it, Will."

Will? Who's Will?

Her face changes. Features melt away until a black, fleshy mannequin remains. The bedroom darkens around me. Reality rearranges itself.

Where am I? Who is this woman?

It's not a woman at all. The person in my grip is a man. He knows me. I know him. Features grow out of the empty face.

Benny.

I let go of Benny's throat and rolled off of him, stricken with a sudden understanding. I wasn't in the bedroom. Never had been. I felt like I'd woken from a nightmare-driven sleepwalk. I looked up to see the police station.

"Benny," I said, "I'm so sorry. I didn't know what…" My apology sagged at the end when I looked back at him and saw his face. He sat up, stared over my shoulder, and pointed. I turned and froze in horror.

The six officers faced us, on their knees, fixed in place. Their arms dangled. Muscles limp. Tears ran from their still, open eyes. Every mouth hung open. Two or three moaned.

I had turned them into Benny.

They were broken, all six of them, staring at their lifeless, floating child. Their traumatized expressions were enough to scar even the coldest heart.

I opened my mouth to say something to Benny, but nothing could follow up what I'd experienced. No words exist in any language that could've communicated my sympathy.

"We have to leave," he said in a somber tone. "They won't stay like this forever."

THIRTY-FIVE

As I stood there in that police station parking lot, paralyzed by the sight of the wilted, helpless officers, Benny sprung into action. He dashed around like a man participating in a life-or-death scavenger hunt, and I only became aware when he finished and tugged my shoulder. I jumped.

"Take this," he said, handing over our CB radio and the key to my cuffs. He put our gun in his belt and flipped through a key ring he'd taken from one of the officers. He looked at the row of cars, all American. "A Jeep. Where's the Jeep? There."

I took one last look at what I'd done, wanted to puke but refrained, then followed him to our getaway car. As we pulled out of the lot, I thought of the squad playing back the surveillance video, wondering what in God's name had happened to them.

We drove a couple miles before Benny pulled the stolen Wrangler into a gas station. He parked it behind the building.

"We'll walk from here," he said. "The hotel should be about a mile that way." Those were the first words either of us had spoken since leaving the station, and the last we would speak until we reached the hotel. Conversation was unnecessary; Benny knew all I wanted to say, and I knew all his responses. The phantom exchange lived in our minds with the same authenticity as anything verbal.

"I don't know what to say, Ben. I can't imagine a worse thing for a parent to live through."

"I could've lost more. I still have my girls."

"…"

"You have a question."

"I have no right to ask."

"Go ahead, Will."

"You killed her, didn't you?"

"I'd give anything to change it. Every day I see my hands on her throat. The light in her face fading away. Every fucking day."

"No one could blame you."

"The jury blamed me. I blame me."

"You shouldn't."

"I should. Tricia wasn't evil, Will. She was sick. I murdered a sick woman. She didn't even know what she did wrong. Can you imagine her last moments? The confusion. Wondering why the man she loved was choking her. How do I move past that?"

"You weren't yourself."

"I should've fought harder. I should've kept control. I deserve those 30 years. I deserve worse."

No – nothing productive would come from bringing that conversation to life. I left it where it belonged.

A stressed-out Cameron waited for us back at our room. She rushed us the instant we walked in. Her hair was tussled from her own fingers running through it dozens of times, and I knew she had been pacing before she heard our key card slip through the lock.

"I've been a fucking mess," she said, hugging us. "I didn't want to leave Keith's, but Benny—"

"You were right to leave," I said, trudging to the bed and falling onto it, face-first. "We barely made it out." Benny sat in the desk chair, leaned back, and closed his eyes.

"Are you gonna leave me with that cliffhanger?" Cameron said. "Or are you going to tell me what happened?"

"I'll fill you in. I just need to lay here a minute." My lower back ached. I stretched.

"We haven't eaten since this morning," she said. "You can tell me over some food."

"We shouldn't be in public right now," I said.

"We can get room service."

I shook my head. "I can't eat."

"We really should get something inside us," Benny said. "It's been a long day. We need it."

"Fine," I said.

Cameron threw her arms up. "Sure, you'll listen to him."

Benny stood. "I'll go down and grab something."

I flipped over and sat up. "Are you nuts? No. The cops are gonna be sniffing the area like dogs. Let's just call down and order something."

Cameron raised her hand. "Hold on. Wait. Did you just say that the cops are on to you?"

"I'll be fine," Benny said, dodging the question. "Really. I just need to be alone for a few. You stay here and bring Cameron up to speed. When I get back, we'll figure out our next move." I knew I couldn't argue with him. If the man wanted to go, he'd go.

"That sounds like a perfect idea," Cameron said. "Being out of the loop drives me fucking batty." She grabbed a couple twenties from her purse and handed them to Benny. "Burger and an iced tea. Unsweetened."

He nodded. "Will?"

"You already know what I want."

"Figured I'd ask as a courtesy."

Even before the door had shut behind him, Cameron began

mining for answers. I found myself walking a difficult line between giving essential information and respecting Benny's right to keep his past buried. She knew I held back details, and of course she tried bringing them out of me. In the end my defenses held up. The recap gave way to a long silence.

Cameron ended the pause after a couple minutes. "I'm sorry about your brother-in-law. It sucks."

"Thank you. I didn't agree with him on much, but all in all, I liked the guy. How can I… How am I supposed to live with myself when this is all over? And I don't just mean Keith. Everything's gotten so fucked up."

"Stop it," she said.

"What?"

"The self pity. Knock it off."

"I can't help how I think. People are dead because of me."

"Tell me something – would you trade any of those lives for your son's?" My sinking eyes answered the question. "Exactly, so stop with the regrets. Your son is worth whatever it takes."

"Your wisdom is a ruthless bitch, you know that?"

"Because it's coming from one," she said. We both smiled. "So you found out where they're hiding. What now?"

I stood. "Now we make sure we don't screw up our chance."

Benny walked through the door as I grabbed my laptop from the table. The room filled with the scent of burnt beef and french fries, and I thought I must have been crazy to refuse the suggestion of food. I sat on the floor with the computer. They both followed. Benny unpacked our late dinner in the center of us.

"Sixteen Corby," I said, opening a browser window and searching for the address. A pin dropped onto the satellite map. "You're kidding me." I turned the screen to show them. "It's less than two miles away. Marcus is less than two miles away."

"I know what you're thinking," Benny said, "but we should—"

"I agree," I said. His misjudgment gave me back my feeling of privacy in my own head. "We should take our time. Do this right." I studied the satellite snapshot. Fences and empty animal pens peppered the property. Forest surrounded it on all four sides. Mountains loomed over three. A straight dirt road, about a half-mile long and mostly hidden under trees, connected the house to civilization. "Looks like a ranch, or what's left of one."

"Any car approaching on that driveway might as well be firing flares," Cameron said before digging into her burger.

I set the computer down beside me and opened my foam container. "Suggestions?"

"We could hike around to the back," Benny said, tracing a path in front of the screen. "Find a position somewhere on this mountainside and set up camp. Then we can scope the place out, learn their routine, and figure out the best time to move in."

"Binoculars," Cameron said with her mouth full. She held up a finger while she chewed and swallowed the bite. "We'll buy binoculars."

"I like that," I said. The optimism I'd needed since embarking for New Hampshire finally caught up to me. "That's the plan then. First thing tomorrow, we'll grab supplies and head out there."

"Can I ask you something?" Cameron said. I nodded. "You know where they are…" *Why not tell the police?* "Why not call the cops and let them handle it?"

"I've come too far, and I have too much to lose. I can't put this in someone else's hands."

"That's half the reason," Benny said.

Just when I thought you were out of my head.

"What's that supposed to mean?" Cameron asked him.

Benny sipped his soda, then wiped his mouth with a napkin. "Will wants to do what the cops won't. He wants to kill Lincoln."

THIRTY-SIX

I closed my eyes that night staring at a hotel ceiling, and opened them in the kitchen of my old apartment. I looked around, nostalgic from all the things I used to see every day – the family pictures, the fake flowers on the counter, the minefield of Marcus's toy cars. My thoughts felt wispy as I ventured into the living room, wondering where my dream would take me.

Julie sat on the couch, facing the opposite direction with her purple wool blanket on her lap. The TV was off, the lights too. She sat in a dim silence, staring at three candles burning on the coffee table in front of her. Beside them sat an empty glass. Somehow I knew it held the last drop of her third round of red wine.

Julie never drank at home.

I heard a shower faucet sputter behind me in the hallway bathroom, then understood where my fucked up mind had tossed me. The wine should've given it away. I remembered the night, twenty-four hours before the robbery, and what had happened after my shower.

I stepped closer to Julie. She didn't hear me, and I wondered if I could even make contact in this dreamworld. The thought of speaking made me want to wake up. *You can't. You need this.*

"Julie," I said. The name tasted like bile.

"Christ!" She jumped and turned in her seat. "You scared the shit out of me." The flickering orange from the candles painted her face with a demonic glow that fit my new opinion of her. "I thought you were in the shower."

"I am," I said. "I'm in there right now, actually."

She looked at me like one would look at a meowing dog. "I'm not in the mood for games, Will. I have enough shit to think about right now."

"Thinking about tomorrow night? About how hard you'll have to swing that bat to knock me out?" Her face desaturated. "Rest easy, you'll get it right."

"Why would you say something like that?"

"Why would you *do* something like that?" She shook her head, confused. I laughed and pointed to the bathroom. "You think I'm that poor bastard in the shower who, as we speak, is thinking of ways to get out of the biggest mistake of his life. You think I'm *Naive* Will. Nope. You see, I'm what Naive Will becomes after you strip him of everything."

She opened her mouth to speak.

"Shut the fuck up," I snapped. "I'm talking. God, it's all so damn obvious now. But you know what they say about hindsight." I turned toward the bathroom. The light from inside and the sound of the water trickled into the hall. "In five minutes, Naive Will will get out of that shower and try one last time to get you to call off the robbery. And you'll say…"

"No," she said.

"Yup, but he won't give up that easily. He'll try telling you what Lincoln said to him, how he threatened to slit his throat. You'll call him crazy. No, that's not it. You'll call him a liar. Much worse. And the two of you will fight because he won't understand why you won't believe him. I know why you won't believe him. Tell me, Julie – how long were you fucking Lincoln before this night?"

She said nothing. No confirmation. No denial. I rounded the

couch and sat in the wooden rocking chair that she loved but I hated. I bent forward to pick up a toy Corvette, then leaned back and tossed it from hand to hand.

"After that," I continued, "Naive Will will say, 'Fuck it, I'm not going tomorrow. You go ahead if you're so set on it. Leave me out the damn thing.' Not in those exact words, but that's the gist of it. And you'll yell at him, and he'll yell louder, and you'll tell him to keep his voice down because Marcus is sleeping. 'You tricked me into this,' he'll say, and, 'I never wanted any of it.' Then you'll blame him. He lost his job. That's why the family is in this position. That's why Marcus is still wearing clothes he's grown out of. That's low, Julie. Real fucking low." I tucked the car into my pocket, hoping I'd have it when I woke.

"And you know what the twisted part is, looking back on it now? The whole time the two of you are going at it, you'll be so full of yourself, because you'll know what you're planning. You're gonna take his son. *My* son, Julie!"

"You're not—"

"I didn't say you could talk. How could you throw me aside like a piece of garbage? I mean, you must have loved me at some point, right? You must have cared. You married me.

"Poor Naive Will. If only he'd seen it. But he couldn't, really. Not something that cruel. Still, he'll beg you to pull out of the robbery. A voice inside is telling him that something will go wrong, and he's terrified about what that would do to Marcus. It's an impossible battle, though, because you, the woman he loves, the woman he exchanged vows with, has already decided his fate. You'll argue more, and scream, and you'll push his patience like you've gotten so good at doing.

"Then he'll hit you."

"You'd never hit me," she said.

"You're right, I wouldn't. But he will. On this night, with all that weight on his shoulders, he'll hit you. And he'll regret it the second it lands, but something about it will feel right, because you've cornered him, Julie – backed him into a crime he has no business doing with a man he has no business knowing, and no matter how much he tries to steer himself onto the right path, you insist there's no other way. It's *his* fault, you'll insinuate for the hundredth time. For weeks you've been hammering it into his head that he's a failure. As a husband, as a father, as a man. And he believes you, you manipulative little bitch."

"Fuck you."

"No, no, no. Fuck. *You.* Now let me finish this touching story." I stood up and stood tall, towering over her. "After he hits you, you'll leave. And he'll stay up all night, knowing you'll come back. He'll pace and drink and think and worry about where he's at, how he got there. You'll return at four in the morning. He'll try to apologize, but you'll stop him. 'It never happened,' you'll say. 'I'll never mention it if you do this for me tomorrow night. Please, Will.'

"He'll think of how much he loves you, and how he wants to provide for Marcus. And he knows that his desperation will only end if he gives up the fight. So he'll submit. Like an idiot. Then he'll kiss you, even though it's clear you don't want it, and when he kisses you, he'll taste the liquor on your lips, but he'll be too blind to see what it means."

Julie stared at me, afraid to speak.

I leaned over the coffee table and blew out the candles. "I'm close, Julie. Just two miles away."

THIRTY-SEVEN

"Wake up, handsome."

I opened my eyes, surprised to find Cameron in my bed. I looked at the other bed, then at the bathroom.

"Where's Benny?"

"Oh, Will," she said, running her finger down my arm from my elbow to my wrist. "You wake up to a prize like me beside you, and the first thing you think about is Benny?" She chuckled. "He took a walk."

"Why would he do that?"

"Because I told him to."

"And why would *you* do that?"

She climbed on top of me, put her lips to my ear, and whispered, "Take a guess." The whisper ran down my neck and through every vertebra. I shuddered. "It's been a long time, hasn't it? I can feel it every time you look at me."

"Too long. Way too long."

She sat up and pulled my shirt off. Then her own. "You could have ended that dry spell yesterday, sweetheart. I was right here, hoping you'd seize the opportunity. Instead, we talked and slept." She slipped off her bra.

"I didn't know this was an option." I put my hands on her thighs, slid them up her skirt, and squeezed the top of her legs. I gave myself a pause to look at her body, which I'd been unable to admire the first time I'd seen it.

"What kind of mind reader are you?" she said. "You couldn't feel how much I wanted this?" She leaned forward and ran her tongue along the side of my neck. "Can you feel it now?"

"Doesn't take a mind reader to" – I flinched as she reached between her legs and grabbed me – "to feel it now." I pulled up her skirt and tugged at her panties. She stiffened her legs and wiggled her hips to help the red lace along, then tossed it aside with her feet. I kissed the center of her chest and worked my way up, peck by peck, past her neck, along her jawbone, to her earlobe. I bit it.

"I can feel you in my head," she said with a quiver. "It's like we're melted together. It's… I can feel every sensation running through your body. It's amazing. Can you…?"

"Yes," I said as her desire rushed through me, from my lips to my toes. Mine reciprocated. The back-and-forth built up between us, with each of us ambushed by the other's internal, once-private sensations. The exchange grew until neither of us could hold out any longer. She lifted her body while I rushed my boxers down my legs, then she lowered herself onto me. I slid inside like we'd given an hour to foreplay. The first thrust put us both inches from the finish line. My excitement raised hers; hers raised mine. With each movement, however slight, our own pleasure intertwined with the other's.

After thirty seconds of this shared bliss, we finished together. Cameron fell forward, body pulsing, breath fluttering. I pulled her tight, pushing further in as she flexed her grip on me. I held her there until the waves passed, then loosened my hold. We lay still for a minute, stunned.

I ran my fingertips down her back, feeling her stuttered inhales and exhales. "I assume you've got some smart-ass remark about my stamina?"

She let out a laugh, made weak by her recovery. "Sweetie…" She nuzzled her face into my neck. "I wish every man could do what you just did, as quick as you did it."

○ ○ ○

When the CB radio on the nightstand chirped, I had just finished dressing after leaving Cameron in the shower. The bathroom door hung open with melodic whistles and puffs of steam escaping every few seconds. I caught a whiff of the hotel's strawberry body wash as I walked over to answer the call.

"Benny?" I said into the radio.

His voice came through at full volume, startling me. "You two done yet?"

I lowered the volume by three clicks. "Where are you?"

"The coffee shop in the lobby."

"Come on up." I let go of the speaker button, but pushed it again. "With two coffees. Black."

When his side came back, it cut into the tail end of a laugh. "Give 'em an inch…"

I poked my head into the bathroom. "Benny's coming back, so you may want to cover yourself when you're done."

"He's already seen the goods," Cameron called back over the water.

A few minutes later, a keycard slid through the reader as I grabbed and woke up my laptop.

"Deleting the video?" Benny said with a grin as he walked in with a tray of coffees in hand. He knew, and I realized just then, that I'd unintentionally recorded the morning's activities in an attempt to catch nighttime phenomena. I stopped the recording and closed the window.

"Nope," I said. "Saving it."

He laughed. Everything about him – his personality, poise, mood – displayed a lighter man, like he had purged a poison from his system. *He has*, I thought, thinking of the previous night. *He's not the sole keeper of his secret anymore.*

"I'm sure it's riveting," he said. "Six hours of you sleeping, then twenty seconds of clumsy embarrassment. Can't wait for the sequel."

"It wasn't that fast," I said. "All right, it was. But is wasn't clumsy. All right, it was kinda clumsy." He shook his head and handed me two coffees. I put one down on the desk and sipped the other. "Ready for camping?"

"Not one fucking bit," he said, pulling a peach from a plastic bag. "Been once when I was a kid. I hated it. Pine needles. Sap. Rain. Fucking bugs everywhere."

The shower stopped. Curtain rings screeched. Benny hated that sound.

"You could stay here," I said. "Watch TV, take bubble baths, and eat peaches while we get shit done." I remembered the Corvette from my dream. I searched my pocket and found nothing.

Benny bit into the fruit. "If I had half a brain, I would. But no, I'll be out there hunting squirrels and rubbing sticks together, or whatever you white people do out in the woods and call a vacation."

"I know you've been away for a long time, Benny," Cameron said, emerging from the bathroom in a cloud of steam, wrapped in a white towel, "but we have things called lighters now. Unless rubbing sticks together is just a prison euphemism."

"Ouch," I said to Benny.

"That's a dig at you, too," she said, walking to the door. "All right, boys – I'll go dress in my room, then we'll take off. Give me five minutes." She walked into the hallway wearing only a towel, then turned left. Before the door closed behind her, she yelled, "And keep your sticks away from each other. We're on a timeline."

THIRTY-EIGHT

"They're everywhere!" Benny said with a rare nervousness, swatting at invisible assailants in the air around him. "These things are fucking with me, I know they are."

Cameron giggled at his overreaction. "You must have sweet blood. They're not biting me at all."

"Me neither," I said.

Benny jogged ahead, trying to escape his tormentors. "Racist-ass mosquitos."

Every so often the ranch that we had gone through Hell to reach showed itself through the foliage. *Hang in there, kid*, I thought. *Just a little longer.*

We'd hiked for about an hour, circling along the mountains at the outskirts of the property. Each of us carried a backpack, each of which bulged from the supplies we bought after an hour at the sporting good store, bickering over what was worth lugging for an uncertain number of miles.

From our position on the slope, when the trees allowed, we had an all-encompassing view of our destination below. At the front sat a two-story, navy blue and beige house. Behind it lay the ruin of a once-functioning ranch. The fences, sheds, and barns scattered on the land showed years of neglect, and the grass alternated between scorched and weedy.

"This should do it," I said, stomping my foot on my chosen spot. "It's as good a view as we're gonna get."

Benny let his pack fall off his back, revealing a sweat-soaked shirt underneath. "I don't think any amount of tree cover will hide this thing." He eyed Cameron. "*Someone* had to get the Cadillac of tents."

"I didn't choose it for the size," she said. "I chose it for the camouflage."

"Yeah, we all believe that," he replied. "Either way, I hope you know how to set it up, because I'm no good with this camping shit."

"I'll show you how it's done."

"I don't wanna be shown."

"Too bad, I'm putting you to work. Unpack the Cadillac." Cameron put her bag down and stood beside me as Benny obeyed with a grumble. Together we observed the ranch. "Who owns this place?"

I shrugged. "Someone Keith knew. That's all I know."

"I can't imagine they're too pleased about hiding a couple of fugitives and a kid," she said.

"And two prisoners," I added, hoping Robert and Heather were still alive.

"Who would welcome that into their house? Keith must have had some loyal friends."

"Lincoln and Julie have diamonds and a lot of cash," Benny said from behind us, fighting with the tent's box. "Enough of that'll sway anyone."

For the next half hour, while Cameron and Benny constructed our tent, I watched the house through binoculars. I had found a comfortable spot against a tree and sat there sucking the salt from a strip of beef jerky. My surveillance yielded nothing. No vehicles were parked anywhere, so I kept my hopeful attention on the long driveway. The lack of activity made me edgy. As the sun began to set, I noticed a faint light from inside the house, but still no movement.

"Is that a light I see in there?" Cameron asked, checking up on me.

"Yeah." I lowered the binoculars and looked up at her. "Doesn't mean anything, though."

"Better than a vacant house."

"I guess."

"Take a break," she said. "Chef Short made dinner." She grabbed the binoculars from my lap and walked away, leaving me no choice in the matter.

When I reached the tent, Benny handed me a plastic bowl full of macaroni and vegetables. "Thanks, Ben. Smells good."

"Tastes good, too," he said, then shut the comically small charcoal grill he had insisted on buying.

"Not bad for a meal cooked in a tin bowl," Cameron said.

"It'd be better with some pork," he said, "but thanks." He sat on the ground and took a bite of his concoction. "My first few years in the box – they weren't real strict back then – I used to make grilled cheese sandwiches right in my cell with only tin foil, Doritos, and a single match."

"Oh God," Cameron said, "please don't tell me you used Doritos as the cheese." She held off on her next bite until she heard the answer.

"No, no, no," Benny said. "If you crush 'em up, they burn pretty good. I used them and the foil as my stove. A few dollars at the commissary would get me all that, plus bread and cheese. Guys would trade all sorts of shit for those sandwiches."

"Huh." Cameron took the last bite of her meal and set the bowl down.

As the leaves crunched beneath her bowl, gravel crunched in the distance. Our heads shot up like a group of gazelles at the sound of a predator in the brush.

"That's a car," Benny said, standing.

I popped up, grabbed the binoculars, and rushed back to my

lookout tree. I peered through the lenses in time to see a pickup truck driving around the side of the house. The dark paint gave up no detail, but the headlights told me it was a Dodge. It came to a stop behind the house, beside the back porch. The engine stopped. Both doors opened.

Benny and Cameron stood beside me, waiting for a report. Clouds blocked most of the moonlight, leaving me unable to make out the figures. The driver seemed to have a masculine walk. Lincoln, maybe. I moved my sight to the much shorter passenger who could have been Marcus. I wasn't sure of either. The two walked across the porch and into the house through a sliding door. I waited for more lights to turn on, but none did. Before long, the existing light from earlier died.

Cameron sensed my disappointment and stroked my back. "We'll get a better look tomorrow."

○ ○ ○

Are you out there, Will? Are you coming for us? I can't feel you anymore.

○ ○ ○

Cameron's prediction came true the next morning.

"Quick!" Benny called, waving me over. "Come here." He had taken over surveillance duty while I made an instant coffee that disgusted me from the first sniff. I needed it, though, and the warmth felt good on my hands.

I rushed to his side. "Got something?"

He handed the binoculars to me and pointed at the house. "That Marcus?"

The truck's doors closed as my vision focused. Through the passenger side window I got a clear sight of the only face in the world I cared to see.

I elbowed Benny harder than intended. "It's him!" The truck started, then drove toward the driveway. "We got him, Ben. We fucking got him!" I dropped the binoculars and the coffee on the ground. Hot liquid splashed our feet as I hugged him.

He slapped my back. "I knew we'd find him, brother. Didn't I tell you?"

"Good news?" Cameron said, investigating the commotion.

I let go of Benny and prepared for another hug. "I saw him."

She let out a wordless shriek of joy and jumped into my arms. My joy overpowered the pain of her body hitting my cuts. I didn't care if the celebration was premature; the morale boost was long overdue. We needed a win, and the validation felt like the beginning of success.

"I didn't catch the driver," I said to Benny. "Did you see him?"

"Yeah. Middle-aged white guy. Dark hair."

"Has to be Lincoln. I bet Julie's in that house right now, alone with Robert and Heather."

Cameron bent down for the binoculars and my cup. "What are you thinking? We gonna make a move?"

"Not yet," I said, summoning every sliver of discipline I had. "We don't know how long they'll be gone, or if there's anyone else in there. I can't risk a surprise. I'm gonna keep watching."

"I'll watch for now," Benny said, taking the binoculars from Cameron before I could object. He lifted his foot to show the coffee I'd spilled on him. "Go pour yourself another cup. Eat something."

"The coffee's garbage, and I'm too worked up to eat. I'll watch."

"Will."

"What?"

"Eat something."

"Goddammit."

○ ○ ○

Heather? Are you awake? Please talk to me.

○　○　○

The truck returned twenty minutes past noon. Benny and Cameron sat beside me at the lookout spot, cross-legged on the ground, playing rummy.

"Bastard," Cameron said when Benny threw down three aces. "I might as well concede now."

He rearranged his hand. "Don't feel bad. I've played this game more in one week than you probably have in your entire life." He followed up with three jacks.

Cameron sighed. "You don't say."

"They're back," I said. I stood and locked on to the Dodge as it barreled up the driveway, throwing dust in the air behind it. Benny and Cameron put their cards down and rose.

"I knew we should've bought more binoculars," Cameron said, shielding her eyes from the sun as she gazed down.

The truck came to a stop in the backyard, on the same brown patch of grass from which it left. The doors opened. Marcus hopped down from the high cab wearing a plain blue sweatshirt, jeans, his Spiderman baseball cap, and a frown. He looked older. That pissed me off; it rubbed my face in the time I had missed.

I panned to the driver. "Yeah, it's Lincoln. Fucking prick."

"What are they doing?" Cameron asked.

"They're walking up the back porch. Hold on." The sliding door opened before they reached it. "It's Julie. She's coming out."

The sight of her left me lightheaded. She looked tired, not at all like a woman enjoying a life full of diamonds and luxury. Her melancholy expression made it difficult for me to maintain my hatred. Benny said something, and Cameron too, but none of it registered over the view of my family.

Julie stopped in front of Lincoln and said something. Her eyes never met his. He pointed an aggressive finger at the house. She nodded and said something else. Then he went inside.

"Lincoln's in the house," I said. "Julie and Marcus are still out back."

"Give 'em here," Cameron said, holding her hand out. "I want to see the Deslars." I passed the binoculars to her. "Oh my God, he's the cutest friggin' thing. And Mrs. Deslar…" *Not bad, Will.* "Not a bad piece of ass, Will."

Benny took the binoculars from her and gazed down. He didn't speak, but I knew he saw his own past in the two of them. He handed the binoculars back to me, and I watched Julie and Marcus throw a baseball back and forth.

Something about the scene bothered me. Their game of catch lacked joy. They weren't having fun, but rather played as if their time together was an escape. They blurred as tears coated my eyes. I pictured myself down there, tossing that ball to my boy, Julie asking what we wanted for dinner, me letting Marcus decide. He'd choose Chicken Mozambique, pronouncing it, "chicken, moose, and beak." He always did.

He threw the ball to Julie. It fell short. She squatted down to grab it, but as she rose she stumbled backward, landed hard on her back, and shot up to a sitting position. Her face showed no pain from the fall, only confusion, like an unsolicited, impossible idea had surfaced in her head. She surveyed the mountains with a squint, and I knew her sweep would stop in our direction. It did. I held my breath.

She can't see us, I thought, and had no doubt of it. A hawk couldn't see us from from that distance, among all those dense pines. *But maybe she senses me.*

A chill ran from the base of my skull to my tailbone. Her stare remained fixed on our position for a few long seconds, after which she stood up and said something to Marcus. He stomped his feet before retreating into the house in front of her. The slider closed, cutting them off from me once again.

○ ○ ○

But don't worry – you'll never have to feel it again.

○ ○ ○

Later that day, Lincoln and Marcus left again. Marcus hated those trips. He pouted all the way to the truck. Lincoln yelled something at him, which only made his pout intensify and his arms cross in defiance.

"I can't wait to see your last breath," I mumbled with Lincoln's face in the scope.

"What?" Cameron said.

"Every time he leaves, he takes Marcus with him. Why? It has to be a pain in the ass."

"Insurance," she said.

"How so?"

"He might be afraid of Julie leaving him. She wouldn't leave without Marcus."

I remembered Julie's earlier demeanor. "I think you're right. It fits."

"Something tells me the situation down there is on the verge of erupting," she said.

○ ○ ○

Can you do one more favor for me, bud? Can you come down to the opening? So I can see you?

Lincoln and Marcus returned a half-hour later with shopping bags. They went straight into the house.

"That's it for tonight," I said to Cameron, judging that the sun only had an hour or so left in the sky. I leaned back against a tree, exhausted from the constant alert.

"Put 'em down," Benny said, startling us. "Dinner's ready."

"Another gourmet meal from Chef Short?" Cameron asked.

"Beans and rice," he said. "I know that don't sound like much, but trust me on this one."

We stood, followed him back to the tent, and attacked the meal like people who had only ever dreamt of eating.

"I don't know how you did it, Benny," Cameron said with a full mouth, then swallowed. "But you've managed to turn canned beans into the best thing I've eaten in weeks."

"It's all in the spices," he said. "I snuck a few into the cart yesterday."

"You didn't sneak shit," I said. "I saw you grab the—"

"If you give away my secret ingredient, I swear to God…"

"Cameron already knows it, just by the taste."

"I do *not*," she said.

I tapped my head. "Yes you do. But seriously, Ben – if you can make something this good out of a can with a twenty-dollar grill, I'd love to see what you can do with a stocked kitchen."

Cameron nodded. "I second that."

"I always wanted to run a restaurant," Benny said, wiping sauce from his lip.

"Did you know that Benny went to culinary school?" I asked Cameron.

"So you cook for real?" she said, then realized how the question sounded. "You know what I mean – like, stuff that doesn't cook over

Doritos and aluminum foil."

Benny laughed. "Yeah, I cook for real. Learned from helping my Aunt Celia. She raised me since I was three and cooked dinner every single night except Thursdays."

"Why not Thursdays?" Cameron asked.

"She played bridge on Thursdays," I said.

Benny laughed. "Yup. And nothing got in the way of Aunt Celia and bridge." He smiled as he remembered her. I caught a quick glimpse of her face, and even though I'd seen photos of her, the picture that existed in Benny's head had an extra brightness to it. "She never had any schooling – you know, for cooking – but my grandfather was a chef. He taught her and my mother. You'd think Aunt Celia was world-class, the way she made miracles in the kitchen. When I was a kid, I'd tell her all the time that she should open a restaurant. She never had the heart to tell me we were too poor."

"Is she still alive?" Cameron asked.

"Oh yeah," I answered for him. "She used to bring Benny all sorts of goodies in prison. Every time she visited, Benny would come back to the cell smelling like a five-star restaurant."

"The woman's an angel," he said. "First thing I'm doing when this is over is going to see her and my girls."

"Aw," Cameron said. "It's so sweet, the way you talk about your aunt like that."

"Yeah, yeah. Don't go telling anyone."

I yawned. "Staring at a house all day really takes it out of ya."

"Turning in for the night?" Benny asked.

I yawned again and nodded. "Nothing else is happening down there, and I wanna be up early tomorrow."

Cameron stood. "I'll go with you."

"I'm gonna stay out here a while longer," Benny said. "It's a nice night."

I used his shoulder to stand, patted it, and walked to the tent.

"Night, Benny," Cameron said.

"Good night, guys."

○ ○ ○

I know what he means to me. I know what he calls me.

○ ○ ○

As I lay there with Cameron's arms around me, my thoughts ran laps in my head.

"Are you happy?" she said.

"Huh?"

"You saw Marcus today. You must be happy."

I kissed her forehead. "Yes, I'm happy. Unfortunately, that's not the only emotion fighting for my attention. I need to end this. I can't handle much more."

She put her hand on my chest. "Soon. I don't care if I have to go down there myself, guns blazing."

"My own personal Rambo."

"You think Robert's really down there?" she asked. "And Heather?"

"Yesterday, when we first got here, I wondered that, and whether or not we're too late to save them. But now I know he's here. It's the same feeling I get when I read those letters. It's like he's part of me. His words and thoughts have been swimming through my head all day. He's still alive."

"I hope so. It breaks my heart to think of what they're going through down there. But it's almost over."

"Almost."

"Good night, Will."

"Good night, Cameron."

THIRTY-NINE

*You told me to let go. You both did. Why did you tell me that?
Why did I listen?*

I won't let it happen again. We can change it.

○　○　○

I woke the next morning to my own voice speaking these words:
"Thank you both. For everything."

I didn't need to open my eyes; they were already wide, already
adjusted to the morning light. Benny and Cameron sat opposite me
with tears in their eyes.

"What's going on?" I asked. "What did I just say to you?"

"He's awake," Cameron said, elbowing Benny, with a spike in her
heartbeat. They both wiped their tears despite knowing it was too late
to hide them.

Through the walls of the tent, I could see the perfect day that
waited outside. The sun soaked the air, birds sang, and I knew if I unzipped the door, I'd see beauty in all directions. Yet a dense despair
filled our enclosed dome, like that outside world didn't exist at all.

"What's going on?" I repeated.

Cameron stood and fled the tent. No explanation. No eye contact. Light burst through the opening, highlighting Benny's somber face. He sniffled.

"Answer me."

"You were talking in your sleep." His speech stuttered several times in the short sentence.

"It was Robert," I said, not bothering to pose it as a question. "What did he tell you?" Benny only looked down and remained silent. "You're scaring me, Ben."

"He told us good news, brother. That's all you need to know. Everything's gonna be fine."

"You don't look like everything's gonna be fine."

He wiped his eyes with his palm. "These are tears of joy."

"You're full of shit."

"It'll be clear soon."

"Make it clear now."

"I can't," he said. "If you see that as a betrayal, then so be it, but you'll look back on this moment someday soon and see the truth."

"This is my life we're talking about. My son's life."

"Have I ever done you wrong?" he asked. I didn't respond. "It's not a rhetorical question. Have I ever done you wrong?"

"No, but—"

"I've killed for you. I took care of you when you were hurt. I stuck by you, knowing that a jump in your blood pressure or some nightmare of yours could kill me. And you still doubt that I'm on your side? Two days ago you doubted me – and what did you tell me when it all went wrong? What did you tell me? You said that you should've listened. That lives would've been saved. Well, here we are again. I need you to trust me this time. I've earned that much."

My jaw tightened. My fists clenched. I wanted to scream and lash out. I wanted to swing at him, to pry out the truth. But I believed him. I knew he was right. And so all the powerlessness and exhaustion that had cut away at me for so long came to the surface in the form of a breakdown I would never allow anyone else to see.

I fell forward and pushed my face into the ground. "Why is this happening to me, Ben? Why me? My mind is falling apart. I don't even know who I am anymore, or what's real, what thoughts are my own, what feelings. I don't know what to do." I felt his hand squeeze my shoulder. "I want this… I *need* this to be over."

"Have faith, brother," he said. "Have faith."

Cameron's panicked voice came from outside. "Guys. Get out here. Right now."

We jumped up and rushed to her, leaving behind the tension of the tent. We stopped when we saw her, fifty feet away, frozen by the sight of something hidden to us. Benny raised his gun, which he had been smart enough to grab on the way out, and waited for the worst. Cameron stepped backward as a figure rounded a large pine. My stomach turned at the sight, and my throat constricted as I tried to speak.

"Julie?"

She walked with her hands clutched in front of her. Timid. Afraid. She wore a tank top and sweatpants, and shivered from the morning's breeze.

"Back up," Benny said as she approached. She threw her hands up and stiffened. Her frightened eyes met mine, silently begging for help.

"It's all right, Benny," I said. "Put it away." He lowered the gun to a 45-degree angle, not ready to let his guard down. Cameron sidestepped over to the security of his weapon.

I made a wide circle around Julie, inspecting the area behind her. I wanted to see Marcus. Needed to. If only he had come trotting out from behind her, my worries would have ended. But he didn't.

"Where's Marcus?" I said, my voice stern.

"He's with Lincoln," Julie said. "They went into town."

The sound of her voice stopped my breath. I took a moment to regain it. "How did you know we were here?"

"I saw you yesterday. No, I didn't see you, I… I don't know how to explain it. You watched us play catch, didn't you?" She brought her fingernails to her mouth, then self-consciously pulled them away. "You did. I knew it. My head hurt. I felt something behind my eyes, like a little pulse. Then I fell, and when I did, I saw myself through binocular lenses. I heard a breath and knew it was yours. How? How did I know that? How did I *see* that?"

"Why does Lincoln take Marcus every time he leaves," I asked, keeping the interrogation on my side.

"To keep me from running away," she said with an almost imperceptible choke. "He knows I'll take off at the first opportunity, and he can't stay here without me. He never leaves me alone with Marcus." The sobbing that she had struggled to keep inside burst out. She looked down, ashamed. "I ruined everything, Will. I know you hate me, I know you do, but we need to get Marcus out of there." She lifted her eyes, but not past my chest. "Lincoln won't let us go. He's paranoid and unpredictable. I'm afraid of what he'll do to us."

Up until that moment, Julie was an enemy. An enemy I wanted to see suffer like I had. But there she stood, suffering in front of me, and I wanted nothing more than to stop it. I hated that I couldn't hate her. That was my fucking right. But that enemy, when seen without my long-festered malice, was a hurt woman. A scared mother.

"Who else is in the house?" I said.

"No one," she said. "We paid Frank – he, uh, owns the place – we paid him to leave until we figured out our next move."

"There's no one in the basement? A man and a woman?"

Her head slanted and her eyebrows scrunched. "No."

"I need the truth, Julie."

She shook her head, not certain of what I wanted to hear. "There's no one there."

I looked to Benny and Cameron, expecting a shared confusion. They gave me nothing.

"We need to move fast," Julie said.

"I assume you have a plan."

She nodded. "I've given it some thought. You see that shed to the right of the old rabbit pen? The one with the tan roof?" She lifted her arm to point it out, but grimaced as she did.

"Are you hurt?" I asked.

"It's nothing. That shed holds our firewood. Every night, Lincoln grabs logs to keep the fireplace going. If you hide inside, you can get a jump on him. It'll be dark by then."

"Why don't we just hide in the house until he's sleeping?"

"I don't want Marcus around when you kill Lincoln. He takes me with him to the shed, and we leave Marcus—"

"When I kill Lincoln? What makes you so sure I want to kill him?"

"You don't?" I couldn't deny it. "He won't stop, Will. I can't risk him ever coming back for me or Marcus. Killing him is the only way to be sure. You wouldn't care about what he's done to me, but Marcus has seen more than any boy should."

"Is he hurt?" I stepped forward to let her know that she had better answer correctly.

"He's fine. But it's only a matter of time. I'm telling you, Will, the shed will work."

I looked to my team for an opinion.

"The plan makes sense," Cameron said. "Assuming you trust her."

Benny agreed.

I looked at Julie. "How do I know I can?"

"Will…" She paused to prepare her plea. "What I did to you was disgusting. I was all fucked up, I was confused, I was greedy and selfish and stupid. But look at me. Look in my eyes. I'm telling the truth. All I want is to get my son away from that man. You do, too. That's all that matters right now."

"If we help you, you won't run anymore. You'll leave Marcus with your mother and do your time. I won't let him grow up dodging police with you."

"That's what I intended to do if I ever made it out of here."

"Promise me."

"I promise."

"OK," I said. I pointed to my group. "This is Benny and Cameron. They helped me get here, and they're gonna help us finish this."

"Thank you both," she said to them, then looked at me. "We have to get you down there." She looked at her wristwatch. Again she grimaced, this time letting out a squeaky cry.

"Did he do this to you?" I asked, putting a hand on her shoulder. A tremor tore through my body as I made contact. The ground spun below me. I fell to my knees, then to my side.

"What's wrong with him?" Julie yelled, then knelt down to help me. Cameron shouted to stop her, but not in time. Julie's once-familiar touch sent another surge through me. My brain pulsed. My skull felt like it would buckle under the pressure. I rolled onto my back and watched the sky give way to Julie's memories.

FORTY

Lexus. Which one is the friggin' Lexus? In the dark, they all looked the same. *Just keep running.*

My legs felt weak. My conscience felt weaker. I wanted to go back for Will, but I couldn't. *Too late. You made your choice.* I knew I had to see it through and live with whatever consequences it brought me.

I reached the first black car and tugged at the door handle. It was locked. I looked at the hub cap. Toyota. *Goddammit, which one is the Lexus?* I should have paid more attention when Will talked to Marcus about cars. Flashing headlights signaled the correct one. I ran to it and jumped in.

"Where's Will?" Lincoln asked, looking back toward The Perfect Cut.

"He's still in there. Drive."

"You better be fucking with me." He looked at me and saw no humor. "Why the fuck is he still in there?"

"Because I knocked him out and left him."

I expected Lincoln to ask why. Truth is I didn't know, at least not in any sense that words can explain. I had felt something inside me rising for weeks. A need to be free, maybe. Resentment. Restlessness. I felt trapped. Then Will hit me – I never thought he'd ever – and I knew right then that I had to get the hell out of that cage. Seeing him fall face-first into that glass-laden carpet was like seeing the lock of my cell snap in two. But there I was, free, wondering if escape was the best choice.

But Lincoln didn't ask why. He opened his door and put one leg out. "We have to go back and get him out of there," he said. Then, as if to laugh at the idea, the store's alarm wailed loud enough to hear from our end of the street. Lincoln pulled himself back in and slammed the door. "Do you realize what you've done?"

"Are you gonna sit here and scold me, or take the fuck off?"

He shifted into first gear, pulled out onto the street, and shifted into second. "We're fucked," he said, clutching the steering wheel hard enough to make veins stand at attention in his forearm. "You fucked us."

"We were going to leave him anyway," I said, seeing the hole in my logic, and knowing he would too.

"Not in police custody." He jammed the shifter into third. "He'll talk. How are we going to get on a plane now? The police will know our names in ten fucking minutes. What were you thinking?"

"I wasn't!" I bashed the door panel. "I fucked up. Is that what you want to hear?"

"We need to move fast," he said. "When we get to your mother's place, you need to go in, get Marcus, and get out of there."

"I have to say goodbye to her."

A light ahead of us turned red. Lincoln cruised through it. "She can't know you're leaving."

"I still have to say bye."

"Keep it quick. I'll leave without you."

"I guess that means we can't stop at my house?"

"You can get new clothes in Amsterdam. I still have to drop off the stash to Craig."

Clothes were the least of my worries. I had a lifetime of sentimental items I'd never see again. My grandmother's wedding band.

Marcus's baby pictures. The copy of *The Bell Jar* my best friend from high school gave to me before she passed. The anniversary cards that Will made me every year.

"What did I do?" I said to myself, or so I thought.

"I told you," Lincoln said, "you fucked us."

○   ○   ○

Blue lights flashed behind us.

No, no. Fuck, no, please. This can't be happening.

"Perfect," Lincoln said. "Fucking perfect."

"Don't swear in front of Marcus," I said.

"Are we gonna see a policeman, Mom?" I turned to the backseat, where Marcus had paused a fight between two Spiderman action figures.

"Yes we are, buddy. Mommy needs you to be quiet and behave, OK?" I faced forward again. I chewed my bottom lip, then forced myself to stop. *Why did I do this? What was I thinking?*

"Do you think they know who we are?" I asked Lincoln. "Do you think he gave us up?"

Lincoln turned on his blinker. "Of course he gave us up. Wouldn't you?" He pulled over to the side of the highway, beneath a sign labeled:

LOGAN AIRPORT
1¼ MILE

A plane, only visible by the blinking orange lights in the night sky, took off in front of us. Lincoln put the car in park and pounded the center console. "Son-of-a-fucking-bitch."

"I said stop swearing in front of Marcus."

"Fuck!" He lowered his window as the officer exited his squad car. "Keep quiet and let me do the talking."

"License and registration please," the middle-aged cop said. I could smell his cologne from my side of the car. Shadow covered most of his face, making it impossible to judge his level of suspicion. His eyes would have told the truth. Eyes always do.

"They're in the glove compartment," Lincoln said.

"Go ahead."

Lincoln reached over my lap and dug for the items. He handed them to the officer.

"You folks heading to the airport?"

"Yes sir," Lincoln responded, his voice calm and even. "Family trip to Europe."

"Getting away for a little R and R?" the officer said.

"That's the plan. Was I speeding, sir?"

"No, you were driving just fine. I just noticed that your tail—"

The radio on his shoulder crackled. A female's voice came through. "All officers be aware – an AMBER Alert has been issued for an adult male and female traveling with a child. Be on the lookout for a black Lexus sedan, license plate number four-two-November-two-whisky-three."

Our plan died with that call.

The officer looked at the registration, backed up three steps, and pulled his gun from the holster. With a stern voice he said, "Step out of the vehicle by putting both hands on the door and opening it from the outside. Ma'am, I want you to put your hands on the dash and stay right where you are. Neither of you make any sudden movements, you hear?"

"What's happening, Mom?" Marcus said, hypnotized by the officer's pistol.

"Everything's gonna be fine, bud. The policeman just wants to talk to Lincoln. Play with your toys." He didn't play. He remained focused on the gun.

Lincoln placed both palms on the door, then slid his right hand to the outside handle. The door popped as he pulled it.

"Good," the officer said. "Now come on out. Nice and slow."

Lincoln pushed the door open, then swiveled to put his feet on the ground. As he climbed out, the back of his shirt lifted to reveal the black handle of his own pistol sticking out of his belt. I wondered if he was crazy enough to use it. I hoped that he was, and I hated myself for it. Marcus gasped behind me. I turned in time to see his eyes light up. His innocent, unfiltered mouth made no attempt to keep the secret. I couldn't stop him.

"Mom! Lincoln has a gun, too?"

The officer glanced at Marcus. Lincoln took advantage of the opening. He grabbed the man's wrist and pushed his firearm to the sky. As a pop sent a bullet toward the clouds, Lincoln slipped his own gun from his belt with his free hand. He brought the barrel to the underside of the officer's chin and fired another bullet to the sky, this time with blood and brain trailing it. The cop dropped.

I shrieked and reached to the backseat to cover Marcus's eyes, knowing he had already seen the worst of it. He dodged my attempt. Lincoln looked in both directions for witnesses, then threw his gun off the overpass. He climbed back into the car.

Marcus was hysterical. "Policemen are good guys!" He threw one of his figures at Lincoln's head and clipped his ear. "Policemen are good guys!"

"Shut the fuck up, kid."

"Don't you ever talk to him like that!"

Lincoln ignored my protest and put the car in gear. The tires screeched as he made a U-turn that jerked me back into my seat. "We won't make it onto a plane. We need to ditch this car and find somewhere to lay low."

I looked back at the flashing blue body on the pavement. Past it, another plane took flight.

"Oh, Jewel," my mother said. "What have you gotten yourself into?" She poured tea into a cup in front of me. Her hands shook. A small splash missed my cup, and I wiped it up before she could. "The police have gone to my house three times since you picked Marcus up Monday night. They told me about Will, about what you two did. They're looking for you."

"I know they are. That's why I asked you to meet me here, and not at your place."

"They said that if I saw you, I should tell you to turn yourself in. They said you'd get an easier punishment."

"I'm not going to the police."

She reached for her cup, but decided that her hands weren't steady enough to pick it up without spilling tea. "Then why are you here?"

"Because I wanted to see you. I wanted you to know I'm all right."

"You're anything but all right. Where will you go? What'll you do?"

"Keith's going to help me. He knows somewhere I can stay."

"You're going to drag your brother into this, too?"

"He offered, Mom."

"That doesn't make it right. And what about Marcus? If you're going to be foolish, then at least leave him with me. I'll take care of him."

"No, he'll be fine with me. I promise."

"Julie…"

"No."

The front door opened and closed with a single swift sound. I heard Lincoln spread the blinds to peek out. We remained quiet while we waited for him to come to the kitchen.

"It's all set," he said with a visible bulge of cash in his front pocket. "We shouldn't stay any longer than we need to."

My mother looked at me as if Lincoln didn't exist. "If you change your mind, I'm here for you."

"I won't." I stood up and kissed her cheek. "I love you, Mom."

○ ○ ○

I snatched the glass of scotch from Lincoln's hand and slid it away on the counter. That got his attention. "You said two weeks. It's been over a month."

"I know how long it's been." He followed the glass, grabbed it, and downed the rest of his drink.

"And? What the fuck is the plan?"

"I'm working on it," he said. "How many fucking times do I have to tell you that?" In the next room, the sound of cartoons blared from TV speakers. Marcus sat cross-legged on the floor, eating cereal.

"You're working on it? That's all you say, you're like a fucking parrot. But I haven't seen you working on shit. Frank's not gonna let us stay in his house forever. Admit it – you're fucking clueless."

He shoved his finger in my face. "Watch your fucking mouth, you hear me?"

"Fuck you. I didn't throw my life away to be a recluse in New-fucking-Hampshire. Do what you want – I'm taking Marcus and leaving."

"I swear to God, if you even think about leaving…"

"Oh, I've thought about it."

"You're not going anywhere."

"Fuck yourself, Lincoln. Fuck yourself with a fucking screwdriver."

He grabbed the glass and slammed it against my face. I heard a crack and tasted blood. The glass shattered on the floor. When I ran my tongue along my bloody gums, I felt a hanging tooth. As I tried to regain my composure, Lincoln's palm hit me in the same spot. The tooth fell out of my mouth and clicked on the tile, surrounded by crimson dots.

"Don't hit my mom!" Marcus shouted from behind me.

Lincoln grabbed my hair and pulled me through the hallway to the bathroom, ignoring Marcus's attempts to save me. "You want to leave me, you fucking bitch?" Strands of hair ripped from my scalp as he whipped me through the shower curtain, into the shower's wall. The impact sent a bolt from my shoulder to my fingers. I cried out as I fell into the tub. He reached in his belt for his pistol.

"Please," I said, curling into a ball and covering my head with my arms. "Please don't kill me. Lincoln, please, I'm sorry."

Marcus stood behind him, swinging with everything he had. Lincoln laughed and grabbed him by the back of the neck. Marcus squealed. "I'm not going to kill you, Jules. I need you." He aimed the gun down through the top of Marcus's scalp. His nostrils pulsed. His face reddened. "But I don't give a shit about this little twit."

○ ○ ○

"Go further, Mom," Marcus shouted. I backed up a few feet, knowing he couldn't reach me. "Further."

"You can't throw that far," I said. I should have known he would take that as a challenge.

"Yeah-huh," he said. "Watch. Back up."

I took another few steps back. He tried his best, but the baseball came to a stop five feet in front of me. I walked forward and picked it up.

"I wanna play catch with Dad," he said with a pout. "Is he coming back soon?" I had a feeling this game would lead to that question. He asked about Will every chance he got. I had hoped that as the months went by, the questions would die down. I could hold him off with vague answers well enough, but when he brought it up in front of Lincoln, fireworks erupted. Will's name made Lincoln furious. The motherfucker was probably listening from inside, waiting to hear how I answered.

"I don't know, bud. Maybe." I threw the ball back to him, underhanded. He caught it, then stopped and looked at it a moment. He seemed lost. *You did this to him*, I said to myself with the same hate I had for Lincoln. *You brought him here.*

"I think he is," Marcus said as he wound up and threw. Again the ball fell short, and again I bent over to pick it up. "Dad's gonna save us from Lincoln."

As I rose, I felt a strange sensation behind my eyes, like an electrical storm bottled in my head. My body went limp. I fell backward, and as I hit the ground, I saw myself falling from far away. From high in the mountains. Through binoculars.

FORTY-ONE

I came back to our camp under the gaze of Julie, Cameron, and Benny. Pine needles stabbed my elbows. Dirt covered the side of my face.

Julie relaxed with relief when my eyes opened. "He's back, guys. He's awake." She moved her hand to touch me, but stopped as Benny and Cameron opened their mouths to protest. "Can you hear me, Will?" She leaned in, blinding me with the sun she had been blocking.

I shielded my eyes and turned my head to the side. "How long was I out?"

"Three or four minutes," Benny said. "Can you stand?"

I sat up. "I think so."

He grabbed my right hand, Cameron took my left, and together they pulled me from the ground. Benny supported me until I found my balance.

"What just happened?" Julie asked me, irritated by her own cluelessness. "They wouldn't tell me anything."

Cameron swatted some nature from my back. "We figured that job was best left to you." Then, with a smirk, she added, "I didn't know how to tell her that her husband's a freak."

"This isn't a joke," Julie snapped. "Why are you all so fucking nonchalant about this? He just fainted." She looked at me. "What's wrong with you, Will?"

"There's nothing to worry about," I told her.

"Liar," Cameron said.

"Thanks. You're really helping me here."

"Well, don't bullshit her."

"I wasn't trying to." I looked at Julie, who had her bottom lip between her teeth. "I'll explain on the way down. You need to get back in that house before Lincoln returns, and I need to be in the shed. How long do we have?"

"Um…" She ran her fingers through her hair. "An hour, maybe."

"Maybe?"

"I can't be sure. He didn't tell me where he was going, but he's rarely gone for less than two hours."

I looked down at the house. "Benny – bring the gun, the knife, the rope, and the binoculars." He began digging through a bag before I finished the sentence. "Cameron – grab water and food. We have a long wait ahead of us."

Benny and Cameron took the lead on the trek down the mountain, giving me the opportunity to speak with Julie.

"I don't know how to explain what happened back there," I told her.

"You're sick, aren't you?" She spoke like a worried wife, a tone I had missed without realizing it. "Whatever's wrong, you can tell me."

"I'm not sick."

"How can you say that? You passed out for no reason. And those two acted like it was a regular occurrence. They just stood there, and when I freaked out they told me to calm down, like *I* was the crazy one."

"Something happened to me. Something I don't understand." I gave my next words some thought, and wished I could just transfer the explanation to her like I had done the first time I met Cameron.

"Blurt it out," Julie said at the sight of my hesitation.

"I saw the police officer at Logan." She halted. I took another two steps, then turned around to face her.

"On the news?" she asked in a low voice.

I shook my head. "I also saw Lincoln put a gun to Marcus's head."

Her lips moved soundlessly until she forced out one syllable: "How?"

"When you touched me," I said.

"That doesn't answer the question."

"Because I don't know how to. I see things in people. I feel things."

"Like a psychic?"

"No. Maybe. I don't know exactly how to describe it. I'm like a conductor, or a channel. I soak in thoughts, memories, emotions – all sorts of shit. And I don't just take these things in. I project my own, too."

"When did it start?" She spoke with acceptance, like it all made sense, and no further convincing was needed. Her vision the day before must have made the crazy talk easier to swallow.

I could have added to her guilt. I could have told her that a certain baseball bat to my head induced my first episode, but my sympathy prevailed. "I don't know."

"Is it happening now?"

I shook my head. "It's not constant. And I can't control it. It tends to happen under stress. That's how you saw yourself yesterday. The sight of you and Marcus out there together – it did a number on me. I must have projected myself into you."

I looked down the slope and realized how far ahead Benny and Cameron had reached. "Come on, let's keep walking."

She started moving again. "Why didn't Marcus feel it?"

"Maybe he did. If I understood how this all worked, I could've avoided a fuckload of trouble." Keith's lifeless face crossed my mind, and I knew I'd have to tell her about what happened. *Later,* I thought, hoping she wouldn't see it. *When we're clear of all this.*

"How much did you see?" she asked.

"Huh?"

"When I touched you," she said, in an almost shy whisper.

"It's more about what I felt."

"What do you mean?"

"You were never happy with me, were you?"

She sighed. "It's not like that. I was never happy anywhere, at any time. But the closest I ever came was the four years I spent with you. I mean that. You gave me stability. My issues, my discontent, all the shit buried inside me, making me miserable all the goddamn time – it all had nothing to do with you. Those are ghosts I've harbored for as long as I can remember."

I opened my mouth, but she stopped me from speaking.

"Let me finish. I've had a lot of time by myself up here, isolated. A lot of time to think. I realize now that no matter where I've been in my life – no matter what I've had – I've always wanted something else. And when I get that something else, I look for something else." Her words got caught in her throat. She cleared it. "I tried being happy as a wife, but I'm not built for happiness."

"Spilling your guts doesn't change what you did to me," I said. "It doesn't make it OK, and it sure as fuck won't wipe the slate clean."

She dropped her chin to her chest. "I know it won't. And it shouldn't." Only fifty yards or so remained to the base of the mountain when she stopped and said, "Wait here a minute."

"What are you doing?" I said.

"Just wait. I'll be quick."

I waved to Benny and Cameron. "Guys. Hold up." They stopped and made their way back toward me while Julie veered away.

"What's she doing?" Cameron asked in a low voice when they reached me. She eyed Julie as she disappeared behind an eight-foot-tall boulder.

"Not sure."

"You're awfully trusting," she said.

"Or just insane."

"That must have been quite the hike," Benny said.

I scratched my head. "Not exactly how I pictured our reunion."

"I envisioned more swearing," Benny said. "Some blood, maybe."

"You're not the only one. I had so much animosity built up, ready to unleash on her, but it's hard to hate someone who needs your help."

Julie returned to our sudden silence, clutching a black velvet pouch the size of a sandwich bag in one hand and a pistol in the other. An alarm sounded inside of Benny, but deactivated when he saw that she held the weapon by the barrel. His hand, which had made it to the grip of his own gun, relaxed.

Julie handed the pistol to me. "Lincoln's paranoid, obsessed with being armed. He always has a gun close to him. This will make it two against one."

I looked at Benny for his opinion. He thought for a moment, traded guns with me, and checked the magazine. He found it full.

"I should've expected suspicion," Julie said, then handed me the velvet pouch.

"What's this?" Before she answered, I loosened the drawstring and saw the contents: a glittery fortune. The mound of diamonds almost stunned me into dropping them.

"Whoa," Benny said, leaning in.

Cameron gazed at the loot with a heavy jaw, like she was trapped in the eyes of the Mona Lisa.

"This is from the safe," I said.

Julie nodded. "Lincoln sold all the jewelry to some thug he knew, but that was peanuts compared to what's in this pouch. Lincoln tells me there's over three quarters of a million in there. He doesn't think I know where he buried it."

Benny shook his head in disbelief. "Jesus, Mary, and Joseph."

Julie continued. "There's a loose plank in the floor of the shed that hides a little stash I've put together in case I ever got the chance to run. Put the pouch there. If our plan goes wrong, at least that prick won't know where his precious treasure is."

"'If our plan goes wrong,'" Cameron repeated, then laughed. "I love the optimism."

"Never had much of it," Julie said as she started walking. "Let's get going."

A minute later, when we reached the edge of the ranch, Benny, Cameron, and I stopped at the threshold. Julie turned and waited as the three of us studied the land, knowing any missed detail could kill us. I saw my hiding spot 20 yards away. The house stood 30 yards beyond it.

"It's a damn shame the owner let this place go to shit," Cameron said. "It'd be gorgeous if it didn't look like the aftermath of a pillage." She smiled at her own analogy. "At least the house still looks good." She changed the subject in light of our silence. "All right then, captain – what now?"

"We'll go with Julie's plan," I said. "I'll wait in the shed. You see those two pines over by the broken fence? You and Benny hide behind them. That should give you a good vantage point. The second Lincoln goes into the shed, move in. When I force him out at gunpoint, I'll need you there for backup. Julie – you go into the house and do whatever you would do normally. Clean yourself up, make sure you don't have any dirt or pine needles in your shoes."

All three nodded.

"Good luck, brother," Benny said, slapping my shoulder. "We'll be close by."

Cameron handed me two bottles of water, a protein bar, and a bag of trail mix. "Ration these. You'll be in there a long time." She wanted to kiss me, but second-guessed the decision. She looked at Julie, then back at me. "Be careful."

I looked at Julie. She chewed on her fingernails as she watched Cameron and Benny walk away.

"This will work," I assured her.

"I know." She forced her finger out of her mouth, crossed her arms, and looked at the sky. "Thank you, Will. For coming here, for helping us. I wouldn't have lasted much longer."

"I'm here for Marcus, not you." The statement had all the blunt force I had intended, but I immediately wanted to retract it. "I'm sorry. That was unnecessary."

"No, it wasn't."

We entered the shed, an eight-foot square with a seven-foot roof. A wall of chopped logs, neatly stacked, rested against the right side of the space. In the center sat a riding lawnmower with thick spiderwebs running from the steering wheel to the seat. Dried grass and dirt littered the ground. More webs crossed the ceiling.

Julie pointed to the back left corner. "The plank is over there. The last one at the back."

"Got it."

She turned to leave, but stopped and stood silent. Then, without looking back at me, she said, "I know you'll never forgive me, and that you'll always remember me by what I did to you. But also remember, even when it's easy to forget, that I loved you." With that said, she left me alone.

I didn't move, but just stood still until her footsteps faded to silence. Then I felt my way through the darkness, guided only by the feel of the wall and the useless bit of light that slipped through the slits in the roof. With each step I took, I imagined walking face-first into a spider's web. I made it to the back corner with no such incident, crouched, and ran my hand along the plank until I found a grip. I tugged at it, almost falling backward when it budged. The board revealed a pocket, dug into the dirt of the foundation, that held a plastic shopping bag. I added the pouch of diamonds without looking at the other contents. A light stomp put the plank back in place. Then I waited.

○ ○ ○

The day took its time passing. I spent that time alternating between sitting and standing, standing and crouching, standing and leaning – always on full alert. Every creak and chirp and whistle of the wind drew me to a firing stance. The stress took a toll on my muscles; my neck and back ached. I lost track of the hours, and only received a hint of the time when the rays of light from above began to dim. I ate my protein bar and trail mix as the sun finished its descent.

Another hour passed, give or take a quarter. I propped myself up against the wall with my gun arm rested on the wood pile. My hairs stood at the end of goosebumps. My stomach growled, unsatisfied. Doubt intruded. *What if he doesn't come, after all this?*

Then I heard the crunch of dry grass. Footsteps. One pair. The crunching grew louder until it stopped outside the shed's door. The rusty metal latch turned clockwise with a low, grinding moan. The visitor pushed to no avail, then put their weight behind the next attempt. The door popped open. Moonlight broke through, outlining a short silhouette.

Marcus.

I wanted to rejoice, to jump up, grab him, and never let go. But I remained a statue, prepared to see Lincoln step in behind him. I listened for more footsteps. I heard none. Marcus squinted into the darkness, then flashed with excitement when his eyes adjusted and found me.

"Dad!" He charged, arms out, and crashed into me. I clutched him tight with one trembling arm while keeping the door guarded with the other. His little body, glued to mine, purged the uncertainty

I'd lived with for so long – that fear of never seeing him again. I had him. Fuck whatever came next. In that moment, I had him.

"Oh God, Marcus, I missed you so much." I backed him up and inspected him. "Are you all right?"

His big head bobbed up and down. "Mm-hmm." His eyes gave a different answer. I ran my fingers through his hair and kissed his forehead.

I gotta be good or Lincoln will be mad. He'll hit Mom. Behave. I need to behave. That's what he says that's what Mom says they both say I need to behave and if I do that he won't hit me but he hits Mom anyway if I'm good or if I'm bad it doesn't matter.

Lincoln was a vivid terror at the forefront of my life. I didn't want to make him mad anymore. I needed to behave.

I slackened my hold on Marcus. Relief from his fear was instantaneous. "Where is he, bud? Where's Lincoln?"

"In the house with Mom." He looked away from me, as if he were afraid I'd be angry with him. "He told me you'd be in here. He said to give this to you."

I felt like I'd been clubbed. Marcus seemed to move in slow motion as he handed me a Marlboro pack. A folded note stuck out from the cellophane wrapper. I took the pack. Something rocked around inside. Blood smeared the package, visible even on top of the brand's signature color. I removed and unfolded the paper, muddying it with blood in the process. A message written in black marker choked me from the center of the sheet.

GET IN HERE NOW OR HE LOSES ANOTHER PIECE

I dropped the note and fought to control my shaky fingers long enough to open the cigarette pack. I saw its contents, gasped, and threw it to the floor. Marcus followed it with his eyes, but I covered them before he saw the dark-skinned ear beside the lawnmower's tire.

FORTY-TWO

"What was it?" Marcus asked, trying to pull his face from the cover of my hands. "I wanna see."

I held him firmly as he squirmed. "Listen to me, Marcus – this is important." He stopped trying to wiggle free. "Go hide in the woods. Somewhere dark, somewhere you can see the house from. If you see Lincoln come out, run. Any direction except for straight back will get you to a road." *Jesus Christ, he's a child. He shouldn't need instructions like this.* "Find an adult and tell them to bring you to the police. Tell the police to come here. It's sixteen Corby Road. Do you understand?"

"Got it," he said, proud and sure.

"Say it back to me."

He used his fingers to count the steps. His thumb popped out first. "Hide in the woods. Run if I see Lincoln. Go to a road."

"Which direction?"

"Any way."

"Any way except for which one?"

"Straight back," he said, happy to prove himself.

"Then what?"

"Find a grown-up. Find a policeman." He started on his other hand. "Tell the policeman to come here."

"What's the address?"

"Sixteen Coby."

"Corby."

"Sixteen Corby." He studied the six extended fingers, then nodded with certainty.

"Good. You did good." I pulled him close and kissed the top of his head. "I love you, Marcus."

"I love you too, Dad."

"Do what I said, OK? Go."

I watched him run out of the shed and turn left. *You'll see him again. You'll see him again. You'll see him again.* I stood, my eyes magnetized to the piece of Benny that lay on the floor, wondering how Lincoln got the upper hand. I couldn't stand around plotting while Benny endured whatever that sick fuck thought up. I had to go in there, vulnerable, with no plan at all. *Marcus is hidden. He's safe.* The thought eased my mind; it helped me muster the will to storm the house with nothing but my hope for the best. I drew my gun and stepped into the moonlight.

One. Two.

Three.

I sprinted to the porch. As I closed in, figures inside the house came into focus through the open slider. Benny, Cameron, and Julie all sat tied to chairs in the center of the adjacent living room. Lincoln wasn't among them. I stopped at the threshold, then entered with my guard and my gun up.

The three of them looked at me with a worrying pity. I sensed something from one of them, or maybe two. An internal dilemma – a desire for me to leave versus a need for me to stay. Benny looked to the side, hiding his mutilated ear. He didn't want me to worry about him. Julie and Cameron appeared unharmed, but while Cameron kept her composure, Julie had fallen to pieces. No one said a word.

"Where is he?" I whispered

"Right here," Lincoln said, entering from the foyer. One hand held a pistol, aimed at Julie's head. The other held a red-streaked straight razor. He walked to Benny and pressed the blade to his throat. "Drop the gun. Now."

I knelt slowly and placed the gun on the ground, locking Lincoln into a stare as I did. *That's not my only weapon*, I thought to him, hoping to connect. *And you can't make me drop the other one.* The message landed, however abstractly, and I saw the subtle twist of surprise in his face.

"Kick it over here," he said, hiding whatever he had felt. I obeyed. "You're just in time, Will." He tapped Benny's remaining ear with the blade. From the opposite side of my best friend's head, fresh blood streamed down over the dark, soaked-in masses on his shirt. Even though his head shivered and his lip twitched from the pain, he remained a rock, refusing to give in to the fear. Lincoln leaned in and whispered something to him. No one else heard, but I knew what he said.

I was hoping for another slice.

"What do you want?" I asked. "Besides another slice." His smirk melted. I could almost see him rationalizing the comment, telling himself that I must have excellent hearing, or that I could read lips.

"What the fuck do you think I want?" he said, believing whatever explanation he had settled on. "My diamonds. Where are they?"

"No clue what you're talking about."

"Stop. This will all unfold smoother without the lies. I haven't made it this far believing every bit of bullshit offered to me."

"This far?" Cameron taunted with a chuckle. Even under the threat of dismemberment and death, she kept her edge. "This far? You made it from Massachusetts to New Hampshire." I'll never forget the bravery and attitude in her voice as she delivered the punchline: "Congratu-fucking-lations, Lincoln. At this rate, you'll reach Maine by Christmas."

Lincoln clapped her cheek with the side of his pistol. "Keep cracking jokes, and I'll break your fucking jaw." She licked blood from her split lip.

"You fucking prick," I said, stepping forward, then stopped at the end of his barrel. "If you don't shoot me now, I swear to God I'll kill you."

He laughed. "Will, Will, Will. I respect your confidence, I really do, but you're not killing anything. Can we please stick to the matter at hand?" He returned his aim to Julie. "I know she gave you my diamonds. How do I know that, besides common fucking sense? I buried a gun with them – a gun I just so happened to find on your friends when I found them hiding in the woods." He stroked Julie's hair with the palm that held his gun. "Not smart, Jules. Not smart at all." Then he looked back at me. "Where are they? You don't want me to ask again."

"Don't tell him," Benny said to me.

"Will you let us go if I give you what you want?"

"Of course," Lincoln said, as if he took offense at the suggestion of otherwise. "You think I enjoy this?"

"Don't tell him," Benny said louder, with more authority.

"I have no choice, Ben."

"You're right," Lincoln said. "You don't. You're all dead if those stones aren't in my hand in five minutes."

"How do I know you won't just kill us when you have them?"

"You don't," he said. "But the possibility of life is better than the certainty of death, no?"

Benny shook his head at me. The movement made him recoil in pain.

Why, Ben? What do you know?

His voice filled my mind. *More than you can imagine. You'll get out of this, and Marcus too, but you can't tell him where those diamonds are.*

"I won't tell you," I said to Lincoln.

"Excuse me?"

"I'd rather die than watch a snake like you walk out of here with a fortune. And everyone here feels the same way."

The refusal caught him off guard. Pissed him off. He was so close, so sure of his success, but I had ripped his prize away. He wanted to put a bullet in all four of us. He wanted to burn the place down and listen to our screams.

But he didn't show his rage; without my ability, I never would have known he was close to exploding. He only sighed. "I had hoped this would be easy. Foolish of me. All right, then."

Julie flinched as he squatted behind her. I heard the tear of duct tape, then her arms came free. She planted them on her lap and sat still, waiting for instructions.

"Stand up," he told her. She did, keeping her hands clutched over her stomach. "Tape him to your chair." When she hesitated, he kicked the chair across the room at me. It slammed into my shin. I fought a reaction. Lincoln grabbed the roll of duct tape from a nearby table, shoved it into Julie's chest, and pushed her toward me. "Do it."

Julie walked with shallow steps and eyes fixed on the ground. She set the chair upright, facing the rest of them, and looked at me for the first time since I'd entered. She carried the guilt of our deaths on her conscience. Her hands trembled as she pried the edge of the tape from the roll. "I'm so sorry I brought you here, Will."

"Don't be."

"You'll all be sorry if no one speaks up," Lincoln said.

"Our answer won't change," I replied.

"Don't be so sure. Sit down."

"Fuck you. It'll take a bullet in my head to put me in that chair."

"If you don't sit your ass down, I'll chop your friends to pieces, starting at their feet." He paused to let us all soak in the imagery. "My patience won't last forever."

I hated it, and I tried to stay strong, but his threat worked. I couldn't allow anyone to suffer for my defiance. I sat and put my hands by my side. Julie stuck an end of the tape to my chest. Tears dropped from her eyes to my lap as she wrapped my torso.

"His legs," Lincoln said.

She wrapped my legs three times before he told her to stop. Then she stood, dropped the roll of tape, and faced him.

Lincoln's gun rose, and as I yelled in protest, I saw the last of its ascent through Julie's eyes. She stared down the barrel with the understanding that somewhere outside, her son was about to hear his mother's death.

A blast tore through the room. Julie's body hit the floor. My mind splintered, like its support had fractured and a single speck of dust could bring it crashing down. I waited and hoped for Julie to move. I studied every inch of her limp body in search of any tiny sign of life. She remained still.

Pulling my gaze away from her felt like an inadequate final goodbye. I lifted my head and squeezed my eyes tight to clear the liquid blur. Cameron's shrieks were dulled by the roaring chaos inside me. She stared at Julie, drenched in tears, shoulders shuddering from sobs. Benny prayed in silence. Above them, Lincoln stood tall.

I pierced him with a stare that carried all my hatred for him, every shred of anger and anguish and pain that pumped through me. He rubbed his temple. Blinked a few times. Grimaced.

You feel it, don't you? That vice grip squeezing your skull. The fear and confusion from that foreign, unexplainable pain showed itself in every muscle in his face. I no longer need to speak. I had broken through his gate. *Your death will hurt*, I told him. *I promise you that.*

"I've…" He tried his best to hide his unease, but despite his confidence, I had shaken him. "I've known that woman for years," he said. "Lived with her for months. I cared about her – loved her – even after her stupidity stranded us here. Even after she betrayed me, and even as I pulled the trigger." He looked at Benny, then at Cameron. "Just think of what I'll do to a spook and a slut that mean nothing to me."

Cameron spit at him, but missed. "You're a fucking worm." She writhed with all her strength, but the layers of duct tape held her.

Lincoln kicked her chair over sideways. Her head hit the floor with a loud smack. She screamed – not from the pain, but from the sheer aggravation of helplessness. Lincoln pressed the barrel of his pistol against the back of Benny's skull. "No more games. I'm going to count down from five. When I reach zero, he's dead. Then I'm moving on to the bitch, and I promise you, I'll take more than five seconds with her."

"Don't tell him, brother," Benny said.

"I won't."

"You can't."

"I won't."

"You *will*," Lincoln said, jamming the metal harder into Benny's skin. "Five."

With any chance of a happy ending long gone, I took the offensive. I dug deeper into Lincoln's mind. I envisioned him shooting himself in the head. The image became clear.

His elbow bends.

The metal meets his mouth.

The back of his head erupts.

I replayed his death. Then again. And again, clearer still. Even with all its vividness, I fail to bring it to reality.

"Four," he said.

I couldn't let it end at that. I'd fought to be there. I'd suffered. My friends and family had suffered. To fail them would be a betrayal of everything they'd sacrificed for me – for my actions, my choices. I knew I could stop Lincoln. I imagined him weak. Numb. Frozen. Catatonic.

Benny saw my plan. "Let it happen, Will."

Lincoln raised his voice. "Three."

Kill yourself. Put the barrel in your mouth.

"Two."

Put the barrel in your mouth and pull the fucking trigger, dammit.

"Don't stop him," Benny said. "Let it happen." He maintained a zen-like calm, like he welcomed the end of the countdown. His eyes watered, but his jaw was stiff and his chin was up. He sat as straight as a soldier, ready and proud to accept whatever came.

Why Ben? You know what I can do. Why don't you want to be saved?

"He doesn't mind dying for you," Lincoln said, "but what about her? Or the brat?" He smiled wide, baring his teeth. "One."

I let out a wild scream. My heart rate rose as I swore and growled and jerked side to side and rocked the chair and made it jump and crashed the legs down onto the hardwood floor.

"Zero."

Lincoln's brain sent the command to his finger to pull the trigger, but the message never reached its destination. He stood still.

I had done it. I had stopped him.

I waited for my relief to be squashed, for Lincoln to move, but he remained a mannequin. Not even his eyes showed life. The last spark in his head faded, leaving him a shell for as long as I could keep it up. But I didn't know how I'd done it or how long it would last or how to make him drop the gun or fall or die.

"Shuffle out of the way, Ben. I think I can keep him still."

"No," he said. "Let go of him."

"What? Why?"

Rivers rushed down his face. "Now!"

"Tell me why."

"Because you trust me."

"For the love of God, stop fucking around and get out of there."

"Listen to Benny," Cameron cried from the floor. "Let go."

"What's wrong with you two?" I said, then put the missing puzzle piece in place. "Is it because of what Robert told you? You were crying in the tent this morning. Both of you. What did he tell you? You can't keep this from me."

"Look at me," Benny said.

I raised my eyes to his. My lips shook, and salty drops curled around the corners of them.

Benny was sympathetic but stern. He spoke to me like an older sibling who knew what was best. "One more time," he said. "Trust me just one more time."

"I trust you, Benny, you know I do, but—"

What am I to you? he thought to me. I looked down, but that didn't mute his voice in my head. *I asked you a question.*

I looked back up at him. *A brother, Ben. A fucking brother.*

Then listen to me. Let go of him.

I don't even know how.

Just let go.

And so I did. I let Lincoln go. I heard the bang. I felt Benny die. His head fell forward into his chest. A ringing filled my ears, then Cameron's screams, and then a boom that could've ripped me in two. White streaks spread across my vision, reaching and growing until the world around me disappeared.

My mind stopped.

Everything stopped.

○ ○ ○

I opened my eyes in a dark room, lying on a bed. I hugged myself and rubbed my goosebumped arms. I sat up and let my eyes adjust. *No windows. Closed door.* I ran to it. *Locked.* I rammed my shoulder into it. *Barred from the other side.* A lightbulb hung at the end of a wire in the center of the room. I pulled the chain. The bulb lit up the wood-paneled walls. I was in a basement; I didn't need windows to know it.

A nightstand stood by the bed. I opened the drawer and rummaged through the uninformative, useless pile of paper. Nothing hinted at my whereabouts. I slammed it shut and moved on to the desk across the room. Inside I found some candy wrappers, batteries, crayons, a pen, and a college-ruled notebook with half the cover torn off.

I stood in silence for minutes, staring down at the empty lines of the paper, trying to remember my name.

FORTY-THREE

Are you out there, Will? Are you coming for us? I can't feel you anymore.

○ ○ ○

Every breath felt like swallowing sandpaper. I needed water. I needed food. I knew I would get neither.

It had been three days since Lincoln (as Marcus called him) stopped our food supply. One day since he hacked up Heather. Fucking monster. She hadn't moved from her bed since. Hadn't spoken. Sometimes she shuffled or turned or coughed or sneezed, and when she did, sharp stabs pierced us both. Her wounds were wide and deep, with no sign of healing. She would never tell me that, but I knew it. They'd be infected soon if they weren't already.

Please come, Will. Don't let us die without names.

I reached into my pocket and felt the two folded letters I had written him. Sometimes the texture gave me a glimpse. I saw nothing then, however, and hadn't since the day before. I had been too weak to write. Too tired, too hungry, too hurt from Heather's torture. Still, I had reached him.

He's on his way, I assured myself. I believed that, I really did, but the belief wouldn't hold up forever.

I forced myself up and walked to the air vent with heavy legs and a hunch. I let the wall beneath it support me. "Heather? Are you awake?" She didn't respond. "Please talk to me. I know you're awake."

She moved somewhere on the other side of the wall. The springs of her mattress squeaked, and she groaned as she picked herself up from it. Her feet dragged on the carpet as she made the slow shuffle to the vent.

"I wasn't trying to fool you," she said, her voice hollow.

"I didn't say you were. You didn't have to come to the vent. I only wanted to hear your voice."

"It's probably best to get my blood pumping a little anyway."

"How bad is it?" I asked, knowing she would lie to comfort me.

"Not too bad. A few small slices, that's all. You have your own wounds to worry about."

"My wounds are nothing," I said. "They're practically healed already."

"Do you think we know where his diamonds are?" she asked. "I mean, do you think we *knew*?"

"He seems certain. There's no convincing him otherwise."

She sighed loud enough for me to hear her breath echo through the vent. "I haven't heard Marcus's footsteps in a while. I'm worried about him."

"I'm sure he's fine."

"The poor thing is terrified," she said. "Terrified of everything but me. You want to know what he said when I asked him if Lincoln was his Dad? He said Lincoln killed his parents."

He's mistaken, I thought. I refused to believe that Lincoln had killed Will, though the radio silence between us suggested otherwise. I hadn't told Heather about him. She didn't know about the letters or visions, or that he was close and coming for Marcus. I wanted to let her in on the whole fucked up truth, but info that heavy and unbelievable can't be delivered through an air vent.

"He's trapped, just like us," she said. "Think of what that boy's been through. What that prick has done to him. If we ever get out of here…"

"We'll take Marcus with us, I promise."

She was silent for a moment, then said, "Has Lincoln fed you yet?"

"No. And I've lost track of how long it's been since I had water. Can't tell time with no daylight. I'm always tired. What about you?"

"He hasn't given me anything, but Marcus snuck me some bread, ham, and juice. He's a sweet kid. He told me he'd bring you something today."

"You should have told him not to. I don't want him to get caught."

"I tried. I told him not to risk it, and that we're fine, but he wants to help."

"Can't say I don't need it," I said.

"The ham was delicious," she said. "The bread, not so much."

I forced a laugh for her sake. "It's strange. I can't remember who I am, but I remember the taste of ham."

"Yeah," she said. "It is strange."

"You must be tired." I said. "You should rest."

"That's what I was doing before you pulled me out of bed." I felt her smile as she spoke.

"I needed to hear that you were OK."

"I know you did. Thank you."

I made the slow stagger back to the mattress. I slept for an unknown period – an hour or two, I'd guess – before I woke to a pair of delicate knocks. I lifted my groggy head and waited. A few seconds later, another pair hit the door. I stood and walked over to it, wobbling the entire seven-foot trek. I used the wall to lower myself to the floor, where I peeked through the opening I took my food through. I saw blue and red pajama pants. I hoped to see the boy's face, but he didn't drop any further than a kneeling position. He reached down, placed something wrapped in a paper towel on the ground, and pushed it through the opening. Then came a juice box.

I took them. "Thank you." He didn't speak. He didn't move. "You don't have to be afraid, Marcus. You can talk to me."

After a moment of consideration, he whispered, "You're welcome, mister."

His voice brought with it a rush of déjà vu. In the same way a word gets trapped in limbo at the tip one's tongue, an understanding teetered on the tip of my mind. A revelation. I knew Marcus. I knew Heather. I knew the animal keeping us all caged. But how? I couldn't grip it. I needed to see Marcus's face. I knew I would recognize him.

"Can you do one more favor for me, bud?" I asked. "Can you come down to the opening? So I can see you?"

"I don't want to get in trouble."

"Just for a second, I promise." He didn't respond. I abandoned my whispering and spoke in my normal tone. "Do I sound familiar to you? Do you know who I am?"

More silence, then, "Dad?"

Dad?

Memories fought to make themselves known. They pounded at the barricade between me and the truth, but couldn't break through. They needed a battering ram. They needed to see Marcus.

"Come down to the opening, son." *Son. He's my son.*

I heard a rustle and saw his two hands press against the floor. He lowered himself to a push-up position and showed me the most beautiful smile the natural world could possibly produce.

"Dad!" His excitement came out as a yell tackled by a murmur.

A sharp zap ricocheted behind my eyes as the revelation I wanted stormed through. My life washed over me in an instant: the roller skating accident that broke my leg when I was six; the questions about my father that my mother dodged for years; her raspy voice speaking from a hospital bed, full of tubes; my stomach turning as I accepted my high school diploma, hoping I wouldn't fall in front of 800 people; Professor Lee leaning over my shoulder, telling me what tiny mistake was responsible for my buggy PHP content management system; my first straight flush steamrolling some guy's smug look after he'd laid down a full house; the smell of Julie's strawberry body spray as I held a coffee shop door open for her, nervous as a child speaking to his crush on the playground; the first time I saw Marcus; the pride I felt every time he called me "Dad"; the loss of my ability to provide for him; my hesitant agreement with Julie's solution; my better judgment screaming each time we met with Lincoln; the alarm buzzing as I lay on the floor of The Perfect Cut, confused, with glass in my skin; the decision to end my own life with tied towels; the relief of Benny's intervention; his terror as rocks fell from the cell block roof; Angeletti's voice in my head – *Take this pig's head off, kid* – invading my mind; Earl's sprayed blood; Phillip's heartbreaking confusion after his partner dropped in front of his raised pistol; the cold, dark river; the sensation of Cameron's wrist snapping; the blast that ended Ted; the slashes; the tub; the shower head eyeing me; the pain; the recovery; the running; the burn of the bullet that killed Keith; the certainty that I'd die at the hands of Lou; the realization that I'd live; the march to another certain death; Benny's rescue before Lou pressed the trigger; our arrest; Trisha; Isaiah's floating body; the zombies in the police station parking lot; Cameron's lips on my neck as her body shuddered and fell limp; the taste of thyme in Benny's campfire beans; the elation of seeing my son through binoculars after so long apart; the joy of holding him close in the shed.

Julie dropping to the floor.

Lincoln's frozen body.

Benny telling me to let go. His head falling to his chest.

Then this.

Robert and Heather.

Me and Cameron.

FORTY-FOUR

Footsteps descended the stairs. They didn't belong to Marcus. Too heavy.

This is it. Do or die.

A day had passed since Marcus brought me the ham sandwich. A day of worrying about Cameron, feeling her wounds fester and the flesh around them darken. A day of keeping the truth to myself, letting her wonder about her own identity while I called her Heather. A day of mourning in silence, replaying the newly-remembered murder of Julie and Benny.

A day of planning and hoping that Lincoln would pick my door.

Cameron and I were both prepared. The only variable that remained in our plan was which of us would have to carry it out. *Me*, I thought. *Choose me*. Sure, I wanted to keep Cameron out of danger, and I didn't want her to know the rain cloud that comes along with taking a life, but I had a darker motive for wanting my own door to open. I wanted to see that fucker's face when I pulled the rug from under him. I wanted to see his eyes widen and his jaw drop when he realized he'd been beaten.

A thud hit my door, followed by the screech of a nail being pried from wood. My hair stood on end. *Lucky me*. Lincoln ripped out the planks that barred my door, one by one. After seven pulled boards, a keychain rattled. The deadlock, snipped and filed on my side, turned. The door opened.

Lincoln stood in the frame with no patience for more questioning. He held a roll of duct tape and a blowtorch with one hand, a black iron fire poker with the other. He intended to make this his last visit, whether he found his stones or not.

I watched and waited, sprawled on the bed like a man inches from death. I let my mouth drip saliva onto my pillow. My eyes darted around, paranoid. I hoped I wasn't overselling my condition.

In my right hand, hidden beneath the bed sheet, I clutched a rubber mallet. Next door, Cameron hid a knife crafted from glass and electrical tape. Marcus had gathered the items in the night while Lincoln slept, under my instructions not to take anything noticeable.

Lincoln dragged a chair in and placed it in the center of the room. "Get up."

"Can't," I told him, adding a dose of hoarseness and strain to my voice. "I'm weak. Can I have water?"

"Pathetic. It's no wonder Julie left you."

"Who?" I asked.

"Still playing the amnesiac, huh?" He held up the blowtorch. "This'll put an end to that."

He had spent the last two days furious, anxious, and fantasizing about the perfect way to make us talk. Even in that moment, his mind was more attached to our misery than it was to the information he hoped to gain. I saw myself in his imagination, taped up across from Cameron. He would alternate between us, forcing us each to watch the other burn. And he wanted the final submission to come from me, with the glowing iron pressed against Cameron's skin. Then he would kill us. Then Marcus.

"Get the fuck up," he said. "I won't ask again."

"I can't."

He slammed the blowtorch and duct tape on the desk. *Come get me*. He stomped his way over to me, poker still in hand. *Wait for it.* He grabbed my arm at the elbow and yanked me toward him. A heartbeat later, he realized his mistake.

I bashed the mallet against his skull, connecting above his left ear. The impact brought him to his knees beside the bed. Even at half-strength, adrenaline let me swing an overhead haymaker that came down with enough force to win a carnival prize. He blocked the strike with his forearm, but plenty of damage reached him. He grunted as he pushed himself away from the bed. I scrambled to stay with him, ignoring my tired, rubbery muscles. I couldn't allow him to put distance between us; a close-ranged fight would render his fire poker useless. I climbed on top of him, swinging like a maniac. I felt the largest of my wounds tear with each frantic blow, but that didn't have a chance in Hell of stopping me. Lincoln held up the iron rod in a desperate attempt to build a defense. Some of my blows struck his shield. Most of them hit his head. My flurry finally broke through the barrier and knocked the poker to his chest. I landed four more direct hits to his unprotected face. He stopped moving. I stopped swinging. I scanned the unrecognizable putty in front of me. It looked dead.

I stood and tossed the mallet aside.

Then his chest rose again.

"Still in there, huh?" I pulled the poker from his hands. He gave no resistance. I loomed over him, holding the iron above my head like a spear. He made no move to stop it. He didn't beg or even seem to notice I had the point prepared for a trajectory to his throat. I tightened my grip and drew back for the kill.

"Dad?"

I turned to find Marcus in the doorway, looking at the scene in horror. I froze, ashamed by what I had almost let him witness. I walked to him. He jumped into my arms. The pain of the hug was worth it.

"It's over, bud," I said, lowering him.

He looked at Lincoln. "Did he die, Dad?"

"No, he didn't die. But he can't hurt you anymore."

"Robert?" Cameron called from the other room with a wary excitement. "Did you do it? Did you get him?"

"I got him," I said. I heard her cry. The sound made my own eyes water. "Hold tight."

I lifted Lincoln's limp body into the chair. He couldn't support himself; only the back of the chair kept him from tumbling out of it. I wrapped his torso and legs with tape, covering the majority of his body in silver strips.

"Come on," I said to Marcus, who had watched the mummification with fascination. "Let's go get our friend."

The first board on Cameron's door swallowed my energy, and even with her encouragement, each extraction became exponentially tougher. It took a short rest and several surges of determination to rip the last plank from the wall. By the time I could open the door, I needed it to stand. I slid Lincoln's key into the lock and turned it.

Cameron pulled the door open with the keychain still dangling from the knob. Without my crutch, I fell forward into her. She caught me and held me close. Neither of us cared about the pain it caused us.

"I can't believe we're free," she said, crying into my shoulder. "We made it, Robert."

I found my footing and pulled her tighter. "It's Will."

She sniffled beside my ear. "What?"

"My name is Will."

"You remember?" she said.

I pulled away from her to reveal my face. To see hers. Her wounds were fresher replicas of my own, the placements identical. Scabbed trails reached up from underneath her stained, shredded t-shirt. Horizontal gashes hid inside slashed fabric from her collar to her stomach. Three more spanned her face, the largest running across her eyebrows. She was still gorgeous.

Recognition skipped over her face, but left before she could complete the puzzle. The seeds of an epiphany were planted, but she struggled to grow them into anything useful. "Who am I?" she asked.

I leaned forward and kissed her. For the first time, I wielded my ability with purpose, knowing the effects it would have. The veil lifted, and when I felt her lips form a smile against mine, I knew Heather was gone.

Cameron pulled away, eyes glazed. "Will. What happened to us? It's all hazy."

"Later," I said.

She looked to my room. "Is he…?"

"Not yet."

"So you're going to—" She noticed Marcus, who had waited patiently through our reunion. "Look who it is. Our hero."

"He sure is," I said, winking at him. "Come here, bud." He stepped closer and hugged my waist. I put my hand on his back; I felt his heartbeat underneath my palm. "Marcus – this is Cameron."

The sight of us together made him uneasy. He wanted his mother. From the protective cover of my legs, he said, "I thought your name was Heather?"

Cameron knelt down to his level. Pain made her movement awkward. "I was only Heather until you rescued me. You're a brave boy, I hope you know that." She let her arms fall, leaving herself open for a hug. I waited, unsure if he would accept. He released me, and the trust that Cameron had forged with him as Heather became clear.

I watched the bittersweet embrace. "Cameron's gonna take you upstairs, OK? I'll be up in just a minute."

She stood and took his hand. "Come on, pal." She led him to the stairs, but stopped at the base to look back at me. *Make him feel it.*

I entered my former prison and faced the warden, the man who had taken so much more than freedom from me.

"Wake up," I demanded. The shallow rises in his chest were the only indication of life. "Lincoln. Look at me, you fucking scumbag."

With a slow effort, he lifted his head high enough to let it fall backward. Only his left eye showed through the mallet's destruction. It focused on me. Red. Bulging. He said nothing.

I snapped my fingers in front of his face. "You in there?" His eye followed my movements. "You see me?" I put up my middle finger. "How many fingers am I holding up."

"Fuck you," he said through his crooked, broken jaw. He wanted to spit at me, but knew he couldn't. "You going—" He recoiled in pain. "You going to kill me?"

"Why shouldn't I? You killed Benny. And Julie."

"A nig—" He choked. Blood dribbled down his chin and jumped from his lips as he spoke. "A nigger. And a gold— A gold— Digging bitch."

I knelt down for the fire poker. I took the blowtorch from the desk. "You put a gun to my son's head."

"*Your* son?" He let out a weak chuckle, but couldn't form the smile to complement it. "Stop. Stop acting like you're that kid's father. It's— It's pitiful."

I thumbed the lever on the torch and pressed the red trigger. A seven-inch-long flame blazed through the nozzle with a soothing hum.

"I'm not going to debate the definition of a father," I said. "I know what he means to me. I know what he calls me."

"All this—" He grimaced and let out a tiny squeak. "For a pesky little shit who's not even yours."

I held the tip of the poker to the flame and twirled it. "I'm going to put this poker through your heart, Lincoln. It's mercy, really. You deserve worse. I should make you suffer. But that 'nigger' and that 'gold-digging bitch' and that 'pesky shit' wouldn't want that. Not even for you. They'd tell me not to go the route you'd take."

I could see Julie and Benny's face in the blue and orange stream as it wrapped around the iron. Tears blurred my vision. The intense color of the torch streaked as I blinked away the water. Pride mixed with my sadness when I remembered Benny's stoic sacrifice. Fear joined the fray when I envisioned a future Marcus asking about his mother. Then anger came.

"You put a gun to my son's head," I repeated, still lost in the flame. I licked a salty drop from my lip and snapped out of the hypnotizing brightness. I removed the flame from the glowing iron and dropped the torch.

I had spent many days and nights preparing for that moment. The final confrontation. In my dreams I had always delivered one last statement before killing him. Something he couldn't ignore. Something that would break him. I wanted that closure. I wanted him to die knowing the weight of the pain he'd caused. The pain of my son growing up without a mother; of Benny's girls, robbed of the best man I'd ever known; of Maureen, both of her children gone. *You did that. You.* I wanted to bring together some combination of words that could make him feel it. All of it. But I couldn't. I just stood there, sobbing, fixated on the orange iron point. No speech could deliver the justice I hoped for. Knowing that, I gripped the pole like a spear once again, closed my eyes, and readied myself to slay the beast.

Then the beast wept.

When I opened my eyes, the left side of Lincoln's face was wet with tears. His breathing shuddered. Mucus ran from his nose. I looked into his eye and saw my own grief behind it. My final statement hadn't needed words.

"You feel that?" I said. "That's something human beings feel. That's loss and tragedy. That's hopelessness."

He sniffled and closed his eye. He knew.

I drew back my spear. "But don't worry – you'll never have to feel it again."

FORTY-FIVE

I glanced at the door of my cell, then down at my mattress.

They're burying Benny right now. Right now. His girls are crying in his aunt's arms, and you have the nerve to feel sorry for yourself?

I lifted the cushioned slab. A white chain of towels hid underneath, ready for a second try.

You know who you should feel sorry for? Marcus. He had to face his mother's funeral without you. Go ahead, congratulate yourself for saving him, like that burns the blame. You're the reason he needed saving in the first place. You really think he'll ever be right? After all he's seen? Fuck, you might never see him again without that glass partition.

I checked again for onlookers. I knew I had a short window before Dean returned from the showers. Ten minutes, tops.

And Cameron. She'll never look into another mirror without remembering that dungeon you led her to. All those scars. And she's actually waiting for you. Why the fuck should she wait for you?

I tied one end of the cloth chain to the foot of the bed, then ran it through the steel frame of the top bunk.

Maureen. Both of her children – murdered. Her grandson – a constant reminder. She hates you. She'll be at the trial, too, listening to the DA accuse you of killing Keith.

I climbed to the top bunk and sat on the edge. I tied the free end of the chain into a slipknot. I placed it over my head. Tugged at it.

And if you do get out – what then? You're a walking grenade. Three people hospitalized in the past four days. How many guys in this cell block do you think want to off themselves right now, just because you're in a pit of self-pity. How many wish they had your collection of towels?

You could kill Marcus with a mood swing.

I pulled tighter.

You can't risk that. It's your responsibility as a father, as a decent fucking person, to make sure no one else gets hurt.

I closed my eyes and saw all the lives I had ruined.

The world will go on spinning without you, safer and happier.

I leaned forward and looked at the concrete below.

Keep your legs limp. It won't take long.

I let myself plummet.

Benny can't save you this time.

I fell a couple of feet before the slack ran out and my body jerked upward. I had hoped for a clean break, but the short fall wasn't enough. My heels hit the ground. I pulled them up, kept my knees limp. I couldn't breathe. I wanted to reach for safety. I wanted to put my feet down. I kicked my legs to keep them from stiffening. The cell blurred. The dozens of conversations from the common area hushed to white noise. I felt a zap. That fucking zap. The harbinger of death, taunting me from behind my eyes.

Darkness took over.

I opened my eyes to a green fabric roof and sucked in an unexpected gulp of oxygen. I touched my neck, expecting the towels. I felt only stubbled skin. I sat up in a panic and looked around. I was in a tent. Cameron slept beside me. Benny stirred a few feet away. I almost jumped back at the sight of him. *Did I do it?* I thought. *Am I dead?* A breeze hit the side of the tent, and when the fabric rippled, Benny opened his eyes.

He ignored my shocked stare and checked the watch that lay beside Cameron. He groaned. "Nine already? How the hell did I sleep so late?" His voice put a knot in my throat. I couldn't speak. He sat up, yawned, and stretched his arms upward. "You gonna go watch the house? I can do it if you wanna eat something first."

"Watch the house?" I asked. Then it came to me; I realized where I was. Not in Heaven or Hell or any other fairytale post-death kingdom, but the mountainside behind the ranch. The morning Julie showed up. The day it all went to shit.

It doesn't have to, I thought, seeing the end to all my problems. *Benny's alive. Right in front of me. I can save him.*

"Cameron," I said, grabbing her shoulder and giving it a light shake. "Get up."

She rose with fear in her veins, then dropped back to her pillow when she saw no danger. "You ruined my dream, you bastard. I was in my own bed. I miss that fucking bed."

"Both of you need to listen to me. I don't know how long I have, and we're all in trouble if I don't get this out."

My urgency brought them to full attention. Cameron sat up. Benny leaned forward. They waited.

"Will is still asleep," I said. "I'm projecting through him."

"You're Robert," Benny said.

"No. Not anymore."

"I don't get it," Cameron said. She looked to Benny for an explanation, but he kept his eyes on me.

I noticed myself tapping my knuckles on the ground. I stopped. "The Will you went to sleep with last night is going to lose his memory in less than twelve hours. He'll wake up, trapped in a room, not knowing his name. He'll reach out to a man he feels connected to, thinking he'll be saved. And he won't know that that man is himself."

Benny chuckled as he considered my explanation. "So Robert's your future self? That's original, Will. I mean, I'll believe pretty much anything at this point, but shit…"

"I'm not joking."

He laughed harder.

"Look me in the eyes, Ben."

"Get outta here, man."

"Look at me!"

The humor left his face when our pupils met. Doubt left his mind. His solemn stare soaked up the truth. "Holy shit."

"I'm Will, two weeks from now," I said, preempting the question forming in his head. "After he escapes from that basement. I know it doesn't make sense."

"It makes perfect sense," he said. His mind sped through the events of our journey. "It explains everything. But that means…"

"Things go bad down there. Real fucking bad."

"This is insane," Cameron said, then lost herself in thought. When she spoke again, her voice was low and hopeless. "Heather. I'm Heather." She knew it, but dreaded my confirmation. When she saw the answer in my face, she lost all strength. She hunched over and buried her face in her blanket. I wanted to console her, but I let her be.

"What about me?" Benny said. "Your letters never mentioned me."

I just looked at him.

His eyes widened. "Fuck."

"You—" Sorrow bubbled in my throat. "Lincoln killed you, Ben. I felt the shot. I felt you die. I could've stopped it, but I let it happen. I'm so sorry."

Benny put his face in his hands. I didn't feel what he felt, but I hated it like I had. Their silent grieving called attention to the wind-blown leaves and the knocking of a woodpecker outside. I waited.

Cameron emerged first, and we gave Benny time.

When he pulled himself from his hands with moist eyes, he said, "What happened? After what you told us in the letters?"

"I thought Cameron and I were gonna die down there. But I killed Lincoln. We escaped. Marcus, too – we got him out of there."

"Where did you come from? Where are you in two weeks?"

"I'm back in prison."

He twitched like a bug had flown into his face. "Please tell me I didn't just see what I think I saw."

I looked down, ashamed.

"It's true," he said. "Fuck, Will. What the fuck?"

"What did you see?" Cameron asked, afraid of the answer.

"I'm hanging myself," I blurted out before Benny could. "Right now. I'm hanging from my fucking bunk."

She covered her mouth with her hands. "Why would you do that?"

"Why the fuck wouldn't I?" I yelled, startling her. "I'm dangerous. I spend every second in fear of the next freak accident. Julie's dead." I looked at Benny. "You're dead." I stopped Cameron as she opened her mouth to speak. "He tortured you, Cameron. He cut you up. I can't stop hearing it and seeing it and thinking of it. Marcus lost both of his parents. I'm in a cage, and they're gonna give me more time for what I've done out here. You and Marcus are waiting for me. I'm a burden.

"I lay in bed every night in that fucking cell and I think about what I could have done differently. How I could have kept everyone safe. I stopped Lincoln from pulling the trigger, Ben. I froze him. I fucking did it, he couldn't move. But you told me to let go. You both did. Why did you tell me that? Why did I listen?"

My silver lining came back into focus, and I smiled through the sadness. "I won't let it happen again. We can change it."

"No," Benny said.

"What?"

"Where's Marcus?"

"With his grandmother."

"Safe?"

"Yes."

"Then why change anything?"

"Because you're going to die. We can do better."

"Marcus is safe," he repeated.

"You're not," I said.

He swallowed and cleared his throat. "A fair trade."

"It doesn't have to be a trade. Everyone can make it out of this."

"Go back to your cell, Will."

"Please listen to me," I begged.

"No," he said with authority. "You listen to *me*. We came all this way. All this fucking way. For what?"

I couldn't speak. My body shook.

He raised his voice. "Why are we here?"

"For Marcus," I said. The words barely reached him.

"Exactly." His chest rose as a dutiful anger took over his voice. "You just told me he's safe, waiting for you to get out. Mission accomplished. I'll be damned if I risk that boy's life by doing anything other than what I know will put him in good hands."

I appealed to Cameron. "Please don't let it happen. Don't tell me to let go of Lincoln."

She looked at me like I was a wounded deer. She wanted to help, but she wouldn't. She'd allow nature to run its course. "He's right," she said, then hugged her knees. "And if I have to suffer to save Marcus, then so be it." She put a hand on Benny's shoulder. "We both lost a son, Will. We won't let you lose yours."

"He killed Julie, too," I said. "What about her?"

"Would you die for Marcus?" she asked.

"Of course."

"So would Julie," Benny said.

They're right, I thought, hating the concession. *Marcus is safe, and I'm risking his life trying to change what's over and done.*

"This is what's gonna happen," Benny said, unwilling to accept disobedience. "You're gonna go back to that cell, and you're gonna stop yourself from making an orphan of your son. Be proud that you kept him safe, and that you did exactly what a father is supposed to do. Finish your damn sentence and be with him." He gestured to Cameron. "Be with her. And be thankful they're both waiting for you."

"I'll wait for as long as it takes," Cameron said as a drop fell from her chin and disappeared into the blanket on her lap. She put a hand on my knee.

What if I hurt more—

"Learn to control it," Benny said. "You have plenty of time."

"Your daughters, Ben."

"When you get out, find them. Tell them I love them. How much I talked about them." He exhaled a stuttering breath. "Tell them how often I looked at their pictures."

Tears flowed from every eye in the tent. I remembered waking up that morning to find the aftermath of the conversation. Cameron running from the tent. Me begging Benny to tell me what Robert had said. I remembered their secrecy. Now I knew the need for it.

"I love you, Ben. There're no words for how grateful I am."

He smiled through the rivers. "You don't need words."

"I'll see you when you get out," Cameron said. She kissed her hand and placed it on my wet cheek.

"Thank you both," I said. "For everything."

ABOUT THE AUTHOR

Robert Sadler is an author, graphic designer, and fine artist living in Massachusetts with his wife and a half-cat, half-squirrel, half-kangaroo creature. His favorite things are: great stories, art in any medium, peanut butter, books, music, beer, orange (the color, not the fruit – though the fruit isn't half bad), coffee, and anyone who has appreciated this book or any of his other creations. Oh, and writing lighthearted "About the Author" blurbs to top off serious novels.